# Still With Eyes Closed

DeWayne Watts

Copyright © 2014 DeWayne Watts

All rights reserved.

ISBN- 10:1502381249
ISBN-13: 978-1502381248

# DEDICATION

To my beloved wife Cj; to whom I desire to me married to for all eternity.

# ACKNOWLEDGMENTS

First to my wife for allowing me the time to write this.

To William Gordon for his help as editor.

This book is a work of fiction. Names, characters, places and incidents either are products of the author's imagination or are used fictitiously. Any resemblance to actual persons, places or events wither living or dead is purely at the extrapolation of the reader and is entirely coincidental.

# CHAPTER 1

The August sun filtered through the dirty glass of the dining room window. Dust particles danced and fluttered through the air as though having life within them. The once starched white lace curtains were now covered and darkened by the dust of time, neglect had settled upon them. A corner table spilled over its catchall contents, much of it now settled in piles on the once spotless floor. A home that was once bright and clean now stood sad and silent, waiting – for the passage of time.

Jim's gaze was fixed past the curtains and through the window to some distant time, now only in memory. The edges of his mouth curled in those memories of happiness, his eyes glazed in the present thoughts of despair. He brought the coffee cup to his lips, giving the black liquid a gentle blow. Swirls of steam forced him to squint his eyes; it was still too hot to drink. He carefully placed the cup back on the table.

Strewn before him were mountains of envelopes, bills, notices, and well wishes; most left unopened. There was a time when the table was clear, a fresh bowl of fruit sat at its center, but that time was now forever gone. He riffled through some envelopes wondering if he should read some of the cards, but knew there was no point to it, all hopes of 'get well soon' were now faded. He picked up the coffee cup and went outside.

The morning air was humid and stuck to him; he knew Jennifer would not be able to take the heat that was becoming day. As he sat down he pulled his pocket watch out and looked at the time, seven thirty, he would have to wake her soon, morning medications. He took a sip of coffee, closed his eyes and enjoyed the warm liquid as it permeated his body. It was a pleasure his wife could no longer feel. The warmth of the rising sun, the aroma of fresh coffee, the sounds and joys of life, it was these things that Jennifer was no longer able to share in. A wave of guilt washed through Jim's mind. Guilt that he could still enjoy these things that he once took for granted but his wife would never enjoy or feel again.

His heart cried for Jennifer, it had long ago broken and crying was all that was left. He allowed himself to sink deeper into the blackness of his despair. In the rush of the morning he heard sounds of happiness, children and parents starting their day and somewhere in the distance the bark of a puppy. His eyes snapped open, they had waited too long to try for children, and now there was no hope of any part of Jennifer continuing. He tossed the reminder of his coffee over the railing of the porch and went to gather the medications that kept his wife alive.

Three times a day, every day he had to sort out her medications. Each assortment of doses was different; pills, patches, and liquid's, requiring three lists. He had made a mistake before using the list, a mistake that nearly sped up times take on his wife. When he had her morning medications properly measured out he poured a glass of orange juice, cup of coffee and dished out some peach cobbler from the refrigerator. He picked up the tray of his assorted goods and made the routine morning trip to her room.

He paused in the doorway to take in the sight of his beloved; still asleep as if she would always be there; be here with him. His breath was deep and painful, his heart ached knowing the pain she was in, and what lay before her. He felt a wave of helplessness wash over him, as her protector there was nothing he could do to save her from this fate.

When she was forced to spend most of her time in bed Jim rearranged the bedroom and had additions made to make her life easier. The bed they shared had been removed and an adjustable multiple position bed put in its place. The head was positioned three feet from the wall to allow full access from all four sides. Behind the bed was a window that faced east, to allow the morning sun to beam in and awaken them, which was their hope when they built the house. To his wife's left as she lay in bed was a small table. On it sat medical items that she needed on a daily basis; it was also the table at which Jim ate most of his meals. Next to the table sat a breathing machine that provided her with a supply of fresh oxygen. In the corner, behind the table, a small red cushioned chair was pushed. It was his chair whenever he spent time next to her bed. A few footfalls from the same side of the bed, was the master bathroom. The doorway had been widened and grab bars installed to assist Jennifer as she descended into death. The once oversized walk in shower had been replaced by a step in tub with a waist guard to prevent her from slipping under the water. Through an easy access control panel she could summon jets to massage her at any place her body ached. To the right of her bed was her closet and dresser, containing clothing that had been altered to allow Jim to dress and undress her easily as well a supply of Depends to allow her to maintain her dignity in her last remaining days.

He entered the room and placed the tray on the table next to the bed; the sound caused her to stir. He opened the curtains allowing the morning sun to be a part of their new day.

"Bright!"

He turned and looked at his wife who squinted her eyes to block the morning sun.

"Ya, hot and humid again today."

"I want to go to the park."

"Think you're up to sitting in the heat?"

"I want to."

"Then; to the park we shall go."

He helped her to sit up and pulled the red chair next to the bed, keeping the tray to his side.

"So what did you bring me?"

"Some whites, blues, one yellow, coffee, orange juice and peach cobbler."

"Skip the first three?" She said giving him a wryly smile and shifting her eyes back and forth.

"Can't do that, I need to keep you here with me; at least for a bit longer."

Her smile became tight, they both knew that bit was going to be short, and they were still waiting to learn how short. With gentleness and patience he fed his wife small bites of cobbler, and brought the coffee or juice to her when she asked. The tremors in her hands made holding liquids impossible and when she tried to feed herself the spoon would shake so violently that the food never found its way to her lips. He never conveyed the idea that he felt burdened or that she took too much time, she was his love and he wanted to do all he could to make what time she had left the most precious time they had.

"I'm done." She said dragging the back of her hand across her mouth.

"Okay. I'll go run your water; then we will set the compass

for the park."

Jim stood and pushed the chair back to the corner, its small brass castor rollers squealing on the hardwood floor. After the chair was back in its resting place he turned and faced his wife pulling his watch from his pocket. He flicked open its cover to look at the time.

"It's eight thirty. You'll have to shave some time off your bath in order to go to the park."

"You'll buy that boat after I'm gone." She tilted her head left so she could look up at him where he stood next to the bed.

He closed his watch and stuffed it back in his left front pants pocket.

"Don't think so. That was our dream, not mine. When you're gone all our dreams will be gone as well. How can I think about our hopes and dreams when you'll no longer be with me?"

He pivoted on his heal turning from her, hoping to conceal the tremors in his voice.

"You'll carry what you remember of me. You don't plan to forget me do you?"

"You know the answer to that. But I – to be honest after you're – I don't know what I'm going to do? What is there for me after? You're my life." He looked at the floor studying the wood grain, redirecting his mental energy to avoid breaking down. When he felt strong enough he turned back around to look at her, his eyes red and swollen from fighting back tears and emotions.

He moved closer to the bed and leaned over kissing her forehead and then left her alone to consider all that would change after she was gone. As was the pattern every morning he ran her bath water, it was cold for most people; but it needed to be for her. While the tub filled he placed two towels over the warmer and squeezed some toothpaste on her brush and laid out her hairbrush and hand mirror. When the depth of the water was where she liked it he returned to the bedroom, she was still sitting up in bed, but crying.

He looked down at her, his face a reflection of the life that was being taken out of her. He softened his voice and knelt beside the bed, gently stroking her hair.

"Why the tears?"

"You. If I'm your life, when I die what will your life be?"

He let his head drop on the edge of the bed and sighed.

"I'll have to wait to see what happens. That'll be a different chapter, a new page. I'm sure I'll go on after – but I'll never give my heart to another." He raised his head and smiled.

"You can't say that Jimmy. You might find some sweet young woman that takes your breath away, sweeps your off your feet, melts your heart."

"How many clichés you gonna' hit on?"

"Just sayin' you can't say you won't fall in love again."

"Right now you have my full heart, my whole life."

She gave him a playful smile knowing that he meant what he said, but at the same time realizing he would have to move on, he would have to let someone else take his heart. He folded the covers back off her and removed her Depends and carefully cleaned her. Then he gently placed his left arm under her knees and his right arm behind her shoulders and carried her to the bathroom, he slowly lowered her in the bathtub.

"Ah! You got the water perfect, nice and cool." She said, letting her approval show on her face.

Jim returned the loving gesture and smiled back.

"You're welcome. Enjoy, if you need anything press the buzzer."

"You know I will."

\*\*\*

Jim shifted the van into park and started the lift that would allow Jennifer to exit out of its side. After she was diagnosed as terminal Jim applied for all the handicap aid and benefits that he could obtain for his wife. It had taken nearly six months to get the approval for the van, but he was determined to give his wife the freedom to continue to go where she wanted. As he walked around to the passenger side of the van the side doors gently opened and the lift lowered, positioning itself even with the van floor. He used a side step and entered the van coming up from behind his wife. Her chair was securely locked in place to prevent movement while the van was in motion, so he reached down and released the locking clamps, allowing the chair independent movement. Jennifer then used the arm control to roll the chair back to the opening of the van and onto the ramp platform.

"Ready for drop." She said in a childish playful tone, flicking back what remained of her sandy brown hair.

Jim pressed a button allowing the ramp to slowly and gently lower his wife to the ground. When the ramp stopped he unlocked the safety gate, giving her the freedom to move about wherever her chair was able to go. She rolled off the ramp and then stopped giving time for Jim to lock the van and set the alarm.

"Ready to roll?" Jim asked.

"Let's roll."

Jim walked as she maneuvered the power chair next to him. It had been seven months since the last time it rained and the late summer grass was brown and dry, crunching under the wheels of the chair. They made their way to a tree they had shared for the past twenty one years.

*** 

Jennifer just turned ten and her parents brought her and her friends to the park late one summer evening for her party. The young girls spent their time under the evening sun exhausting themselves with games until they were too tired to run. With sweat covering their bodies they collapsed under a tree in the cool shade to rest. Unknown to the girls, and Jennifer in particular, was a boy of twelve who noticed when they arrived and watched as they played. The boy watched from a distance, too shy to approach the girls and ask Jennifer her name. He continued to watch as she tossed herself back on the grass under the tree, exhausted from the hard play she had been in. Jim realized if he did not act quickly she and her friends would leave and he may never know who she was. From deep within himself he found the strength he needed; swallowed hard, wiped his brow and started the walk across the field of thick green grass to the tree. As he approached he could hear her laughter and the sound of her voice. To him it was the sound of a symphony of strings and wind, more than music, and it caused his heart to leap. When he stepped into the shade of the tree the other girls grew silent, Jennifer was lying on the grass, still with eyes closed.

"Name's Jim." The boy said. He stood tall and erect with his left hand placed in the palm of his right and kept them folded behind his back.

With fear inside him and confidence outside he watched as she opened her blue eyes and propped herself up on her elbows, her sandy brown hair tangled around her shoulders.

"Jim; is that supposed to be important to me?' She said

shifting her weight to one elbow and shielding her eyes with her other hand.

"It needs to be. See I saw you when you arrived and well, I would like to be your boyfriend." Jim said. He pulled his shoulders tightly back and pressed his chest forward.

"I don't know you and you don't know me. I don't even know what school you go to." She sat up and wiped her hands together, knocking the dust from them.

"Yorktown Academy;" Jim extended his hand to her, "Name's Jim." He cheeks dimpled when he smiled at her and his emerald eyes appeared to glaze over.

"Ya you said your name was Jim. I caught that." Jennifer stood up to be face to face with this boy who took it upon himself to crash her tenth celebration party.

She took her time studying the boy before her; she could see the confidence in his emerald eyes, a future man of strength and purpose.

Jim was stocky for a twelve year old boy, the build of a boy who spent more time in physical activity than in front of a television. His dark hair was well groomed and parted to the left side. Even his stance gave the impression of trust and power under complete control.

"Yorktown Academy; that's a rich kids school, I'm just an average poor girl, I go to Westside." She took Jim's extended hand in hers giving a firm handshake. "Name's Jennifer." She said returning his smile.

"So now that I know your name and you know mine, and we know where each other goes to school. Would you like to be my girlfriend?" Jim allowed his posture to relax, his shoulders dropped and he resumed the appearance of a boy.

"Don't you think I have a say in that?"

The unknown voice startled Jim; it came from behind him and was the voice of Jennifer's mother. Jim spun around on one heal, extended his hand, and gave Jennifer's mom a dimpled smile.

"Hello ma'am, Jennifer's mother I presume?" Jim said, projecting his smile.

"You do so correctly. What were you asking my daughter?" Her tone was sharp and had a matter of fact demand.

"I wanted to know if she would be my girlfriend. I will be happy to give you my phone number and address so you and your husband can meet my parents and learn more about me." Jim said. Before she could answer he reached in his back pocket and removed a small tablet of paper and pulled a pencil from its spiral binding.

"Well I must say young Jim, you are indeed bold. Have you ever met my daughter before?" She folded her arms across her chest to increase her visual size, a mother protecting her child from possible danger.

"No ma'am. May I ask your name please?" Jim asked. He kept his smile on and allowed his long curved eyelashes to catch her notice.

"You are respectful as well. My name is Kassidy. How do you know that she does not already have a boyfriend?" Kassidy asked. She hoped the question would be enough to send little Jim on his way.

"I would suspect that if she did; she herself would have informed me upon my first proposal." Jim said. His answer came across sarcastic although in his mind he was presenting a point of logic.

The word 'proposal', forced Kassidy to raise her eyebrows and a turn of surprised etched across her face. For a moment words escaped her as she fought her desired reaction to form a reply.

"Did I say something wrong?" Jim asked. At twelve years old he still held the innocents of a child and was unaware of the weight of the word 'proposal'.

Kassidy swallowed hard and cleared her throat. When she started speaking her words were slow and carefully spoken.

"No Jim, nothing's wrong, just the choice of your words at such an age." Kassidy answered.

Jennifer was still standing behind Jim and unaware to him she mouthed the words to her mother to get his phone number. Kassidy did not see any danger in the young boy and thought that in time the two would play out their childish dating game then part and move on to more serious things in life.

"Well Jim; I'll take you up on the offer of the phone number and address. But mind you, Jennifer's father and I will call your parents." She said.

By her posture and tone of voice Jim know it was not a threat, her words were a promise, she intended to protect her only child.

"Yes ma'am I suspect so."

***

Since that first meeting twenty one years ago the two have continued to come to this park and sit under the same tree. They were married under it when Jennifer turned eighteen. From that day as children it had become their spot.

"This is fine Jim." Jennifer said as she brought her chair to a stop.

Jim unfolded a lawn chair and set it next to her power chair. The sun had reached its halfway point in the sky and was now on its decent when they made it to the tree and he knew she was exhausted. He took out her noon medications along with some drinks and a light lunch; it would provide her with some added strength. Jim sat their lunch on a small table he had unfolded and noticed Jennifer was transfixed on the children that were playing.

"Does it upset you Jim?" She asked.

"What's that?"

"That I put wanting kids so long."

"If you had known what we know now, would you have put it off?" Jim asked. He stopped setting up their lunch to give her his full attention. He hated having these discussions, but knew she needed to have them. With the passing of each day, she was filled with more regrets of putting life off.

"Of course not Jimmy." Jennifer said. She brought the corners of her mouth up attempting to smile but instead made an upside frown.

"What I mean Jen, neither of us knew what we now know. How many things would we have done differently if we had? Kids, that trip to Europe, the boat. Our whole lives would have been different. But we did not, nor could we have known what our future held, so no regrets, okay." He reached over to stroke her cheek with the back of his forefinger.

"Do you regret our first meeting here?" She asked. It was a question she had held for the past year, she needed to know that he had no regrets that he had been happy with what she had given to him.

Jim's eyes flooded over with tears at recalling their first meeting, and the corners of his lips curled in a mischievous smile as he remembered his introduction to Jennifer and her mom. He knew the value of his boyish looks, emerald eyes, dark hair and dimpled cheeks had gotten him many things, including his wife.

"Oh no, never. Jen from our first meeting and when we married, I've been the happiest man on the planet, in the universe. I would not exchange one fraction of one second of the past twenty one years with you. In fact I would do it again, even if I did know what we know now." He leaned over and gently kissed his wife on the lips.

They remained in the park until the setting of the sun, from time to time Jennifer dozed off, and Jim let her sleep. She would always wake to new children and fresh shrills of joy in the air, which would cause a wave of smiles to wash across her face. As the evening started to surrender to the night Jim knew their time at the park was over, he still needed to clean her and allow time for her to soak in a cool bath. He packed up the remaining bottles of water and carried their trash to a nearby trashcan. After dropping their trash in the can he thought about picking up the paper and empty bottles that lay on the ground. It was such an easy act to throw something away and it kept the park clean for everyone. It was only a few that ruined it for the many. Realizing it was useless to try and change the way people felt about the world around them he disregarded the trash on the ground and walked back to Jennifer. When he was finished cleaning up their spot he unlocked the wheels on her chair and they made their way back to the van. He reversed his earlier movements when he let his wife out, and when her chair was locked in place he climbed in behind the steering wheel and headed home. He pulled the van into the garage and repeated the steps of letting her out, he walked next to her as they made their way in their home.

When they entered the house Jim went to start her water

while she stopped in the living room to watch the evening news. She rolled to the arm of the couch and picked up the remote from where he had left it. With her left hand she pressed her right arm against the arm of her power chair to keep it from shaking as she fingered the buttons. After pressing the power-on button she turned to CBS in time to catch the narrator introducing the broadcaster.

*"This is the CBS Evening News with Ted Daniels"*

Jim cut a path across the front of the television as he made his way to the kitchen to prepare her night time medications. As he did so the attention grabbing music played from the speakers. As the camera zoomed in on the news desk the narrator read the headlines.

"What did he say?" Jim stopped working on the medications, picked up a dish towel and walked to the edge of the living room.

"I know, and it's the first story, hurry and sit down." Jennifer said. She tilted her head to the couch to encourage him to sit next to her as they presented the story.

Jim tossed the hand towel on the table and rushed to the bathroom to turn off the water and just as quickly made his way back to the living room in time to hear what he hoped was good news.

*"In a medical breakthrough; scientist believe they have found a way to slow, if not reverse the ageing process, while at the same time curing many diseases. With us here in the studio is our CBS medical news consultant Doctor Emily Thomen. Welcome Doctor Thomen.'*

*'Thank you for having me.'*

*'So exactly what is this breakthrough? Is this the elusive answer to all of humankind's illnesses that we have been longing for?'*

*'We can't say for certain Ted, yet, but we are hopeful. It was discovered quite by accident and because of the ethical issues involved the process is still being kept in the lab. But what I can tell you is how it was discovered. Recently a man*

in his late seventies presented his doctor with a case of leukemia. Now given his age, most doctors would have simply attempted to extend his life and made attempts to increase the quality of life he had remaining. However his case proved to be unique.'

'In what way was his case different from that of another person in his age group?'

'You've heard of location being important, in his case it proved to be most important. He happened to live in an area with one of the largest cancer research facilities in the world, and at that facility they just happened to be testing a new serum, which by the way, has not been approved for human trials nor has even been approved for stage one testing by the FDA. But a doctor there, with the patient's permission, made the gamble to test it on him.'

'And the results were unbelievable I presume.'

'Yes, in fact the FDA gave post approval, but no further approval due to the ethical questions involved. But in this single case, the man's leukemia not only went into remission, but thus far no trace of reoccurrence has been noted, but there were unexpected results. At first it was believed to have been a clerical error, until more in-depth testing proved otherwise. His aging process appeared to, at first, to have stopped. It did not stop but was drastically decreased. As to the ratio of the decrease, that is still being determined. The man also had scar tissue from years of smoking, that also cleared up, along with several other age related complications.'

'If I understand you correctly doctor, this process not only cured his leukemia, but slowed his aging process and reversed the effects of age related illness?'

'That's correct Ted. But there's more to it. Doctors feel that this is the cure for all cancers, AIDS and other diseases that affect all humankind. The slowing of the aging process and the reversal of age related complications is a side bonus.'

'And a major side bonus at that. Thank you Doctor Thomen.'

'You're welcome; and again thank you for having me here to share this.'

'As noted by Doctor Thomen there are some very serious ethical concerns with the serum, questions that must be dealt with before the FDA will allow stage one trials to begin, so this is something that is still decades away, even after the ethical questions are answered. Join us here on CBS tonight at nine Eastern eight Central for a two hour in-depth special report into this remarkable discovery.'"

"Jim?" Jennifer's cheeks flushed a dark rose and tears gently flowed down them.

"I *will* record it. I promise." Jim said. He leaned toward her to stress his words.

Jim leaned over the arm of the couch and kissed her on her tear stained cheek and then returned to the bathroom to restart the water. For the past two years they had both put their hope and faith in cures and promises that never manifested, only to be cruelly dropped off the edge of despair. They knew discussing anything would only feed hope; hope that could later turn to discouragement. So conversations dealing with any hopeful cures were intentionally avoided. He sat on the edge of the tub and let his hand dangle in the water, feeling the coolness wash over him as the current passed from the spout. Inside his heart he could feel hope starting to build, but he knew not to allow it. He wanted to scream at the cruelness of the world, at how hateful life could be to offer him, and more so his wife, hope only to have it yanked away time and again.

From the day the doctor informed them that she was terminal he had grown to hate life outside his wife and it was his plan to end his after she was gone.

He did not notice when the water passed the safe mark for his wife. He reached over and turned off the tap, then allowed the water to drain until it was low enough for her. With the water at a safe level he attached the extra handrails and placed washcloths within easy reach.

Jennifer enjoyed her bath time, it was a time her body could float free, and pain and pressures were eased. It was not unusual for her to remain in the bath for an hour or more, it seemed as if the cold water took away the burning sensations. When he had completed preparing the tub area he went to the sink to wash the tears away that had slid down his cheeks. With his nerves settled he returned back to the living room and his wife.

"Did they say anything else about the cure?" Jim asked. He dragged the sleeve of his shirt across his cheeks to ensure any reaming tears or water was removed.

"No. Jimmy I was thinking? I can put my medications off until, say about thirty minutes before the show ends? I want so bad to stay up and watch it. What do you think?" Jennifer asked. Although she had promised him not to put hope in anything they heard, she could not resist the hope within her heart.

"I think it's a good idea. But…" Jim said.

"I know you don't have to say it. But I will. We can't talk about it until we talk to Doctor Ellis, and we can't let hope build." She cut him off in mid-sentence having heard his lecture on hope so many times in the past two years.

"And you know that's easier said than we have ever been able to handle." Jim said.

"I know. But I promise no words of hope until we talk to Doctor Ellis." Her words were spoken as a promise, but her eyes were filled with hope.

"Let me take you to your bath."

When they were in her bedroom he lifted her from the power

chair to her changing chair. After securing her in place he started undressing her, being careful not to pull or snag the port tubes in her chest, or inflict undue pain. When he finished cleaning her up he carried her to the bathroom then gently lowered her in the cool water. She let out a sigh of relief as the water flooded over her body; she then laid her head back and closed her eyes to the burning pain that was starting to subside. Jim quietly exited the bathroom and returned to the kitchen to finish her medications and prepare the evening meal.

Most of the information presented in the special report was a rehash of the evening news, except with added interviews, charts and a projected timeline of approval, if the ethical questions were cleared. It was those ethical questions that interested Jim and Jennifer the most, and the reason why they had watched the entire late version of the presentation. However it was the one topic not mentioned in the story. As Jim had expected Jennifer fell asleep as the story grew into its second hour, he had the recorder running, knowing that she would want to see the remainder in the morning. When the newscast was over he stopped the recorder and tenderly carried his wife to bed.

They had stopped sleeping together shortly after she was given the diagnoses; his turning in bed caused movement which in turn caused her pain. He hired a contractor to remove much of the wall between the master bedroom and an adjoining bedroom. Then he set up his bed in the newly created space and let her have the master bed. Months later the master bed was removed to be replaced by the hospital bed. Although not sharing a bed, they remained in the same room.

With the rising sun he followed the same routine that he had for nearly two years, except for one difference, before waking his wife, he made an appointment with her doctor. He knew she would ask and the earlier it was made the earlier they could get in to see him.

As with every morning the two started with talk of – after – she was gone, but this morning he cut it short by letting her know he made an appointment to see Doctor Ellis at eleven o'clock. This early time altered their routine so they now had to hurry their morning schedule, a hurry she did not mind. After she was dressed he positioned a floor mirror in front of her so she could give approval, once given he sat on the bed next to her and started brushing her hair.

Chemo had taken its toll on her once full beautiful sandy brown hair, most had fallen out and what was left was dry, brittle and course. Its sandy brown tone no longer had shine to it; it now had the appearance of sun baked grass from the heat of a summer's day. When they were in the van and en-route to the doctor's office the conversation of hope started, as he knew it would.

"Jen, this is dangerous. We, you have been let down so many times…" He kept his tone tender, but firm in hopes of sidetracking the conversation.

"Jimmy its different this time, it works. Whatever the ethical questions are I'm sure that someone *is* doing testing, with or without FDA approval." Jennifer said.

He could hear the pleading in her voice, the begging for hope, and hoping that he would share those same feelings.

"We can't do this. We can't think or talk like this. Let's wait and see if Doctor Ellis knows anything about this." He kept his voice firm, but this time removed the tenderness. He felt the same hope within his heart, but they had been dropped so many times he felt it necessary to press it deep inside.

She turned away from him and locked her gaze out of the passenger window. She was not mad or upset with Jim, but she knew he was right, it was wrong to hope. The remainder of the trip was in silence, each alone with their thoughts and feelings.

When they arrived at Doctor Ellis' they did not have to wait and instead of being taken to an exam room they were taken to his office. His office was large, with oversized plush furniture; his desk was also oversized and made of cherry wood. The walls were covered in English tiled wood panels and a deep red accent of colors completed the look. The wall opposite the desk was lined with shelves of books, ranging in topics from medical to physics. The room conveyed the impression of knowledge and authority.

"I thought I would see you today. How's my favorite girl, and guy – well couple?" Doctor Ellis asked as he entered his office. He approached Jim and Jennifer, leaned over and gave her a kiss on the cheek and extended his hand to Jim. Jim stood and took the doctors hand, returning the firm handshake.

"We're fine – well no we're not. Did you see the news last night?" Jim asked. His tone carried insecurity and disbelief, unsure if what he saw was not a hoax. He stepped backward and sat back down.

A couch and two chairs were positioned in the middle of the room and a large oversized coffee table that looked like a stack of books sat in the center of the furniture. A single large rug covered the hard wood floor under the table. Doctor Ellis was sitting on the couch across from Jim and Jennifer.

"I can only imagine how you feel after seeing that report. And yes I did see it, but there's more to it." Doctor Ellis said. He shook his head up in down when he spoke to affirm his statement.

"Are you speaking of the ethical question?" Jennifer asked.

"There's that; but I'm part of the research team." Doctor Ellis said. He spoke the last statement with hesitancy, unsure if he should reveal his position.

'*REALLY!* Oh Jimmy; I told you so; I told you this time it would be okay to hope." Jennifer's voice pitched high and quivered. Her blue eyes glazed with tears of hope and joy, her cheeks flushed deep rose.

"Jen, back down. We don't know anything yet, we have to hear him out." Jim said. He placed his hand on her shoulder, as if pinning her back to the Earth.

"He's right Jennifer, there's that blasted ethical issue. I can't tell you what it is, but I'm aware of it and it's extremely complicated. No matter the benefits to all humankind from this serum, if we can't find a way for medical science, the American and other governments to see past this single issue, this is something that will never come to fruition. The ethical issues surrounding this are way beyond cloning or stem cell research. In fact congress would approve stem cell usage long before they would even consider ever looking at the data on this. I'm on the ethical board and I've already tried to lobby congress and the FDA, they will not allow us to enter stage one testing, and that's all in lab testing, no human trials at all." Doctor Ellis said. His body slumped in the chair, resigned, his statement was laced with frustration and when he retold his efforts that frustration seemed to be aimed at Jim and Jennifer.

"I own you two an apology. I'm sorry for letting my frustration out. It is so – I don't know how to express my feelings about the regulations of this country. People are dying needlessly why the bureaucrats of this country debate unrealistic possibilities." Doctor Ellis sat up on the couch and leaned forward to stress his apology, when he leaned back he pushed the bridge of his glasses with his forefinger.

"So what's the hang up, what's the issue with ethics?" Jim asked.

"Jim I *can't* tell you, I know it has to be frustrating for you, and more so for you Jennifer, but everything they said on the news is true, but – it's the means we use to obtain the serum and no one alive feels that the ends justify the means of collecting the cure, not even me, at the present time. We're looking for a better method, but I see nothing on the horizon, nothing for decades." The frustration was still evident in his voice, but no longer aimed at his patients.

"I'll be gone long before then." Jennifer said. She turned and buried her face in the pit of Jim's arm. Both men remained silent until she was able to bring her sobs under control.

"I shouldn't bring this up, because I know if I do you're going to want answers right now, but I've gotten close to you two over the years." Doctor Ellis took off his glasses and wiped the lenses with the tail of his shirt. He held them to the light to inspect his cleaning, then put them back on, pushing the bridge with his forefinger until they were tightly on his nose.

"What?" They both said at the same time. Jim leaned forward in his chair to impress his impatience on Toby Ellis.

Toby again pushed his glasses back with his forefinger, and then ran his fingers along the arms of the glasses and over his ears, to ease the pressure they placed on the sides of his head. His hair was parted down the center and feathered along the sides and his glasses were wire-framed, he gave the impression that he was still in nineteen eighty five.

"There may be a second option. Because the serum looks to be decades out, maybe even as much as seventy or more years. And due to that delay the committee is considering a second option for some candidates, Jennifer you're on the candidate approval list. However we wanted time to get final approval and setup done before mentioning it to potential candidates, but you two have forced my hand. I won't go into detail at this meeting, but I do have a committee meeting tomorrow, at which time I'll mention your case again and if approved I'll give you and Jim a call to come back here so we can go over the details. But I can't tell you more than what I've already said." Toby's tone was firm and definite; he did not want to be asked questions.

"I understand Doctor Ellis, and I'll keep Jen as level as I can until you call. So does all this have a name yet, the cure or committee oversight?" Jim asked. His question was intended to direct the conversation away from the second option, and prevent Jennifer from asking questions of her own.

"Thanks Jim. No, no name yet. We'll pass that motion tomorrow as well. We're reluctant to call it anything; there's serious doubt of getting any kind of approval to move forward. The committee feels that giving any part of this a name instead of a number will create false hope, for us and any who hear a name. I'll give you a call to set up a meeting as soon as a decision is made, okay?" Toby said.

"Thank you doctor." Jennifer said her voice shaking as she held back a surge of emotion.

"Hold on this time Jennifer, this is a real hope, and I'm sure that you'll be approved for the second option. This is the most complicated medical and ethical question that has even been faced by doctors and governments. I believe that it will somehow be approved, but I don't see how it will be, yet." Toby said.

"Thanks again Doctor Ellis." Jennifer said through tears and sobs.

"Jim, you've done a wonderful job taking care of your wife. I've never seen such devotion and love. I have continued to use the two of you as examples of what love can do. As you know Jennifer, when the leukemia in you got the upper hand, I figured you had only six months to live, that was two years ago. I truly believe that the love between you two has helped you to endure. You're an unbelievable couple. Keep that love strong, because somehow I feel that this will work to your advantage." Toby Ellis said as he stood up to indicate the conversation was over. He walked to the door and held it open, first Jennifer and then Jim exited. He watched as they approached the lobby exit then shut his office door and removed his cell phone to make a call.

When they were in the van it was Jennifer who broke the silence.

"Jimmy; what do you suppose the second option could be?" Her voice was soft and full of wonder, as if she was ten years old again and holding his hand as they walked through the park to sit under their tree.

"No idea; I was sitting here considering that myself." He answered. He reached up and dragged his right hand through his hair, flicking his fingers as the last stands of hair filtered through.

"But; what if the insurance won't pay for it and the cost is too high?" Jennifer asked.

When Jim turned to look at her, a look of panic shrouded her face, hope gave way to fear.

"You already know my answer; can you put a cost on life on living? No. There's always a way. We have managed thus far, we'll continue to manage." Jim said.

The remainder of the drive home was in hopeful silence.

# CHAPTER 2

Jim awoke the next morning, keeping his same routine, however while sitting at the table he started to open the cards of well wishes. Some were intended to be cute with kittens, puppies or other lovable creatures, others were funny and occasionally he came across a card with a serious tone. He continued reading, taking in the hope and letting it build in him; the more cards he read, the greater his hope grew. In his mind he continued to tell himself that hope was useless, but his heart allowed hope, this time. When he heard the chimes of the grandfather clock strike eight he pulled his watch from his pocket and flipped it open, it confirmed what he heard. He got up leaving behind years of cards still to be opened, believing now he would have the time to do so.

As on all mornings he religiously followed the dispensing of prescriptions for his wife. He prepared orange juice and coffee, but instead of peach cobbler he prepared eggs and toast. He arranged the tray, including a bouquet of summer flowers from the yard and went to his wife's bedside. He paused at the entry to her room, a smile lit across his face; he knew she would be there tomorrow, and for the rest of his life. He placed the tray next to her bed and pulled open the curtains to allow the sun to join them on this new day of hope. The morning sun streamed through the window and its rays shimmered off her hair, he now looked forward to the day when it would be as lush as it was in her youth.

"Good Morning." Her words were a chorus as she spoke them and her voice was bright and cheerful knowing that this day brought on a new hope. She pulled herself to an upright position by the renewed strength, her face beaming with delight.

"You're Wonder Woman now? Be careful, we still have to take things day by day." He said. Although he too felt hope, it was overlaid with caution.

She looked at the breakfast tray next to the bed, seeing the usual items and then the eggs and toast.

"Day by day? Then why toast and eggs?" Her expression changed to a childish smirk with a playful tone of sarcasm.

"Well let's see, you have to start eating better since you're sticking around a bit longer. No more junk food, you're not exiting this play as soon as we thought." He returned her childish expression, tilting his head and winking his eye.

"Down right bossy now; I see. Jimmy I'm so happy, just the thought of having hope, a chance." Her demeanor and tone turned serious.

"Agreed, let's eat."

They kept the remainder of their schedule unchanged, save with a laid back pace, no longer feeling the rush of death upon them. She spent less time in the bath to have more time to spend in the new day of life. After he had finished brushing her hair they returned to the park to watch the children with a future hope have having their own. When they left the park they went to their restaurant, not that they owned it or had any financial interest in it, but theirs in the language of being a place they both enjoyed eating in the past. It was the day they were told she had six months to live that they ate there last, and this day was a new day for them both. They were unknown to the new maître d' who seated them at the table they requested However when the owner saw them he remembered that night more than two years ago. He approached the table with a bottle of Riesling, a gift for the couple he thought he would never see again.

"Hello Mister and Misses Fuller; may I pour you a glass?" The owner asked titling the bottle back for their inspection and handing the cork to Jim.

"Yes, that would be an acceptable way to add celebration to this day." Jim said. He was looking into her eyes as he said it, and then turned to give a nod of approval to the owner, his face glowing with joy.

"And to what are we celebrating? Life I hope." The owner asked. He reflected the glow of joy emitting from Jim back to both of them.

"Hope and – perhaps life, the only hope for life I've been offered thus far." Jennifer answered. She caught the same glow that was being spread around the table.

"Then this evening's meal is my gift to you." He said; choking back tears, the quiver in his voice apparent to Jim and Jennifer as well as the surrounding guest.

"Thank you Marcus; your gratitude is most appreciated, and I might add, appropriate." Jim looked at Marcus and gave a tight smile, his own eyes starting to glaze over with tears of hope, joy and gratitude.

"Well then, with that let nothing restrain you in accepting my gift, please." Marcus tapped the top of the open menu in Jim's hands to indicate that he meant anything they wanted to order. "I'll leave you two; wave me when you're ready to order." Marcus said.

Jim tilted his head slightly to his left and gave a single slight nod to Marcus, who then disappeared through the swinging doors that lead to the kitchen. The couple of hope sat and studied the menu, Jim holding one open for both of them to read. Inaudible muffles and whispers exchanged between them as they studied various items. Rejecting ones they were unsure of, but wanting to avoid the 'safe' choices, this was after all a time for new beginnings and new experiences. With their choices made Jim got the attention of Marcus who came over and took their order. Marcus spared no expense and ensured all pomp was displayed on delivery.

"Sorry Jimmy; I just can't eat it all." Jennifer said.

He noticed a look of disappointment as it washed across her face.

"Don't fret about it. We can take it with us." He answered, flashing a smile of reassurance.

"Jimmy?" She said his name as a whispered question. "Marcus will be offended." The look of disappointment was now accompanied with worry.

"Then dear, explain why he's bringing you a lovely black Styrofoam box." Jim said.

\*\*\*

The day was too much for Jennifer, after she was secured in the van, she quickly feel asleep. Jim made the trip home in silence and completive thought. The second option, whatever it might be, had opened new doors and new possibilities. His mind formed scenarios of a different future, one where she would beat the cancer and he would not take his own life. Although he deeply desired to live a wave of depression overtook him, he had spent months planning his own exit from the world that the sudden change in the direction of life altered the balance of his thinking. His own life and thoughts had become negative; the switch to a positive outlook would take time, and an emotional adjustment.

She was still asleep when he pulled into the garage and lowered the chair lift. The click of the unlocking clamp woke her up.

"We home?" She brought her hands to her eyes and rubbed the sleep from them, her voice slurred as she started to stretch her vocal cords awake.

"We are." He answered.

"Jimmy? Tomorrow will you take me to the zoo? Remember we use to go all the time before I got sick?" Her voice now awake and the slur no longer present.

"Plan on it." He answered.

He left the chair lift in the lowered position since the van was in the locked garage and walked in front of her chair to open the door to the house at the top of the ramp. Inside the house he followed her to the bathroom, where he turned on the cold water to fill the tub. After undressing and cleaning her, he gently lowered her in the water. Then he left her alone and went into the kitchen to prepare her medications.

The Walton's tune deflected his attention away from the kitchen cabinet. He removed his phone from its belt clip and entered the four digit pass code; he was hoping it was a text from Doctor Ellis.

*"Need to discuss final sale of the company. Can you come by in the morning? Nick"*

He hit reply to answer his lawyer's text.

*"Time."*

*"'Bout noon."*

*"Yeppers."*

*"See ya. TKS"*

Something was wrong; he could feel it and he had no idea what it could be. But the sale of his dad's company was needed to ensure her continued treatment. He knew the unknown that his lawyer did not mention would nag him until they met. He replaced his phone in its clamp and redirected his attention to preparing the medications. Once the task was completed he took the medications along with a glass of orange juice to the living room and sat on the couch. He let his eyes fall on the television remote but picked up the laptop instead. He needed to learn more of the cure mentioned in the newscast; he felt there had to be some leaks on the Internet. Since the days of WikiLeaks and Edward Snowden leaks were now expected, he was hoping his expectations would not lead to disappointment. He sat back and rested the computer on his lap, opened it and tapped the power button. He watched the screen as the Windows logo glowed, then took him to the desktop. Windows 8 appeared to load quickly but it was a farce. Even though the desktop appeared quickly the computer was still booting, it was unusable until the drivers had completely loaded. When at last the computer became usable he opened Firefox to his Homepage. He thought he knew what he wanted to search for, but his mind was blank. He fumbled his fingers across the keyboard, half expecting them to know what to type in. In frustration he flipped his head back on the couch and looked at the ceiling. He watched as his thoughts began to meander, he saw words and phrases flow through his mind, but nothing seemed as if it would return results that would be worthy. He closed his eyes, hoping to shut out all external stimuli. He returned his gaze to the computer screen as he felt his fingers enter context into the Bing search box.

*"Unethical medical cures in 2014"*

The returns were dismal when taken into context. Nothing proved useful or that could result in another search.

*"Miracle cure for patient with leukemia"*

Again the returns were disappointing. Only a few vague references to the same CBS News story with mention of names of different doctors and Doctor Thomen, but nothing useful. He attempted a few more searches, changing key words and phrases, but each search turned up nothing meaningful. Again he let his head fall back on the couch in frustration. With his eyes closed he could hear Jennifer in the bathroom, humming to herself, she was starting to have moments of happiness. His own mind drifted back to happier days, she had always been a hummer when she was happy or joyful. When she saw a funny cat video or cute post on Facebook or Twitter, it always brought her joy. Jim jerked his head up quickly and felt the blood rush forward; he knew a headache was forthcoming. Franticly he typed in the address for Facebook. He had deleted the Bookmarks for Facebook and Twitter when family seemed to always send him links to pseudoscience cures for cancer or a new as yet unknown treatment that the government was keeping from the public. He gave pause when he realized that that was what was happening now, except it was no conspiracy theory or hoax; there was a new cure for cancer and it was being buried by the government. Once at the login screen for Facebook he attempted to remember his password. After two tries he gave up, knowing a third miss would lock the account. He opened Microsoft Word and then a file named *'Shopping List'* a document that held passwords to all his online accounts. In the Social Media subsection he saw what he needed. He left the file open for the Twitter password.

Once logged into Facebook he was barraged with over three hundred notifications of *FRIEND* request and new *POST*. He clicked *'mark all as read'* to remove the notification of new *POST* and dismissed the *FRIEND* request. It was the post he intended to create that took on all importance.

*"Facebook friends. Sorry for the long absence. Not really interested in catching up at this time, but have a need for help. On CBS August fifth two thousand fourteen a story aired featuring a Dr. Emily Thomen. She discussed a man who received treatment for leukemia and was cured, but it also had other effects. The doctor in the story mentioned that the government was not allowing testing at this time due to ethical questions. Jen and I saw Dr. Ellis and he confirmed the story and serum but nothing more. No details or what the blasted ethical issue was. I've tried searching for information on the Internet and get nothing. Has anyone else heard anything different or know anything not in the news story? Please post if you do. The information needs to be made public. Jen is a candidate for treatment and a second option. Although the doctor never mentioned what the second option was. Please post ASAP. Also Jen's spirits are up and hopeful in light of this news story."*

He opened a new tab and typed the address for Twitter. Once the page loaded he returned to Word and copied the password, then pasted it in the password field. Here his typed characters were limited.

*"URGENT HELP: Info on CBS News story about cure to leukemia patient. #CBSleukemia when replying. PLS RT TKS"*

His recall of Twitter shorthand surprised him. With nothing else to read of interest on Facebook or Twitter he returned to Bing attempting a few more searches and as before got no useful returns.

"Jim?" He heard his wife's stymied yell.

He slammed the laptop shut and placed it on the cushion beside him and jumped to his feet and rushed to the bathroom. Inside he noticed that his wife was shivering from being in the water longer then she was accustomed to.

"Sorry." He said as he bent over to release the water. He removed a towel form the warmer and placed it on the bar around the back of the changing chair.

"I was caught up looking for information on the Internet."

"Find anything?" She asked as he helped her to the chair. Given the fact that he lost track of time in research about her made his oversight acceptable.

"No. So I posted on Facebook and Twitter. I'll check after I get you dried and in bed." He wiped the water off her chilled body.

"Bring the computer in the room after you get my med's. I want to know."

His answer was in the form of a smile. After he made her comfortable in bed he returned to the living room to get her medications and the laptop. He helped her with the medications, holding the glass of orange juice as she took small manageable sips. Once she had the medications down he pulled his chair close enough to the edge of the bed so she could see the computer screen. He returned one tab to Facebook and another to Twitter. As with the earlier search results, nothing hopeful appeared in the replies. Most of the replies on Facebook were from family wanting additional information about Jennifer's health. Not a few of which were hateful, accusing Jim of keeping her locked up and away from well-intentioned family. It was not his intent to keep her isolated, but it was her request. Although she knew her family had good intentions, giving false hope from cures ranging from kinesiology to marijuana had taken its toll on her and she wanted to be left alone with her husband at her side. It was those posts they choose to ignore.

"You got nothing with the Internet searches?"

"No. I thought it was really strange that I didn't find a single reference aside from the CBS story."

"Think the government is censoring it?"

"The Internet? They can't, I mean the Constitution – well the first amendment, forbids censorship." He said.

"Something like this, after the lesson from WikiLeaks and that Snowden guy, think the government got the point about how to keep secrets?"

Her statement forced Jim to pause before replying, he wondered if it were possible that the government was now able to censor Internet traffic, perhaps simply by redirecting it to servers that scrubbed content before sending it to its destination. He dismissed the idea as absurd.

"Jen, this is America. If anyone found out the government was censoring anything, the press would eat congress and the president alive."

"Explain the fact that no searches are being returned."

"I can't." His voice resigned with disappointment. The only answer for the lack of returns was the answer he refused to accept. The United States Government would never violate the first amendment; it was as good as written on a stone tablet, but it was also the only possible reason why he was getting no results.

They continued to search Bing in downtime from watching the Twitter feed or posts on Facebook. Inside Jim felt good to be using social media again. It allowed him to feel as if he were a part of something bigger, something outside the world that centered on Jennifer. He was soon lost in thought of catching up with old friends and what he was missing out on in the world outside.

"What is it Jimmy?"

Her voice pulled him back to the reality that had become his life. He shook his head, as if to shake the feeling of guilt from off him, he felt she could see his guilt written on his face.

"Nothing, just never realized how desperate our family wants information. Oh before I forget, Nick texted today. He wants a meeting tomorrow at noon."

"Is everything alright? The sale; still going through?"

"I don't know. He said nothing else. Just set up the meeting. You're starting to doze."

"Ya and loosing fast. So we're still going to the zoo tomorrow?"

"Sure. I figure you can go to the meeting with me, we'll have to skip the park and then after the meeting we can go to the zoo and eat lunch there."

"Sounds like a great plan. See ya in the morning. I love you Jimmy."

"Love you too." He said as he leaned over and kissed her forehead. By the time he returned to a standing position she had fallen into a restless, painful sleep.

He gathered the tray, empty glass and computer leaving her for the night. He placed the computer on the coffee table and returned the glass and tray to the kitchen, placing them in the dishwasher. After starting the washer he turned and leaned against the counter, taking in the sight of the open living area. Tomorrow he would hire a cleaner. He fixed a glass of iced tea and returned to the couch, this time reaching for the remote. Perhaps there might be a follow up story on a twenty four hour news channel.

Redundant news stories continued to run through the night and were still playing when he woke up. His body protested the night on the couch, creaking and popping as he stood. The clock chimed eight, his mind quickly cleared of the nighttime fog; he would be late with Jennifer's medications. The whole day was now set to a pattern of delays. He made shortcuts in his own needs and wants, foregoing his morning coffee and preparing what was needed for her.

He rushed to the limit he was able without causing undue discomfort to his wife and was able to make it to the meeting with Nick at the agreed time. The Barns Firm had been his dad's attorney as well as his grandfathers, his family had used the same firm for the past three generations, and Jim carried on the family tradition. The stately building housing the firm carried the air of power and control, giving the impression that what others failed to do they could. It instilled confidence in Jim, as it did his father. The building itself had been built in the early nineteen hundreds, a firm mixture of concrete, glass and steel. Two large curved windows with individual panes of glass framed in steel stood aside two massive wooden oak doors with the name of the firm etched in black in the center of the right hand door, as if the name had been burned in by the finger of God who granted the firm its power. It was the impression the firm wanted to convey and it was the impression one took in. Inside the weight was heavier, dark reds and heavy oaks with marble floors and large gold light fixtures filled in your sight regardless of where you looked. His Grandfather chose the firm based on the appearance of the building the choice turned out to be wise. The Barns family built the building around their reputation. Jennifer stopped her chair in front of the marble covered oak counter, the top of which came to the middle of Jim's chest.

"Afternoon Mister Fuller. You and Misses Fuller may go on up, he's ready to see you."

"Thanks Christi." Jennifer said as she rolled away, the courtesy seemed to slip Jim's mind.

Nick's office was on the fourth floor, it being the topmost. The first floor housed research, libraries and meeting rooms. The second was for paralegals and junior partners with the third reserved for senior partners. The fourth floor housed only three offices, one for the senior Barns, his up and coming son and their secretary. However Nick's son was still in high school and was being groomed to take the helm when he graduated an Ivy League law school. Nick's office was as impressive and powerful as the entire outside of the building. It occupied much of the fourth floor, steel framed windows joined at the corner. The ceiling towered above at fourteen feet, with four golden chandeliers dropping from the impressive height to light up the entire room. Oak hardwood covered the floor, with oriental hand spun rugs placed under the most trafficked areas. Lining the walls were paintings of well-known impressionist artist. Once more intended to convey money, power and in some cases fear. As Jim approached the man behind the desk he extended his hand. It was gracelessly accepted.

"Glad you could make it on short notice. Let's go to the sitting area."

"What's up Nick, why the urgency of this meeting? Did the buyers back out? I can't afford to lose this sale. We're looking at some hopeful medical procedures for Jen."

"Many questions to be answered. I'm aware of the medical procedures that you're looking at, and I'll get to that in a minute. But first, a bottle of water for each of you?"

"Yes please, for both of us." Jim spoke for Jennifer.

"The sale of your father's company is still on track. In fact the buyers would like to close this Friday, if you're able."

"The reason being? The sale had been slated to close next month. I don't understand." Jim's facial expression conveyed his confusion to Nick.

"The buyers have requested to close earlier. I'm not at liberty to say why. However, Jim, Jennifer, they're willing to add one million to the price if you'll move up the close. I went ahead and told them yes."

"Nick, I don't understand. They're moving up the close and offering us more money? I heard you when you said that you can't give the reason, but I would like to know something." Jim's expression relaxed from its confused state to curiosity.

"The research lab your grandfather built and your dad improved on has great potential for their use. They need the technology that your facilities offer to move forward with their research. They feel that the quicker they can close the deal the quicker they can move their research forward." Nick said.

"Sounds strange to me, and I'm sure Jen would agree. But if you feel that it's all good, then let's move with the close."

"Right move Jim. The sale will sit nice with you two as well. It'll ensure long term funding for your treatment." Nick nodded toward Jennifer. "And also help with – after. I'm sure you understand I mean no ill intent." Again he nodded toward Jennifer.

"None taken Nick. I've been telling Jim for some time now he needs to start planning for that time. But things have change recently Nick. We saw a news story…" Jennifer said.

"I need to cut you off Jennifer. I'm aware of the news story. My firm has been retained by Toby – Doctor Ellis, to get some sort of legal understanding from the ethical concerns with the serum. I'm working on it, dealing directly with the FDA and the Justice Department. But it's likened to smashing my head against that marble table over there." He extended his right arm and pointed to the conference table in his office.

"Why? I mean I don't get it. Why is the government being so stubborn on this? Something that can benefit the entire human race, something that offers the first true ray of hope, not just to Jen, but to anyone with a sick or dying loved one? Is the government of this country full of idiots?" Jim said.

"Jim, the government is full of people of caution. They are concerned about being reelected when the time comes; they have concerns over lawsuits, concerns over ethics. You name it; this scares the very fabric out of them. Toby mentioned the ethical concerns to you, but I take in the legal concerns as well. This is the most promising find for all of humankind, but at the same time fundamentally the most dangerous. The concept itself is shrouded in fear. So this is not a quick fix." He turned his attention to Jennifer. "Jennifer, Doctor Ellis mentioned the second option at the committee meeting this morning, later he'll tell you that you were approved."

Jennifer's eyes filled with tears which in turn spilled over onto her hallow cheeks.

"You're on the committee?" Jim asked. His expression contorted into astonishment.

"Yes." Nick stood and walked over to a shelf that held bottles of various liquids. He poured himself half a glass of rum, knowing not to offer his company any. He turned to face them both. The sunlight coming in from the window shimmered off his jet black hair. His body had been toned from years of care and early morning runs. He peered over the rim of the glass and looked at Jim and Jennifer with his soft blue eyes.

"That's the second reason why the close of the sale was requested to be moved to Friday, I had requested it. As a committee member, and after approving you," he pointed his index finger at Jennifer, "I had to move up the close; otherwise you wouldn't have been approved."

"How does that make sense? What does closing the sale have to do with the second option offered to Jennifer?"

"Jim, I can't discuss that part with you. Current privacy laws about medical care even carry over to me."

"HEPA?"

"Yes, HEPA laws. I was asked to tell you to go straight to Doctor Ellis' office when you leave here, can you do that?" Nick asked.

"Jen wanted to go to the zoo after we left," Jim turned to look at his wife, "Jen? Zoo tomorrow?"

Jennifer gave a simple nod then they left The Burns Firm to go to Doctor Ellis' office. The trip across town to the medical plaza was filled with anxiety and questions. Jim could feel Jennifer's excitement and stress.

"Jimmy? What gives? Do you think Nick and Toby are working together?"

"Nick as much as said that, since he's on the committee, but I think it is counterproductive to speculate."

"There's just so much I don't understand. If people we know, people we're this close to are involved, what can it mean?"

"I don't know any more than you do, but we'll soon have some answers." Jim let the conversation end there as he parked the van. Inside they were taken without introduction to Doctor Ellis' office. He was waiting in his office, having received a text from Nick.

Although Jennifer could not reflect it in her stride, her facial expression carried the thought, she wanted answers. Jim took a seat across from the couch and Jennifer parked next to him. Seconds had bent into minutes, or so it felt, before Doctor Ellis spoke.

"Powerful visit you had with Nick, opened more questions than it gave answers. And I know you two are full of them, questions that is." Doctor Ellis said.

Silence followed Toby's statement. Jim was tired of feeling diverted and this is where the diversion was to end. He locked his gaze, it was Toby who blinked.

"Here it is. As I mentioned, we have no expectation of approval within ten years at most and as far out as seventy. Something on a world wide scale has to change. Attitudes have to change, standards have to change. Some governments that are aware of this procedure are willing to move ahead, but they have neither the resources nor knowledge."

"So this has been proposed to other nations?" Jim cut Toby off in mid statement.

"Some, a few that the United States felt they could trust. As I was saying, many of these governments desire to move forward, but are unable. They have agreed to keep the matter confidential until the world is able to move forward. There are so many catch twenty-twos that no one has any idea where to start to untangle the mess. Even individual rights of nations have to be taken into account. It's the perfect cure, but comes with an imperfect price. But I had mentioned a second option."

Doctor Ellis stood pushing his glasses back on his nose with his forefinger as he did so. He crossed the room to a small refrigerator and took out a cold bottle of Dr. Pepper, knowing not to offer Jim or Jennifer one. Instead he removed two bottles of water and handed one to each of them. He returned to the couch twisting the cap on the Dr. Pepper releasing the hiss of trapped carbon. Tilting his head back he took in the refreshing beverage, allowing the coolness to sooth his throat. Replacing the cap he returned to the conversation.

"I know you're aware of cryogenic freezing?" Toby Ellis said.

"Yes our lab has used it to freeze embryos. We developed a method of long term storage, even to what our techs believed to be hundreds of years…Oh I now see why the sale was pushed up, the new owners wanted the technology. So the buyers are a part of the planning committee?"

"Yes, the new buyers are in fact the committee. We had no idea that the serum would be rejected for human trial. So we had to set up a second option, but it was geared more for the committee. In the beginning we never considered accepting other candidates, until you Jennifer. Jim your family has been friends with my family and that of Nick's for three or four generations, and Jennifer you're now a part of that family. It was my team that developed the serum, and we really believed it would be approved for human trials. That was the only reason we tested it on a person with leukemia. When the FDA rejected the application for stage one lab testing it was a serious setback to me and the entire committee. Which is now called the World Medical Committee, we still have no name for the serum. You two know most of the members of the World Medical Committee. Jim you went to school with most of us. So when the application was rejected for trials the World Medical Committee pushed ahead with the close of the sale for your company so we could acquire the technology to preserve the entire World Medical Committee. We know that at some point in the future the serum will be accepted, but something major has to wake up the nations to make it happen."

"Like what Toby? What has to happen worse then what the world now faces for people to accept the means for the serum?" Jim asked.

"Seriously? I don't know. A major terrorist attack worse than September eleventh, an alien invasion that cost the lives of millions but only after we defeat them, a nuclear war. My point? Something Earth wide major has to happen before the general public will let go of stubborn ideas." Toby's voice was laced with frustration.

"It can't be that serious, parents don't want to see their children die, and no one wants to see loved ones in pain, or die too early. I'm sure this would sell whatever it is; if it is presented correctly." Jim said.

"No Jim it would not. Like I said something serious has to happen to effect change. But forget that. We're here to talk of option number two for Jennifer." Doctor Ellis turned his attention to Jennifer, taking another drink of Dr. Pepper before speaking. "The World Medical Committee intends to be placed in cryo in phases, oldest to youngest. The intent is the youngest member will still be alive when the changeover starts and will be able to wake up the rest of the World Medical Committee. We never intended to include sick or dying people from this age, but you gave us reason to reconsider. As such we are opening the option up to you and other close friends and family that are ill. In order to do so we had to acquire your husband's company earlier than expected and triple the size of the storage facility. We believe at this time we have the ability to do so, even though we have exhausted many resources in the process. We also feel that you should be a part the foundation of those cured, since it was Jim's technology that pushed us ahead. So there it is that's the second option."

Nothing filled the air, no words, no sighs, and breathing was only audible if focused on. Toby picked up his Dr. Pepper and walked to a window, looking out at the late summer day. Leaves had turned brown from dryness and the ground was parched due to lack of rain. Global warming, he was sure the World Medical Committee had the answer for that as well. He imagined a world without sickness, children born disease free, and people living long enough to see their tenth generation born. He had the power to make this happen for all people, what was long considered an unreachable dream was now within the grasp of mankind.

"So I'll be frozen like a popsicle?" Jennifer broke the long silence.

"Um, what? Excuse me? I'm sorry Jennifer I was lost in thought. Please say again." Nick said.

"So I'll be frozen like a popsicle?"

"Well, ya I guess you could put it that way. Jim is fully aware of the technology, and it's safe for human use, the FDA has approved us that much."

"Toby; we only tested it on chimps, we never took it to the next level, we never tested a single human subject."

"But we *did*. I know what I'm about to tell you opens me and the entire World Medical Committee up to a lawsuit if you were to choose to do so, but given the situation, I'm electing to tell you. Since the sale of the company was going to take place, Nick released your labs proprietary technology to the World Medical Committee, using that knowledge we tested it on a human for one year. There was no residual effects, or damage to the body, brain or thought processes."

Jim felt the first tinge of betrayal, anger started to rise from the pit of his inner being.

"Jim, stop. If they didn't explore that option it would not be presented to me." Jennifer had noticed his cheeks turning red and the tension in his jaw as he grinded his teeth.

"You don't get it Jen." He turned his anger toward Doctor Ellis. "What if the experiment failed? Would your blasted WMD or WNC or World Medical Committee whatever, have gone through with the close?"

"Yes." Toby could tell the answer was not the answer Jim was expecting. "Regardless of the outcome your technology was the only reliable and stable solution as yet known to us. In time, if something had gone awry we knew we had the ability to work out the bugs, even if it meant hiring you to oversee the work."

The irony of the statement was not lost on Jim; he would have sold his company, and still managed to keep his company. He anger washed out of him.

"So the test subject, was it one and the same as the man with leukemia?" Jim asked.

"No. Justin volunteered."

"So he's on the World Medical Committee also? He was always a risk taker. I'm surprised he's still around." Jim said.

"You've been out of the loop and away from your friends more than you thought. But it's understandable."

"So then, you've told us this much. What's the ethical question?" Jim asked Toby Ellis.

"That Jim is something I'll have to take to my cryo bed. And I'm serious. You two take time to talk this over. Give it some serious consideration. Jim you have to take into account the letting go of Jennifer earlier than expected, but you can still look in via a live cam. There's a great deal for you two to hash out. Take your time; you must be sure about this. No turning back once done. Okay?"

With pleasant goodbyes the two left Doctor Ellis alone in his office. They had much to consider.

# CHAPTER 3

It was late in the evening when they arrived home, discussion would have to wait until morning. Regardless of how good she felt, Jennifer still required a certain routine to keep her alive at present. She rolled to the bathroom with Jim in tow to prepare for bed. He started the water and then seated her in the changing chair, carefully undressing and cleaning her. The two exchanged no words as he watched the water level rise. When it was deep enough he gently lowered her in and excused himself to the kitchen. There he prepared her nighttime medications along with a glass of orange juice, which he took to her bedroom. He sat in the chair next to her bed to give thought to the changes that awaited him.

His future plans had altered considerable in the span of a few hours. A few days ago he faced death at his own hand once Jennifer had passed, but now she would be gone, but still here and yet he would still be alone. It was a paradox that frightened him. Could he face a future with his beloved in it, but not in his life? Could he accept that after he died, at some future date she would be awakened in a new world, able to start a pain free life with a new husband? His mind raced with questions that no one had the answers to, questions that allowed a new form of depression to take hold. What if the new world change occurred while he was still alive, but older? Would

Jennifer accept that she was married to a man old enough to be her grandfather? The future that stood before him frightened him, and he feared for his own life, a life apart from Jennifer in a way he had never contemplated. He failed to notice his tears, as his thoughts continued to meander their way through time, a time without the two of them together. He felt pain in his chest, his heart ached at the thought that she would still be here and alive, but forever out of his reach, out of his love. He longed to see her healthy again, to see her running through the park and her sandy brown hair flowing gracefully in the wind. He desired to see her blue eyes glazed over with the joy of holding a child, their child. He ached to make love to her, if only one last time. She would have all that again, and much more, a long and full life, but without him. His tears flowed unabated, and his sobs carried to Jennifer's ears.

Jennifer felt she knew why they came. She had loved him from the day of that bold introduction under the tree in the park. Even though at ten she may not have understood what romantic love was, she understood what she felt for him at that time. She also knew from the years of him caring for her that that love was fully returned. She knew the two could never be apart, now or in the future. What was presented to her, a perfect future free of this sickness that ravaged her body, was not a future she wanted if it was apart from him. There had to be a third option, the first was not going to happen and the second was unacceptable, there had to be a third.

"Jim?" Her voice pitiful and strained as she raised it to be heard by him.

Jim sniffled and snorted the mucus back in his nose, dragging the back of his hand across his cheeks to dry the tears.

"Stop snorting, and leave the tears. I know your crying and why you're crying. Come get me out." She said.

She had only been in a short time, but what she needed to

present to her husband was more important than relieving what was now temporary pain. As he entered the bathroom he removed a towel from the warmer and draped it over the changing chair. After drying and dressing his wife for bed he carried her out of the bathroom.

"Before you give me my med's I want to express my feelings about this second option. This way you have time to consider them tonight. The FDA is too afraid to allow stage one testing and option two is just not fair, not for you now and me when they wake me up. So I want an option three." She was sitting up in bed and her body stiffened when she made the demand for a third option.

"Jennifer, there was no option three…"

"There is now Jimmy. We;" she waved her quivering finger back and forth between them; "have the final say over the sale of your company. They can't move forward without it. Forget the extra million, sign the whole thing over to them, the house and land with it."

"Woman; have you gone out of your mind. I will need – wait; what are you suggesting?"

"You get your own cryo bed. Don't sell the company to them. Appoint the World Medical Committee as trustees including the propriety technology so they can do what they need to do. Sign the deed to the house and land over to the World Medical Committee as well. They get to sell the house, land and all our worldly goods and use those resources, and the entire facility and lab as well as the technology as long as we both get a cryo bed and get to go to sleep at the same time." Jennifer had been spinning the idea since Doctor Ellis first proposed the second option; it was when she heard Jim crying that the final pieces fell together.

"Jennifer; that is the most insane loving idea you've ever had.

I don't need time to think it over. The thought of being apart from you frightens me. It frightens me in a way I've never felt. So my answer to option three is a resounding yes. I don't think the World Medical Committee will disapprove. But let's hold off until Friday to tell them. They'll all be at the close and we can tell them all at the same time. So if they have to meet in committee they are already there to meet. I love you, you perfect woman." He leaned over the bed and gave her a kiss full on the lips. She reciprocated, not having opportunity to remove the oxygen tube.

Jim returned to the chair and sat by her side until the medication took effect. Once she was in a restless sleep he took the empty glass to the kitchen and started to clean. He spent hours on the kitchen and dining area. The main living area of their home was without walls to separate the rooms. The kitchen flowed into the dining area and they both were open to the main living room area. In the past they had entertained friends, family and business partners, but in recent times it had become a collection of discarded memories. He removed the curtains from the windows and ran them through the laundry to remove the years of settled dust. While he waited he rummaged through the remaining cards, sorting them to be read to Jennifer at a later time. Instead of a graveyard full of memories, he needed to sort the contents of their home to be stored and opened at some future unknown date. It would be the largest time capsule anyone had ever assembled. Both of them would be a part of that capsule. He felt purpose in his life again; he felt life moving forward; what once was stagnating was now flowing. With the kitchen and dining area cleaned he retired to the couch, exhausted. As the clock chimed the one o'clock hour he drifted off to a restful sleep.

The seven a.m. chime woke him from a lucid dream of the future. He saw his beloved, free of the cancer that was stealing her life and in her arms their first child. They waited until they were in their two hundreds before trying, to ensure all traces of chemo had drained from her system. He saw she was happy, and the world around him was at peace with itself, being free of illness and early death. The dream ended with him and his wife sitting under their tree in the park watching their own children play, they had passed on the life they enjoyed to a new healthy disease free generation. He awoke from his dream contented, ready for what the future held.

He started the coffee and set out Jennifer's medications then turned his attention to a better breakfast. He prepared buttermilk biscuits from scratch and as they baked he set the table. Seeing it cleared and the drabness of the room removed, a family breakfast was what they both needed. The curtains remained opened to allow the entire living area to be flooded with the bright morning sunlight. He set the oven to warm and went to his wife. As every morning he bathed her and dressed her, and then he placed her in the power chair which she maneuvered to the dining room table. The table had been set with a center piece of Bachelor Buttons of blue, pink and white, and two place settings. Jim poured his wife a cup of coffee and placed it in front of where she pulled to the table. The aroma drifted up to her in puffs of steam, filling her nose. She knew he had placed it there for that purpose, and that he would hold it for her while she drank. After completing the breakfast menu of bacon and gravy he took his seat beside his wife and the two enjoyed family breakfast at their dining table again; it had not been used for such a sitting in over two years. Breakfast took longer than they were accustomed to, since he was feeding them both, but he never complained, or felt his time was not well spent. After they were done and she had taken her medications he cleared the table, loading the dishes in the washer and the two went outside on the porch to watch the day start.

As with every summer morning the air was alive with the sounds of distant people starting their day. Jim heard the same little puppy; he wondered who in this area had gotten a dog. One day before cryo he thought he would seek it out, just to see what kind it was. He looked at his wife and wondered if it was simply hope that caused her to look better, to have the look of life in her eyes again. It appeared that she was putting on weight, he would ask Doctor Ellis to weigh her the next time they were at his office. It also appeared that the shakes in her hands had stabilized somewhat, but he felt his own hope could be blinding him to a truth that what he was seeing was what he wanted to see. From the house he heard the clock chime nine.

"Did you still want to go to the zoo?" He asked.

"I would like to. I doubt I'll be able to see all the places you use to take me. But to be there, watching the children looking in at the animals. That alone is worth going." She said.

The look on her face reminded Jim of the wonder of a small child, exploring the world around her. Although, in the past, they made regular trips to the zoo, this would be their first trip in more than two years.

"Well then let's get loaded in the van. Did you want to take a picnic lunch and eat in the jungle park, or buy something once we're there?"

"We'll just get something there."

Jim helped his wife settle in the van and they left for a day at the zoo. The drive took them through downtown and across the city. Along the way abandoned stores lined the streets. Stores that once were founded on dreams and hopes now lay empty and dark. Trash cans that were placed on street corners spilled over and littered the sidewalks. As Jim drove he dodged pot holes and complained about the lack of care for the city's infrastructure. The city focused its resources on the downtown area, a fact that did not escape his notice. Skyscrapers of glass and steel appeared to reach into the clouds, reflecting sunlight back to the Earth and the concrete below.

The drive to the zoo was full of conversation and anticipation of new additions and changes that had been planned years ago. They wondered if all that was planned then had been accomplished by now. Arriving at the zoo they paid their entry fee and started their tour down the wide brown cobblestone path. All around them swirled families with children of all ages and sizes. Jennifer soaked it all in, watching with excitement as fathers pointed to different caged animals, explaining to their sons or daughters the habits of each. Not a few times she heard the question asked 'why did they keep the animals locked up in cages or exhibits'. Jennifer heard fathers and mothers attempt to explain that it was for people to see them without getting harmed. Some children expressed confusion at what they perceived to be an injustice to animals that should be allowed to roam free; some even stated they felt the animals looked sad. Jennifer had always shared those same sentiments, even when she was a young girl. It never seemed just to cage a bird that was intended to soar in the heights above. Did the caged bird sing sad songs, songs of despair? In the wild, lions roamed over miles of territory, here they had only a few acres. Did they lie around because they were depressed? Questions such as these had always plagued Jennifer, and she could hear those same questions being asked by the current generation of children now surrounding her. She felt relief that others saw the injustice of stripping animals of their freedom, only to be caged for humans to peer at. Although she felt it an injustice to cage an animal, seeing them in a zoo was the only place she and most people would ever get to see them. Others around her knew that as well and somehow that made the injustice acceptable. But it was not only the animals that drew her to the zoo; it was the interaction of children with their parents, watching the world come alive through the eyes of little children. Seeing the wonder of understanding as they learned something new about the world around them and the animals they peered at. She longed for children of her own, and regretted delaying having a child. She wanted time to bond with her husband, and that was acceptable, but she also wanted time for herself and she felt that was selfish. She and Jim had bonded and had gotten close during the first three years of their marriage, during the fourth they had started discussing children, but she opted to wait. She wanted time to explore her own desires and goals, and felt that children could come later. She never contemplated sharing her goals and desires along with a child. Only now did she look back and realize that she could have passed on all she had learned and shared with her child, desires that for a time she felt she would carry to the grave.

Now that has changed. As she watched the children flow around her chair she knew that when she woke from her deep freeze she would mother a child, a child that she could love and pass knowledge to. The two continued their tour of the zoo and when they reached The Jungle, Jim ordered and they took their food to a nearby tree to eat in the shade.

"I would hate to see their water bill. It looks so green and lush. With the drought they have to be using a lot of water." Jennifer said.

Jim opened her food and set it before her, but within his own reach.

"I think a large part of the water comes from a nearby river. We pass over sections of it on the tour path. They're not allowed to dam it up, but they can draw from it." Jim said.

He cut her food into small manageable bites and then started to unpack his own food.

"I thought that was a fake river, part of the manmade exhibit. Well – where does it start, what river is it?" She asked.

"It's the Walnut River. It feeds two lakes in the state and goes on to feed other lakes in a couple of other states. It's a big river, one of the biggest in the country."

"Ya, ya, I know the Walnut, just never realized it passed through the zoo. That explains the amount of water and how they keep it so lush here. Friday is only two days away Jimmy, are you worried about the presentation to the committee?" Jennifer asked.

Over the years he had grown accustom to the abrupt changes in conversation.

"Nope, I think they'll accept the purposed change, it saves them millions. But I don't know how they'll accept the part about me going into cryo with you." Jim said.

"They can't have one without the other. Making the World Medical Committee trustees saves them millions in purchasing the company, money they can put toward research and development, and in exchange all they have to do is freeze you along with me."

"That's how we see it Jen, but will they see it the same way? If they open up a cryo bed to me, will the wives of the World Medical Committee expect the same, or others who are not on the World Medical Committee, but are aware of the program, expect a bed?"

"I doubt that the members of the World Medical Committee are going to forgo their wives a place. As for anyone else, there has to be a limit in place. But if they do not have to pay for the company it opens that money to be used for more beds." Jennifer said.

"It all makes perfect sense to me and you, but I wonder if they'll see it the same way? Ready to head to the house?"

"Yes Jimmy, thanks for bringing me today. I really enjoyed it." Although she was exhausted, the smile on her face reinforced her words.

"Even seeing the poor little creatures caged up? I know it's the whole experience. You're welcome my love."

As they made their way to the exit Jennifer watched as new faces of excitement passed her. Children danced around parents, their voices radiating with questions about the animals kept in cages. In many cases the default answer was 'because' or 'that's the way it is' and even 'oh the animals don't mind, they have it better here in the zoo than in the wild'. She knew the answers were defacto, in many cases the parents wished they knew the real answers, but they also realized that they did not want to know the truth about the caged animals. Truth was better kept in the hands of the few, and the public told what they wanted to hear about the caged of the world.

Once her chair was secured in place, Jim helped her with the noon medications, although over an hour late, and they started the trip home in thoughtful silence. They felt they had said all that could be said in regards to the presentation Friday, and any further discussion would be pure speculation.

"Jimmy! The park. Let's stop for a bit."

"The zoo and the park? Think you may be taking in more than you can handle?" His voice pitched up when he spoke the words 'the park'.

"If I'm going to be asleep for the next fifty or so years, I want to have some fun first." She flashed him a playful smile and flicked her hand through her hair.

"You'll not even be aware of the passage of time. As soon as you close your eyes you'll open them and be free of the cancer and in a new world and time. Think of it as time travel, except plausible."

"Next thing you'll be telling me is we'll get an assignment aboard the U.S.S. Enterprise when we wake up." The laughter in her voice echoed in the tightness of the van.

"If the World Medical Committee could accomplish that – well that's just dreaming *too* big. We need to keep our feet grounded in reality when it comes to what they *are* able to do." His tone carried the weight of seriousness.

"Jim, Jimmy I was not serious. I should know better than to bring up anything to do with Star Trek. It gets you too excited, too logical. You still remind me of that twelve year old boy showing off his model of the Starship Enterprise when I went to your house for the first time. I don't believe there was a spot in your room or on your wall that did not have some sort of Star Trek display. For that I love you even more, never grow up and lose that quality."

"Lose my love for Star Trek? That World Medical Committee would have to do more than cure all diseases."

When they got to the park they made their way to their tree and Jim spread a blanket on the ground. Then he lifted her from her chair and sat her on the blanket, propping her back against the base of the tree. He found his place beside her and they passed the rest of the afternoon watching the children play.

"Why do you suppose so many of their parents let them bring smart phones and tablets to the park? Here they should play with each other and run around, free themselves of tethers to the outside world." Jennifer said.

All through the park children as young as eight were sitting at tables and on benches with smartphones or tablets. The playground equipment was occupied by children too young to be drawn in to technology.

"I was thinking the same thing. It would not surprise me if half the kids here in the park are texting the other half. I wonder if they have real life social skills." He answered.

"I can't see that they would. Everything they know about interaction with others takes place with some sort of device. Although Facebook, Twitter, Instagram and other sites like them have been useful, I think it would be better for people if they went away, or never existed. This generation of children needs to learn how to interact with each other in real life. It's such a loss, a waste of a whole generation. They have nothing of real value to contribute to the whole of human society. I think Nick and Toby were right, something serious needs to hit the Earth to wake this generation up." As she spoke she moved her head back and forth, as if saying 'no' to the technology that now surrounded her and Jim.

"I remember when I was in school. My dad bought me anything I wanted. Of course we did not have cell phones, well we did, but not like today. I did have a beeper I carried on my belt. Those kids that had them in public school were mostly drug dealers, but in Yorktown all the kids had them. It was a status symbol. My dad never wanted me to feel left out."

"We were too poor. My video game system was my imagination here at the park. I had to dream up my own dragons to slay, or – well whatever kids play on those systems. But I never knew I was without. I never felt deprived, as if my parents were holding something from me. I was always happy, more so after I met you." As she spoke she turned her head to him and smiled a sexy quirky smile.

"Ya, I did have that affect. I'm just glad you didn't shove me off that first day."

"In reality, when you had your back to me telling my mom you would give her your name and number I was begging her to take it. I thought you were cute, but I really liked your boldness. You showed no fear in front of the other girls or my mom. I wanted to get to know why."

"I'm glad you did. But I never knew that you did that. Thanks for sharing that with me. You ready to go home?" Jim stood and brushed his backside, although he was sitting on a blanket it was a reaction to sitting on the ground.

"Ya, it's been a long day and I want to turn in early. Tomorrow let's just sit around the house. No plans, no going out, just lounge around watching television or ticking off family on Facebook. I know; post on there that we tried some of those homeopathic treatments and they killed me right off."

"Jennifer! Some people believe in that pseudoscience, we can't go playing with their minds, they'll just run off to their practitioners to get a fix for that as well. Besides it would be very unkind to tell them you died, albeit funny."

Their laughter brought unwanted looks from people in the park; they ignored them and continued to laugh as they made their way to the van.

When they entered the house the clock chimed six, they had spent a longer day out than intended. Jim ran the bathwater and lowered her in, allowing the cool water to soothe her burning body. Although the burning sensation was only felt through the central nervous system, the coolness of the water seemed to help ease the pain, real or not. After he was sure she was settled he returned to the living room and set about cleaning it. He did not have enough time to finish the night before, so he took advantage of her bath time. When the clock chimed seven thirty he returned to the bathroom and then helped his wife to bed. The day's activities put her to sleep before the medications had time to take effect. He turned and took a moment to look at his wife before exiting the bedroom for the night.

In the living room he finished cleaning and took in the sight with pride. It had been over two years since the house had been this clean, and he was sure Jennifer could have done it better. But what lay before him was a task he had never done, so anything he could do was acceptable. Exhausted he poured himself a glass of iced tea and took his place on the couch to watch television.

He turned on Netflix and scrolled through the science fiction listings until he found *'Star Trek – Into Darkness'* then click play on the remote.

*"If Kahn was here and it was really that easy to cure his wife, a serum from Kahn's blood, would the world be full of Kahn's?"* He thought to himself.

He managed to make it through the movie again without falling asleep. After the final credits he turned off the television and went to his bed.

Thursday they had done just as Jennifer requested, lay around the house watching television. He pulled out the DVD set of *'Little House on the Prairie'* for her to watch. As much as he enjoyed *Star Trek*, she enjoyed *Little House*. They made the day a marathon of the old seventies show. In his opinion *The Walton's* were a much better family then the *Ingalls* could ever be. He wondered what would have happened if *The Walton's* ever met the *Ingalls*. John would kick Charles' butt. He let out a chuckle; Jennifer was too engrossed in the show to ask why. The day ended with a family dinner at the kitchen table. He was unsure how to properly cook fried chicken so he picked up a complete dinner from Kentucky Fried Chicken, and that became their late night feast. Afterword he helped his wife with the nighttime routine and they went to bed early, Friday was going to be a difficult day.

The alarm did its job Friday morning with the second most annoying sound in the world, the first being a hair dryer. He woke at six; taking extra time for himself then helped his wife get dress. They ate a light breakfast at the kitchen table, and then drove to the meeting that would forever alter their course in life. The meeting was held in the conference room at The Barns Firm on the first floor. It was intended to be convenient for Jennifer; however they also needed the largest room in the building. When Jim entered he noticed the entire World Medical Committee was waiting, Nick Barns, Toby Ellis, Emily Thomen, Justin McCloud, Steve Troy,

Daniel Walker, and Greg and Carla Watts, the only husband and wife on the committee. Toby had been correct; he had gone to school with most of the people in the room. It was the Watts' and Doctor Thomen that he did not know. He had seen Doctor Thomen on the CBS news story, and he knew the Watts' were from Germany.

"Do I need to introduce anyone to you two?" Nick asked Jim and Jennifer as they entered the room.

"Jen may not know everyone, but those that I didn't attend school with I know from other sources." Jim answered.

Nick obliged and introduced all present to Jennifer, in turn he introduced Jennifer to the assembled committee. They took their seats and two attendants handed out beverages and took orders for lunch. After they left the room it was Nick who started the meeting.

"I know we've ordered lunch, I did that hoping that a solution could be worked out quickly."

"Solution? Has something derailed the entire cryogenic freeze?" Jim asked.

"Yes; money Jim. When we spoke last I mentioned that we had put a lot of or resources into the project. Most of those resources were in the form of funds. We have to have funding to keep the facility running for the next seventy years, so what we have in the bank must stay in the bank. When we did the calculations we're coming up short to pay you for your company." Toby explained.

"So the short of it is, if we pay you what you are currently asking for the company, then we'll run short of keeping the project going, should the longer time frame need to be met." It was Emily that laid out the disparaging news.

"Jim? Tell them." Jennifer was pounding on his shoulder with her clinched fist in desperation for his attention.

"What? Do you have something we've not considered Jim." Toby turned his head back in Jennifer's direction in surprise as she attempted to get Jim's attention.

"I believe so. But it comes at a price, but not what you would expect." Jim said.

Jim explained Jennifer's idea to the World Medical Committee, making it as simple as he could. He had prepared a PowerPoint presentation along with some graphs and charts, and captured the attention of the entire committee. He was offering a cost free solution to a problem they perceived was a death blow. As he delivered the presentation he noticed members of the committee nodding their heads, a few smiles and not a few aha's. He felt he had offered a solution that could not be rejected.

"Jim that's perhaps the most ingenious solution we've had suggested." Toby said.

"Of course Toby, it does open us up to others who may want a 'ticket' as it might seem." Greg offered. His German accent punctuated his English as he formulated his words.

"Somehow we have to close the loop." Justin said.

"Jim; we could appoint you as an adviser to the committee. Not on it because we have to get presidential approval, and I just don't feel like dealing with those bureaucrats in Washington right now. We can appoint advisers, and we can attach a level of importance to those advisers. Also since you're no longer selling the company to us, but appointing the committee as trusties, then you have to be appointed as an adviser to assist us in our proceedings." Nick turned his attention to those around the table. "So we need to take a vote, and I must make it clear, the vote must be unanimous. I make a motion to appoint Jim Fuller as a level one adviser to the World Medical Committee, do I get a second."

"I second the motion." Toby said.

"All in favor say aye." Nick instructed.

Aye was returned from all committee members.

"All opposed." Nick asked for legal purposes.

Silence echoed in the room.

"The aye's have it by unanimous vote. Well that turned out to be easier than I thought it would." Nick said.

"Does this mean you get a cryo bed?" Jennifer asked her husband.

"Yes Jen it does. When we wake up in the new world I will be with you to enjoy our new cancer free life together."

With the delivery of lunch meeting was adjourned.

# CHAPTER 4

The World Medical Committee gave Jim and Jennifer two weeks to complete their final arrangements. Nick was to oversee the transfer of the trusteeship of the company to the committee as well as the transfer of deed to their home and land. Jim hired a company to pack up the items they wanted to store, forgoing asking family for help to avoid unwanted questions. During the meeting two weeks seemed to be more than enough time, in reality it was not. Along with personal family mementoes they packed the remaining unopened cards, and pieces of furniture that had been in their families and the laptop. They transferred important documents and photos to the laptop to conserve room in storage, the computer now contained the largest volume of items they intended to keep. What they decided not to keep went to auction, including the car and van. All proceeds from the sale went into their savings account along with all other liquid assets they had; money they would need to start their new life. Since Jim retained ownership of the company it would remain an asset, one he could collect on once the serum was approved.

Jim did not understand the ethical question about the approval process, but he knew it was only a matter of time before it would be approved, something that benefited all of mankind would not continually be denied. He had grown up with most of the committee members and over the years he never had reason to doubt any advice they gave him, likewise he had no misgivings about the ethical issue. He placed his entire family fortune into the hands of the World Medical Committee, and he was about to place his life and that of his wife's. This also gave him no doubts or fear, the only remaining unknown concerned politics and world conditions.

Valdemar Putin (AKA Czar Putin) of Russia was pushing his troops into Ukraine, while President Obama was pushing back with words. Putin continued to push the west by shooting down a passenger airliner as well as offering "aid" to those of eastern Ukraine. Putin secured greater control within Russia by limiting religious groups if not enacting new bans. He also created the Department of Media, a means to control all social media access and sites as well as having full access to ISP's and their subscribers. The Taliban was once again in control of Afghanistan and had established itself as a formidable power able to garner trade with other countries, including the United States, albeit though a third party. Iraq and Syria was losing ground to control of ISIS and all the blood spilled during the war was runoff in the ditches of the desert. Throughout the northern continent of Africa countries were falling due to social media; both Twitter and Facebook playing a key in the demise of Egypt, Liberia, Syria as well as several other countries. In western Africa several nations were under the grip of an outbreak of Ebola. North Korea was breathing war with South Korea with China as its backer. China feared the influx of social media and watched as other countries and powers were toppled due to free and unrestrained access. To suppress its people the government of China blocked popular social media sites and created its own, under the watchful eye of its ruler. Although the United States presented itself as a nation that respected freedom, it continued to gain greater control of the Internet through laws that 'protected' copyright content. These laws in reality restricted public access on the Internet and gathered intelligence on American's as they posted to social media. In the news, the office of the White House and Congress reassured the American public that the runaway antics of the NSA was behind them, when the fact was; language of their work had been rewritten. The entire world stage was on the verge of exit, nothing seemed stable to survive the years it would take to get the serum approved. Seventy years may well have been seven thousand years if something worldwide did not bring the human race to a stop on its path of self-destruction. With current world conditions Jim had no hope in the leaders of the world; he believed they would leave the Earth uninhabited in less than thirty years. It was a fear he kept to himself and from his wife.

Two days before they were to be placed in cryogenic freeze the two opted to go on vacation, away from their home, friends and all they knew. They took the necessary medications and drove to a cabin they had in the Cherokee Mountains. The cabin had been left to Jennifer by her grandfather. She never changed the name on the deed after she and Jim married, it was a choice they made together to leave it as it was.

August of two thousand fourteen was coming to a close and the peaks were clear of any year round snow pack. The ski resorts had closed for the last time several years back; there was never enough snowfall to attract skiers. The naysayers of global warming had long fell silent and the nations were now in a scramble to undo over one hundred years of Earthly damage. Regardless of all the other issues that humankind faced, they were losing the battle to save the planet. Jim wished the World Medical Committee had a cure for all the problems that humans face. What benefit was it to live in perfect health for nearly one thousand years if the average yearly high was ninety degrees? Perhaps, he thought, it would be better to let death take them both before they saw the only planet in the universe capable of sustaining life destroyed at the hands of man.

But for right now that was a future date that awaited another generation and another Jim and Jennifer. Here in the mountains in their cabin he was with his wife, it was to be the last two days they would spend together in the old world. If for some reason man did blow the whole thing up, he would never know, he would continue to sleep, at least from his perspective. The deck of the cabin overlooked a mountain lake that had fallen far below its normal water level. Around the edge were white marked etchings in the stone face, each displayed a new water line, leaving behind minerals as a tale of what once was. He wondered what lay at the bottom; there might be some long forgotten sunken treasures. Around the globe many remarkable finds had been discovered with the drying of rivers and lakes. Even the Mediterranean and Black Seas were surrendering secrets of civilizations no one knew existed. The oceans rise and gain more salt, while the fresh water lakes and rivers deplete leaving little for man to drink. All the sunken treasures of the world could not undo the damage man has done, the only treasure left was an end to what man is doing.

"Do you think when they wake us up all this," Jennifer waved her hand through the air suggesting the damage to the Earth "will also be fixed?"

"I was wondering that myself. I don't really see how they can undo the damage. I wonder if we'll ever wake up."

"If we don't, at least we went to sleep together, and neither one of us had to let go of the other." Jennifer said.

"True enough. But – if somehow they manage to fix the mess of this world, we'll be awakened to a new lease on life we never could've dreamed of. I want ten kids, five of each." Jim looked at Jennifer and smiled, showing his teeth, hoping her reaction would not be retaliation.

"You can want all you want. You don't have to push them out. Although I've not had to yet, I can't imagine it being easy. I mean considering." She returned his look and raised her eyebrows to allow the glare of her eyes to penetrate as deep as possible into his eyes.

Jim was grateful she restrained her response.

"Well what did you have in mind, how many?" Jim asked.

"Let's start with one and go from there. I would be happy with one perfect child."

"What if we have twins?"

"Then two perfect children. Just short cut it and make it a boy and girl combo. I do want our own children Jimmy, but not the pain with having them. You would think I would be used to pain by now." She said.

"I don't believe anyone ever gets use to pain."

"You really knew all those people on the World Medical Committee?"

Jim looked intently at his wife, his face drawn with confusion. After years of marriage and being her only source of conversation he thought he was use to the abrupt changes in topics.

"What? Before you switch subjects so abruptly, let me know. I get wordlash." Jim said.

"Wordlash, Jimmy that's not even a real word."

"It's like whiplash but with words. I didn't know everyone. Of course we both know Nick and Toby. I went to school with them as well as Justin, Steve and Daniel. Doctor Emily Thomen I didn't know but she was the one we saw on the CBS news program. Doctor's Greg and Carla Watts are from Germany, Toby told me they are specialist in epigenetics."

"Epi; what?"

"That's what I said when Toby said the word. He explained it to me and I'll try to explain it. You're aware of DNA and how it looks like a ladder with rungs in the middle. Each of those rungs has a code across it, it's the code of us, and the edges are the chromosomes, our makeup. For year's scientist thought that that was all there was, but it turns out there's more, a lot more. In epigenetics there are switches. Doctor Ellis made it simple for me. Picture a long electrical line. On each side of the line are light bulbs. The line goes on and on. Each of us has that line of bulbs that line is what determines certain behaviors, likes, and dislikes, if we have large hands and even if we are going to get cancer. Some epigeneticists even feel that mental health is predisposed as well as deviant or criminal attitudes. It's also believed that those 'bulbs' and the order they are switched on contains the memories of past relatives, like our parents and maybe even some from our grandparents."

"So they think that all information is in those bulbs? How?"

"I asked the same question, I only hope I'm getting all that Doctor Ellis said correct. But something during our development triggers certain switches to turn off or turn on certain bulbs, personally I think it sounds more like binary code, but something causes an on or off switch to flip. It's the certain combination of on and offs that make us what we are. As we make decisions in life and grow through life those choices and changes in behavior can alter the switches. Many of the switches are preset when we are born, like I mentioned, some are determined by the choices we personally make in life and still others are flipped by our environment or even outside forces. That's the field Doctor's Greg and Carla is in."

"So they must have figured out how to flip those switches manually, that must be the cure." Jennifer said.

"I don't think so Jen. If it were that easy there would be no ethics issues that are upsetting the world. I also asked Toby that. He said that is goes much deeper than flipping the switch from an on to an off position or reverse. I tried to press him but he changed the subject."

"It has to have something to do with epigenetics or those two doctors would not be on the team. What is Doctor Thomen's field?"

"The answer to that surprised me. Doctor Ellis said she is the world's leading pediatric doctor."

"WHAT! That's the craziest. Unless they need her to ensure all new children are born healthy. Well regardless it sounds like Nick and Toby pulled together the best doctors in the world. I know Justin is the best geneticist, and let me see if I can remember what Steve and Daniel do. Steve had something to do with blood, and Daniel; what did he focus on?"

"Geriatrics."

"Ya elderly people. So the World Medical Committee covers the entire spectrum of the medical field. I suppose if you intend to provide a cure for all of the sicknesses that man is dealing with, you have to cover all your bases. I hope they can work out the issues they're having." Jennifer said.

They sat in silence looking out over the dying lake, each in deep thought as to the future. Together they had arrived at some conclusions; apart they kept their fears turned inward. To express them would release them, once released they could never be retracted. Would their fears stop the other from moving forward?

*** 

"Morning, ready to get back to the city and be put to sleep?"

"Almost sounds like we're being put down, sure. Jimmy, make me look my best, so when the doctors wake me up I'll be beautiful."

"You've been and always shall be beautiful to me, you can look nothing else."

After kissing her on the forehead he carried her to the bathroom. They never made the time to equip the cabin for her limitations so he remained with her while she soaked in a tub of cool water. After dressing her they went to the table on the deck and ate a light breakfast and then made the drive into the city. They made a farewell pass by their home, and then stopped at the park, saying goodbye to their tree. Jim took his time on the drive to Fuller Laboratories.

"Here we are. You scared?" Jennifer asked.

He was bent over unlocking the wheel clamps on her chair.

"Yes, in fact I'm more afraid of waking up than going to sleep."

"Me too. But I don't want to back out. I hope the world is still here or at least a working version of what we have now." She said.

"If they don't burn the place down I'm sure something will be here. Regardless, we've run out of hope."

"That scares me the most Jimmy; we have run out of hope. It's not just us; all humans are out of hope."

"The World Medical Committee may be that new spark of hope we need. With the future we're facing now, total ruin, total damnation; I don't think the ethical question will be a question when entire world governments are facing their own end. If China, Russia, England, France or America were to face their own end I believe it would be an anything is acceptable law. I can't see the U.N. Security Council allowing an end to the world as they see it over some little ethical issue."

"What if the issue is not little? Remember Stalin, Lennon, Jackson and Hitler? What if the ethical issue is major and feared more than anything they did? What if it is greater than anything any government has proposed in the past?" Jennifer said.

"I can't see that happening. All those men you named allowed inhuman experiments on people in the name of eugenics or ethnic cleansing. Man has moved beyond that, we have grown; we're not prone to repeat mistakes of that magnitude. At least I don't believe so."

"Can you be sure Jimmy? Can you be sure that – maybe they found something in some old fallen empire in some dusty book that is the cure and maybe the fix to our problems. Remember it was the Soviet Union that invaded Berlin; the Americans let them have it as revenge for the invasion they suffered. Suppose the Russians have kept some Nazi documents hidden all this time and the cure is based on something horrible they did to people in those camps?" Jennifer said.

Jim could hear the fear and uncertainty in her voice. He too felt that the ethical question was a question of human morals, he pushed his fear aside.

"Never, never." Jim said.

"You can't say that Jimmy."

"Yes I can. Did you see one Russian on the entire World Medical Committee?"

"No, but there were two Germans." Jennifer said.

"Ouch, got me there. I still don't think it's anything like that. I think it's more modern and has something to do with tinkering with the genetics of humans, maybe before we're born. It has to be something to do with complicated genetics, otherwise why have all of those specialists? I don't think we can expect another Nazi invasion; the world is safe from that kind of ethical issue. Let's go in and go to sleep, we'll have time to worry about this in seventy years or so."

When the ramp lowered Jennifer to the ground Jim placed her crutches within arm's reach. She carefully wrapped the soft straps of one crutch around her right forearm and fastened it tightly in place. She did likewise to the left crutch. With her crutches in hand she slowly stood and started her four legged creature walk into the laboratory. When it became apparent that she would need assistance walking she had started out on crutches. Jim teased her about the stance she made, hunched over and leaning forward, he told her she looked like a strange four legged creature from an old science fiction movie. As she made her way up the ramp and into Fuller Laboratories Jim walked closely behind, his hand extended toward the small of her back, in the event she needed braced. As they approached the private entry the two glass doors pivoted open on their off center rest. Jennifer entered followed by Jim, inside the World Medical Committee was waiting.

# CHAPTER 5

The morning sun scattered shadows across the brown cobbled walks of Fuller City. The few streets remain void of vehicles since no emergencies demanded their presence. Street lamps resembling lanterns from the eighteen hundreds started to dim and turn off as they emerged from the darkness of the night. Throughout the city people came from their homes and apartments to begin their daily activities, some either biking or walking to work, others were using the elevated rail line. Some people were going to the local grocer or starting a relaxing day in leisurely pursuits. The mood of the city was relaxed and its pace slow. No one was rushing, shoving or annoyed by the presence of others. An air of peace blanketed the city and enveloped it, encasing its people and reflecting in how they treated each other. As the people of Fuller City passed each other they nodded their heads as a greeting or took the time to stop and talk. Few things distracted them as they started their day. No one could be seen with a cell phone texting or held to their ear and benches were not filled with people holding a tablet or laptop. Gone were the skyscrapers of steel and glass that towered over the city, beaming down with the bright glare of reflected sunlight. Standing in their place were buildings made of brownstone, brick or overlapping wood planks, a throwback to a past century. Unsightly billboards and flashing neon signs were nowhere to be seen. Signs of simplicity rested in windows advertising local products or letting potential customers know if a store was open or closed. A group of people waiting to board the elevated rail watched an electronic information monitor that displayed arrival and departure times to points all over the city. In the lower right hand corner of the information monitor the morning news was broadcast from the central office of the WIO, World Information Oversight. People sat on benches in front of the broadcast, those that were unable to sit stood nearby. Several people shifted position as Doctor Emily Thomen was introduced to read the morning list of names, some hoping a name they recognized would be among those mentioned. After the reading was completed the crowd resumed a relaxed stance and started sharing congratulations or mentioning if they knew someone listed. When the train arrived at the station the morning crowd quickly and orderly boarded to disappear in the distance. With the departure of the morning crowd the cobbled walks were swept clean by local store owners as they opened for the day. They swept the nightly deposit of leaves into a pile and deposited them in trash cans placed every ten feet along the city pathway. The trash cans were ornate and had an attractive charm. Heavy gloss black paint over heavy metal with hunter green etchings noting the street and nearby address, the heaviness kept them in place during gusts of wind. The cans matched the color and style of the street lamps above them. The decor of each street was similar with slight variations in colors and architecture, but they retained the same old world charm and stately appeal. The city was silent and free of the roar of traffic or cars, no horns blared to disturb the calm that permeated the city, causing tempers to flair. Fuller City had devolved and evolved into something grander than what existed in two thousand fourteen. In its prior existence it was a city full of tension, frustration, and the existence of people who rushed through their short lives. In its modern day incantation it was a city at rest, peace and full of people enjoying the moment they were in. Two blocks from Central Square was one of the oldest remaining buildings comprised of two large arched doors and massive steel and glass windows. Few buildings of this style were allowed to remain after the city transformed its image, but The Barns Firm comprised the people who redesigned and reshaped the city, therefore its demise was waved. Inside on the fourth floor the World Medical Committee members sat facing each other around a large heavy cherry table. At the head of the table was the president of the World Medical Committee and the UWN, United World Nations, Nick Barns.

"So we're all in agreement?" Nick asked.

The members of the World Medical Committee and United World Nations were all known and unchanged since their first meeting prior to the sleep of two thousand fourteen.

"Aye."

Was the unanimous reply from those present, Toby Ellis, Emily Thomen, Justin McCloud, Steve Troy, Daniel Walker, and Greg and Carla Watts. No objections were raised.

"Alright; Doctor Thomen, instruct your team to begin treatment of Jennifer Fuller. Doctor Ellis you and Doctor Greg Watts start the procedure to wake up Jim Fuller. I want Jim awakened first, I want to bring him up to date on what has happened since they were put to sleep." Nick Said.

"Be careful Nick. Too much too soon could prove too much for him to take in. Give it to him in small doses." Steve said.

"I agree, but would like to also add another caution. Withhold much of what had to be done to get past the ethical question. Before he was put to sleep we had a difficult time gaging him, if he were to learn what had to be done to bring about this world, it could be the catalyst to tear it apart. We have to play him carefully." Daniel added.

"Play him?" Carla asked. He German accent punctuated her

English.

"Yes. Feel him out slowly and methodically. After his wife is cured and awakened try to get a feel for how he feels about having her back; complete. If his feelings are, well, ecstatic we may be able to open up to him and tell him the truth, but if not we dare not expose what we had to do. This city was renamed after him, the cure was named after him, and the new world constitution was named after him. He is considered the George Washington of the new world. If we tell him too much before we know we can trust him with full knowledge; he might attempt to tell the public. The people would give a listening ear to him, even if we did stop him, some would already be tainted with his ideas if he opposes what we had to do." Daniel said.

"I hate to agree with you Daniel, but I do so reluctantly. I've known Jim my whole life and I can't see him turning a blind eye to world peace and the end to sickness and longer life spans, especially after he has his wife back in his arms, whole and well. But we'll proceed with extreme caution with the information we allow Jim access to." Nick replied.

"I think under the circumstances it's what has to be done. As far as I'm concerned there's only one man alive that can destroy this entire worldwide project and that man is currently asleep in a laboratory across town. When he wakes up he becomes the most powerful man in the world, and that makes him the most dangerous man in the world. And that's due to the fact that we gave him that power by telling this new world that it was created on his concepts, his ideas. If he becomes aware of how much power he can control, we lose control." Daniel said.

"President Jefferson never officially appointed him to this committee, he therefore has no controlling power in the United World Nations, and Jim's only an idea." Justin Said.

"And a dangerous idea, you forget Justin; the President was assassinated in twenty fifteen, the Vice President had not been briefed on the project and as a consequence was – how should I put it, replaced by judicial action requested by this committee. Before the Speaker of the House was sworn in we made him aware of the project but" Greg cleared his throat. "we never told him how we were appointed or where we get our authority to rule. We also never included that information in the United World Nations Constitution. Only those present in this room, the ruling body of the United World Nations and a few Generals in chosen military forces around the world know this body's authority. When we wake Jim up for all intents and purposes the world and the rulers of the world will believe this world, our world, is his creation, his construction. Daniel is correct; Jim will be the most dangerous person in the world once is he awakened. He can be a force for our good or he can destroy us. We must proceed with extreme caution, but we also must be ready to – remove Jim if the need should arise." Greg said.

\*\*\*

It was July fourth twenty fifteen when President Jefferson stood before thousands of gathered veterans of the first and second Iraqi wars, the first to repel the invasion of Kuwait, the second to topple Saddam Hussein. The soldiers before him were dressed in their finest uniforms, the summer sun beating down on them without mercy. Behind the President rose the dome of the Capitol with its majestic Lady of Freedom facing the city of Washington, her back to the President. Since the early part of twenty fourteen ISIS pushed toward Bagdad but was then repelled, and the shoving has continued. The sand soaking up the blood of thousands of combatants on both sides; as well as innocent men, women and children. Fear gripped the few remaining troops loyal to the government of Iraq; yet many had dropped their weapons and deserted. Over that same time period President Jefferson continued to promise American's that he would not put boots on the ground, American troops would not be sent back into the nation of Iraq. It was rumored that this speech, on July fourth twenty fifteen, to the gathered veterans of the first two wars was to solidify that promise; he was to assure the families of America that no more American's would die in the dunes of Iraq for a third time. As the first black president of the United States approached the pedestal a clasp of thunder was heard in the distance, many looked to the skies in desperate hope for rain, but knew it would lead to despair. The Secret Service moved closer to the man whose words the entire nation waited patiently to hear.

*"My fellow American's."* His words were interrupted as thunder rolled across the sky, as if canon fire once again filled the streets before the Capitol. Black clouds started to gather behind the President and Capitol, creating an ominous backdrop. *"My fellow American's, everyday ISIS is moving closer to Bagdad and everyday it is feared that the capitol of Iraq will soon fall and be in the control of extremist, a fear that will soon be realized. You who sit and stand before me have spilled your blood on that soil and many of your buddies lost their lives to gain freedom from a former dictator. We as American's, the governors of freedom, peace and the right to self-rule cannot let that happen. We who value the right for each individual and each nation to choose its own course cannot sit by while another self-imposed extremist movement forces its will on a nation that does not want it. I know I promised that I would not order troops back into combat, however..."*

For a fraction of a second the Secret Service did not move, the gunshot sounded like another roll of thunder. Many in the gathered crowd thought the President had stopped speaking to allow the echo of thunder to subside. However the President did not resume speaking but instead he reach up and grasp the podium with both hands, clinching tightly to remain standing. As the first of several Secret Service agents approached a CBS news cameraman realized what that sound of thunder was and zoomed in tight on the stage. As he did so the camera focused on the face of the President, a face etched in terror and pain. All America watched as blood trickled from the corner of the President's mouth, appearing for a moment as if he were going to continuing speaking. He reached up to wipe away the warm red liquid with the back of his sleeve and when he released his grip from the podium he fell back into the arms of an agent who lowered him to the stage floor. Linda attempted to run to his side but was covered and dropped to the ground by several other agents. She watched as her husband took his last breath while she was whisked from the platform.

The gathered soldiers recoiled at the sight of the fallen Commander in Chief; then chaos swept through the crowd as the hunt for the assassin began. Throughout the entire mall Capitol Police and Secret Service agents fanned out, many moving in the direction from which the bullet was believed to have been fired.

In the distance, from his vantage point one thousand feet away the gunman disassembled his rifle and handed the individual parts to the four men who waited behind him. When the last of the parts had been distributed the men left with their own weapons drawn and their agent identification badges hung from their necks. The gunman then pulled his own badge out from under his shirt drew his holstered weapon and assisted in the search for the assassin.

It was three weeks after the assassination when it became clear that the Vice President would not continue the World Medical Committee's project; congressional leaders who had been involved with the project from the founding waited that long before starting the proceedings of impeachment. Evidence was discovered that implicated the Vice President as taking part in the assassination of the President. During the impeachment hearings the World Medical Committee started closed door meetings with the Speaker of the House, wanting assurances that if he were sworn in as president he would continue to move forward with the World Medical Committee's project and a new form of worldwide central control. When the Speaker had sworn his allegiance to the World Medical Committee, he was sworn in as the forty fifth President of the United

States. The groundwork to ensure passage of the serum had been laid.

***

"NOW WAIT! What do you mean 'remove Jim if the need should arise'? Are you suggesting that — I can't possibly believe that you're suggesting we have to be ready to kill Jim? He's Jim." Toby said.

"That is just it Toby, *HE'S JIM*! Not if he learns the truth, but when he learns the truth, he can assert control of this body, and then move to control the United World Nations, and dissolve the entire *Fuller Lives Project*. I can't and won't allow that to happen. What is the death of one man when we are talking about saving an entire world? Why is his death any less important or more significant then what we did to achieve what we now have? Many have fallen for us to reach this point, what is one more Toby, Nick?" Daniel tried to reason with the members of the committee and help them to understand the need to protect the project, even if that meant taking the life of another.

"Daniel, Jim is different, Jim is our friend. I've known him since I started school, all my life as far as I'm concerned. I couldn't kill Jim; I could never hurt him or Jennifer." Toby replied.

"If the need arises I could, I would do it. I had known there would be issues when we got around to waking him, but I never considered the ramifications of those issues. I could 'remove' him if the need arises." Nick answered.

"My word; let's hope the need never arises, and let's hope we never have to have this conversation again." Carla's accent was heavy as her emotions reviled her distain for taking a human life.

"Daniel you go with Doctor Ellis and Doctor Thomen to wake up Jim. I'm assigning you as his shadow. You're to be a reflection of his every move until we can be certain that he can be trusted." Nick turned to Toby. "Toby; I know he's your friend, he's mine as well. But we can't sacrifice the world for one man. You know that, you helped build this world and write the United World Nations Constitution. I know Jim; he'll see things our way. His love for Jennifer will see it no other way. Chin up old man, it'll work out for the best, trust me. A while from now and we'll all be sipping white wine together again." Nick said.

"I hope you're right." Replied Toby Ellis.

***

In preparation for the awaking a four story wing was added to Fuller Laboratories. During its first stage of life it was to be used as a recovery center for those that were awakened from cryogenic sleep. In its second and succeeding stages of life it would be used for testing and recovery rooms for the Fuller Life Serum. The first floor was used for administration offices and areas for research and development. The second floor was devoted to treatment and surgical rooms. The top two floors were patient rooms, where the cryo beds were placed and self-contained life support systems were in each room. The entire facility had its own source of power that was independent from the city or other outside sources that could be tampered with or hacked. Attached to the outside wall of each room was an array of solar panels that fed into a small adjacent room full of batteries and continued a circuit to the cryo bed. If the monitoring computer detected a drop in the main power feed it redirected the flow to the bed from the storage batteries. Once the main power levels returned to normal the computer switched back to the main power source.

Each patient room was arranged in the same manner. From the door to the left was the cryo bed, above which was a monitor that displayed the life support status for the patient. Between the display and outside wall was a door that led to the power storage room, through that room you could enter the next patient room which was a mirror image. Across from the bed was a built-in storage unit for personal items and bedding. A small bathroom was between the unit and opposite outside wall.

A glass wall separated the room from the main hallway, for privacy the glass could be tinted with the wave of a gesture. Display monitors were embedded in the glass wall near the door. From the monitor medical personal could alter room temperature, monitor life support and alter the settings of the cryo bed. As with the tint in the glass, the display responded to specific hand gestures. The hallways of Fuller Laboratories were wide, bright and spacious. The floors were covered with a white sheet of a non-porous semi-glass translucent substance. The same material comprised the walls but each section of each floor was embedded with a different color, from which soft amber light emitted. It gave the appearance of a translucent glow of many subtle hues. Embedded within the walls and floor were tracking devices that were in constant sync with the identification badges worn by everyone working at Fuller Laboratories. The Central System, developed by Hewlett Packard, monitored all personnel as they entered, went about their activities and at the end of their shift exited the building. In the event a person attempted to access areas they were not allowed the computer stopped their progress by locking all doors in their path and alerting security.

As Doctor's Ellis, Thomen and Daniel walked down the hall a light pastel blue emitted from the wall, casting it colorful hue throughout the north end of the fourth floor. The three came to a stop outside of room number forty eight. Doctor Ellis and Doctor Thomen stood for a moment watching the information as it displayed on the embedded monitor outside of Jim's room. Doctor Ellis made a gesture which altered the readings that were synced to the Android tablet that Doctor Thomen held. A few minutes after each gesture the life support readings altered. As the cryo bed temperature increased the room temperature adjusted so it would be comfortable when Jim finally woke. While Doctor Ellis continued to alter the cryo bed Doctor Thomen monitored Jim's life signs. Slowly his heart rate increased as well as his core body temperature. The process continued over the next thirty minutes.

"Where we at?" Doctor Ellis asked.

"Body temp holding at ninety eight, respirations at sixty, heart rate at seventy five bpm. He's ready." Doctor Thomen replied.

Daniel made a half circle hand gesture in front of the glass door which then slid effortlessly on a track offset and behind the glass wall. He walked through followed by the other doctors. The room temperature still had a chill but the opening of the door would allow a quicker warming transition.

"Twenty cc's of FLS."

Before breaking the seal of the cryo bed Doctor Ellis injected the Fuller Life Serum into the IV that fed into the sealed bed and then into Jim's arm. The doctors turned their attention to the monitor above the bed, watching the readout with familiar anticipation.

*"Heart rate eighty five beats per minute and rising; core body temperature one hundred degrees and rising; respirations eighty two and rising."* The soft spoken female voice stated from the speakers embedded in the wall next to the display.

Doctor Thomen gestured in front of the display and the monitoring voice muted. Through the glass of the cryo bed the three committee members could see Jim's cheek's twitch and his eyes start to move rapidly back and forth. He went into a state of REM.

"He appears to be ready for the future." Doctor Ellis stated.

"But is this future ready for him? Precede doctors." Daniel

instructed.

Doctor Ellis held two fingers together and made a half moon gesture in front of the display, the room was instantly filled with the hiss of escaping air and fog as it exited the cryo bed and drifted to the floor. The computers preprogrammed settings increased the room temperature to eighty degrees; it would assist Jim from shivering. The lid to the cryo bed continued to slide down along the length of the bed until Jim was exposed to his knees.

"Grab him a robe from the closet if you don't mind Daniel." Doctor Ellis said.

Daniel walked to the closet, removed a robe and quickly returned to stand next to Doctor Ellis. The World Medical Committee members watched as Jim's eyelids fluttered and then opened, the computer dimmed the lighting to an ambient setting.

"How, how, how long?" Jim's teeth chattered as he clinched his jaw.

"How long since you were put to sleep?" Toby knew that's what Jim was referring to, however as part of the wake up routine the patient was always asked questions to gage their processing abilities.

Jim shook his head up and down, indicating yes.

"You were put to sleep in late August two thousand fourteen, this is twenty eighty." Again instead of giving the answer in years asleep it was presented in dates, to allow the patient to process the difference.

"Sixty six years?" Jim replied as a question still chattering his teeth.

"Yes Jim; sixty six years. Here put this on." Daniel extended the robe to him.

Jim started to rise from the bed but was suddenly slowed by a hand on his shoulder.

"Slow old friend. Don't move too fast. Let the blood fill your veins a little at a time. Too fast and it will cause problems." Toby said.

Jim used deliberate force to slow down. In his heart he wanted to bolt from the bed and find his beloved and embrace her now perfect body. When he reached a full sitting position he remained sitting for five minutes, it was preprogrammed to prevent a rushed departure from the cryo bed. When five minutes elapsed the side of the bed near his waist slid down and disappeared into a recess enclosed in the bed itself. He bent his legs toward him then lowered his feet to the floor. When his feet made contact with the floor he quickly recoiled, he felt as if he stepped on a bed of needles.

"It'll pass in a minute or two. Your nervous system is firing back up. The pressure of the floor against your feet over loaded it." Doctor Thomen explained.

"Will it be like that with everything I touch?"

"The first few touches with each part of your skin, including when you slip on the robe, you'll feel it on every part it touches." Doctor Thomen added.

Again Jim placed his feet on the floor and forced himself to keep them there until the needle pricking sensation passed. When he was sure it had he pushed himself up with the palms of his hands, feeling the needle sticks in them as well. He forced the pain from his mind. As he stood he staggered and swayed but retained his balance. When the doctors woke the first few patients they assisted in stabilizing them, which turned out to cause a delay in awaking the nervous system. Realizing their mistake they allowed the patient's own inner ear balancing system to do its job.

"Woozy." Jim said. "Let me guess it'll pass."

Toby smiled at him. Jim took a few steps forward then turned left, stopped turned around then turned right. When he came to a stop a second time he was standing in front of Daniel who still had the robe in hand.

"Turn around let me help you put it on." Daniel offered.

"Thanks, but I'll do it. If what Doctor Thomen said is true I want my system fully functional before we go to Jen's room. We're going there next right?" Jim tied the front of the robe covering his nude body and then turned to face the three doctors.

"We need to talk about that..." Toby started.

"Don't tell me something happened, I can't..." Jim's voice quivered and he knew if he could shed tears they would be flowing down his cheeks.

"NO! NO! Nothing like that, no Jim. I'm sorry, I should have thought before I opened my mouth. Come on let's go. We have a receiving area for new Wakes. You'll be given a special protein mixture to drink to restart your digestive system. We can talk there." Toby put his arm around Jim's shoulder and took the lead in escorting him to the receiving area.

As the four exited the room something caught Jim's attention. He stopped and turned around and watched as a panel in the wall slid up and a small machine rolled out of a nesting bin and into Jim's room. The room became filled with a bright light and a mist emitted from the machine and covered every part of the room, even reaching the crevices. When the misting stopped a hissing sound followed that spilled over into the hallway. When that cycle was completed the machine exited and returned to its nesting bin.

"What in the world was that?' Jim asked.

"It's a sterile bot. We call them S-Bot's. When a patient exits a room for the last time the S-Bot enters and sterilizes everything that remains." Doctor Thomen said.

"Won't the computer get damaged or the cryo bed? What about the wood and clothing?" Jim asked.

"The displays are a part of the wall, embedded in the wall. There's no exposed electrical or outlets; power is wireless. There's no wood either it's simulated, so no damage. Now that the S-Bot is done the cleanup crew will enter and remove that unneeded items and prepare the room for its next intended use." Toby explained.

Jim dragged his hand through his hair, stopping midway and rubbing it in disbelief.

"If that surprises you, prepare to be amazed. Welcome to the year twenty eighty." Daniel said

"I hope I'm ready."

The committee members gave each other a knowing smile and continued to escort Jim to the receiving area. The room held to the same décor as the rest of the wing. The floor retained its translucent white and emitted the same white glow as it did throughout the facility, but the walls turned to a soft hue of emerald green as they approached the receiving area. The translucent emerald green continued into the receiving room which was vacant except for two tables with four chairs each at its center and a small section with four cushioned chairs in one corner. Toby made his way across the room and took a seat in one of the four cushioned chairs, the others followed. Although Jim still showed concern for his wife the anxiety had subsided, the emerald green hue was having the desired effect. After they were seated a nurse approached and handed Jim a large glass with a milky colored substance. As he took the glass from her he gave Toby a puzzled look.

"The protein drink I mentioned earlier. Of course it has other needed nutrients and electrolytes to assist in your body's ability to 'wake up'." Toby explained.

Jim cautiously took a sip, dragging his tongue across his upper lip as he pulled the glass away. It was not chalky or gritty as he expected, but smooth and tasted like a vanilla milkshake.

"Not bad. So about Jen?" Jim asked.

"Yes. She's fine and we have started her treatment to remove the cancer, but it will be ninety days before we can start her wake cycle." Doctor Thomen said.

Jim squeezed his eyebrows together, drawing them toward his nose, twisting his face into confusion. Before he could ask the question Doctor Ellis responded.

"You had no terminal illnesses so we could wake you up in one complete cycle. Prior to waking you we administered the Fuller Life Serum, but only as a means to start your body's process of DNA and cellular rebuilding. Since there was nothing life threatening to reverse there was not need to keep you in cryo. Jennifer's cancer has to be reversed slowly, and cured before we wake her. Unfortunately we learned this mistake the hard way, and it took three times before we realized what we were doing wrong. Jennifer will be our twentieth patient to awaken from a terminal illness, so she's not a lab rat, so to speak." Doctor Ellis said.

"Ninety days. That's a long time alone. You named the serum after me?" Jim asked.

"Yes it seemed the appropriate thing to do, after all without your donation to the project and making the World Medical Committee trusties of Fuller Laboratories this new world would not have been possible. As for the ninety days, look at it as time to get assimilated into the new world and new expectations. Much has changed, the entire world has changed. It will also allow time for you to get set up in your new home and learn your way around" Toby paused and glanced at Daniel who gave a nod of approval. "Fuller City."

"You renamed the city after me? Why?" Jim asked.

"As Doctor Ellis mentioned a lot has changed Jim, a lot. Much of the city was – destroyed and rebuilt in the aftermath of the events of late twenty fifteen and through two thousand twenty two. When the rebuilding started it was decided to rename the town after you. As was mentioned, if not for you this new world would not be here." Daniel was careful to control the information given to Jim.

"Was there a war?" Jim asked.

"Time for that later. You'll have three months to catch up before Jennifer is awakened, and then you'll have a lot of information to share with her. Let's get you fitted with some clothes and then I'll give you a ride to your new home." Toby said as he stood.

"Doctor Thomen would you escort Jim to the fitting area and then I'll meet you downstairs?"

"Sure Doctor Ellis. Jim; please follow me."

Daniel waited until Doctor Thomen and Jim exited the room and was several paces down the hall before turning his attention to Toby. Toby extended his arm and held the palm of his hand toward Daniel.

"No need; I know what you're going to say." Toby stated before Daniel could speak.

"I know you know. Also keep in mind that all conversations in public and in private are monitored, and we'll know if you attempt to take him to a secluded place." Daniel reminded Toby.

"Daniel although he's my best friend and I've known him most of my life I have no intention to betray my loyalty to the United World Nations and more importantly to the World Medical Committee. I don't want to see Jim disposed of, but if I feel he's a threat I'll be the first to expose that threat. I don't believe one man can bring down what we've achieved, but I do believe that Jim can cause a great deal of harm to us and the world in general. My loyalty is without question." Toby said.

"I don't doubt you Toby, but make sure it stays without question. Anyone and I mean anyone that attempts to harm or betray the World Medical Committee or the United World Nations will be disposed of. I mean anyone." Daniel locked his eyes with Toby's as he stressed the last statement.

"I understand. But as I said, my loyalty is without question." With that Toby exited the receiving area and made his way to the elevators.

Daniel stayed behind and called Nick to update him on the current status of Jim, and Toby.

# CHAPTER 6

Toby and Jim exited Fuller Laboratories into the busy walkways of Fuller City. He turned right toward Central Square and indicated for Jim to follow by a gentle tug on his elbow. They started the six block journey walking down clean brown cobblestone pathways to an apartment that had been prepared for Jim and Jennifer. Over the past sixty six years the city had changed its look and feel, and as they walked Jim took in the changes as would a small boy. The air was filled with muffled talk, people stopping and greeting one another or catching up on the events of their lives, but no on yelled or raised their voice. The walkways were clean and free of clutter, not even a cigarette butt could be seen in the crevices. The people they passed were not smoking nor did anyone smell of cigarette smoke. Jim titled his head back to look up into the sky and noticed its deep blue appearance, no haze or brown filter to block the bright yellow sun. The buildings around him did not tower to the clouds and none was taller than four stories. When Jim turned his attention back to the people around him he realized no one had a cell phone or tablet, he now understood why a low chatter filled the air, people were talking face to face. They had covered a distance of three blocks when it dawned on Jim they had not crossed a street or seen a car.

"Toby?"

"Yes Jim."

"Where are the cars?"

"And so it begins. I was wondering how far we would get before you started with the questions. Cars? Let me think just how to explain this. The Transition Period was a difficult time for the United States, in fact the entire world. It started in twenty fifteen with the assassination of President Jefferson. For the next several months the American government was in chaos, the succession of powers failed to be smooth. The Vice President tried to enact dictatorial powers, and in so doing it was discovered he was behind the assassination of the President. Congress started the impeachment process, but the bureaucrats were moving too slow. The Justice Department went ahead and charged the Vice President with murder and soon thereafter the Speaker of the House, Turner, was sworn in." Toby paused to allow what he said time to sink in. As they approached a bench Toby gestured for Jim to sit down.

"This is getting to my question about cars?" Jim asked.

"Yes; I wanted to explain how The Transition Period started. Without knowing that bit of history, trying to explain the answer to your question would be too difficult."

"Then continue." Jim said.

"After the Speaker of the House was sworn in as President the chaos settled quickly, but America was hit with a new chaos. As you may remember before you were put into cryo the weather due to global warming was spiraling out of control, extremely severe hurricanes, tornados, earthquakes and tsunamis, many of these taking place in areas that had never seen such weather. As more of the ice at the polar caps melted the weather continued to get more violent. By late twenty sixteen the United States and other countries could no longer deny the cause of the severe weather patterns. The nations turned to the UN for answers. A special committee was ordered to look for solutions; President Turner was aware of the Fuller Life Project and the World Medical Committee and he purposed that the World Medical Committee oversee the project. We, the World Medical Committee, already had a plan in place and Nick addressed the assembled nations at the UN. No one, no nation liked the presentation or the solution, well the first phase of the solution, but it was adopted."

"First phase of the solution?" Jim placed his hand on Toby's knee to draw his attention when he asked the question.

"We could not present all of our proposals to the United Nations at that time, too radical and it would never have been adopted. What needed to be done had to be presented in small doses or phases. The first phase was to stop the out of control effects of global warming."

"All this global warming stuff has to do with the approval of the Fuller Life Serum? I thought the serum was the only purpose of the committee. Not the science of global warming." Jim said.

"Let's stay on topic Jim. All this will lead to a complete understanding, but in due time."

"You're dosing it out to me little by little? Aren't you?" Jim felt like a child sitting in a classroom listening to a teacher giving step by step instructions to a math problem. He shifted his position on the bench, crossing and then uncrossing his legs.

"Yes I am. That first proposal Nick presented was for the elimination of cars, worldwide."

"A little at a time of course, right?" Jim asked.

"No. Every step, every phase had to be radical and severe.

People in every nation had to turn in their cars for recycle the day after the proposal was adopted. Not all nations agreed of course, but I'll get to that at a later time. The five nations making up the Security Council did agree, two were reluctant but saw no other way. The car manufactures either had to switch to making electric cars or scrap their company, GM, Ford, and Chrysler did not survive. Their boards did not believe the United States would ever let them falter and they failed to accept the new guidelines. Today the leading car manufacture is Tesla, there are some smaller companies, but Tesla is the worldwide distributor of cars for personal use. Until a complete world change took place the governments and military of the world still used combustion vehicles. Manufacturing plants also had to make serious changes."

"So why don't I see any or streets?" Jim asked.

From what Toby had just explained, if some people had personal electric cars then where were the streets on which to drive them? Not everything he was hearing from Toby was in agreement with what he was seeing.

"As part of understanding the effects of global warming the proposal explained that paved or concreted streets contributed greatly to the warming of the planet. Pavement itself was toxic to the environment, and it absorbed heat that was transferred to the ground as well as reflected back into the atmosphere. It took some time to figure out a solution that the five Security Council Nations could agree on, but in time they did and most other nations accepted that decision. The major Interstate system in the United States was kept, and one single major highway to larger connecting cities. Similar highway structures in other nations were kept. Smaller rural highways were scraped up and the pavement recycled. Streets within cities were also scraped up and recycled. Electric elevated rail systems were built to transport people over long distances, for local travel we walk or use bikes, some use electric bikes."

Toby continued to explain the transition the world made away from combustion engines and factories to wind and electric generated power. He explained that with the elimination of combustion engines and coal production the global mean temperature of the Earth started to drop, allowing the planet to start to cool. A worldwide funding project was created to educate people about waste and the absolute need to recycle; it was part of The Transition Period. In the beginning of The Transition many people fought the requirements, but as Toby explained, an incentive program was adopted that motivated people to accept change. With the education and incentive programs in place the worldwide Transition was quickly adopted and when people changed the world changed.

"It all sounds noble, but producing electric modes of transportation creates carbon waste." Jim said.

"In the past that would have been true. But the nations always had the means to clean up production but did not implement those changes due to cost. The Transition Period eliminated the cost factor, the world had to change or it would die. There was no longer any choice in the matter."

"Well it seems to have worked and I don't see that people are upset about not having a personal car. But I've noticed no one has a cell phone or tablet, why?" Jim said.

"Not all at once Jim, we have to dose this out little by little as you mentioned. Too much too soon will cause some confusion. You need to absorb your surroundings a little at a time."

Jim hung his head and sighed, he knew Toby was right, but he wanted to know more about The Transition Period and what event took place worldwide that forced people to accept changes that they never would otherwise. Jim decided once he was settled in his new apartment he would research the changes on his own through the Internet.

"Okay; I understand. Is the park still there?"

"Yep, but with a few changes. Let's walk over there." Toby stood and waited for Jim. As they walked they kept their pace leisurely.

Toby continued to explain some of the minor changes in society as they walked to the park. In the decades since The Transition Period people had to relearn how to interact on a social level. What was once considered normal behavior, talking face to face, had become an unknown skill to most. Since the reestablishment of personal social skills violent crime steadily declined until it was eliminated. People getting to know each other on a personal level had other effects as well, kindness and a willingness to consider others first started to spread worldwide, that in turn affected change in acts of barbaric terrorism. The school system in the United States regressed back to focus on life skills and physical interaction, which in turn eliminated the need for mind altering drugs to keep restless children seated for six hours a day. In other nations the schools were open to all people, boys as well as girls, and opportunities were withheld from none.

"No offense; but the world sounds like a Utopian Society." Jim said.

"Not Utopia; reality." Toby said.

As their conversation continued Jim became more intrigued and he asked more questions; questions that Toby deflected to another time, another conversation. Jim's own suspicions from the evasive maneuvers that Toby used continued to grow. Although he knew the World Medical Committee was capable of many things, he felt they were not able to affect worldwide change. But he also remembered before being put into cryo that the World Medical

Committee had continued to state that something dramatic would need to happen before the world would accept the ethical questions surrounding the Fuller Life Serum. Was the World Medical Committee capable of creating a worldwide situation that forced people to accept changes they did not want to accept? Jim's mind started to create scenarios; scenarios that were haunting and disturbing; he shook them from his mind and turned his focus back to the conversation with Toby.

"Reality, that from my point of view seems to be fantasy. I don't know Toby; it all seems too rich, too perfect."

"Nothing is perfect, this world is not perfect. What we as the World Medical Committee and the United World Nations have achieved is not perfect, but it's not far from it, in my opinion."

"And the cost Toby? What price did the people of Earth sixty six years ago have to pay for the world around us today?"

"Well here it is your park." Toby waved his hand in the direction of the park, a gesture meant to deflect Jim's question.

Jim noticed the arched sign above the entry, *'Fuller Park'*.

"They named the park after me?" Jim asked.

"Well, you and Jennifer. Jim, if you had not appointed the World Medical Committee as trustees back in twenty fourteen this world would never have come to be a reality. Although it took millions of hands to build it, it was one man who designed it. Once you and Jennifer were put to sleep the World Medical Committee went to work on getting the serum approved and for the first few years of The Transition Period we put all of our financial resources into the project. If we had paid you for Fuller Labs we would never have succeeded. Your single contribution set into motion the changes you see around you, those within your body and the changes you're not aware of throughout the entire world. So in every nation and in every city there's something named after you, a park, school, an art institute, something. You're the hero of the world."

"I don't believe I can carry that burden." Jim said.

"Not a burden Jim, an honor."

Jim looked at Toby and pulled his eyes together to challenge the statement. He did not feel honored and it did not feel right to accept any honors based on his limited knowledge of this new world.

"I doubt our tree is still standing." Jim said.

"It died long ago. The Earth's temperature had risen too high before we implemented serious change and much of the vegetation died off. When we got the temperature back under control a worldwide re-planting campaign was started. It took several decades before some trees and plants got a strong foothold. Where your tree once stood, now stands a monument to you and Jennifer. Part of the monument has an overhang to create shade as your tree once did. Not the same, but it's permanent."

"Well, until the next Transition Period." Jim said.

"Next Transition Period? There won't be another." Toby repositioned his body to face Jim, both in a stance of defense and to challenge.

"Toby, if history has taught us anything it's that mankind is never happy with what they have. They always want more and change is the path they take. Either slow or forced, change is inevitable."

Toby stepped through the arch to be followed by Jim, once inside the park they continued walking side by side down the cobblestone pathway.

"With the Fuller Life Serum I don't believe we'll ever see that kind of change again. The ruling body of the planet will remain the same for hundreds of years. When a member of the ruling body is reaching the end of their ability to rejuvenate a new member will be appointed, decades if not a hundred years in advance. That new member will be groomed and their thinking altered to keep things the way they are. I can't ever see the day that what we've achieved will be done away with." Toby's voice carried in it the assurance and conviction of his statement.

His words caused fear in Jim. Fear that the world he woke up to had been forced upon the people of Earth without their consent or ability to have a part in the decision making process. Was it possible that a ruling body could act as a dictator? Was the World Medical Committee that dictator presenting itself as a savior to the world? Again Jim shook the thoughts from his mind. He had very little information to form opinions and to do so with what little he had could lead to tunnel vision. As he learned more facts his mind would force those facts into a preconceived idea. He had to exercise caution if he wanted to arrive at the correct conclusion.

As they walked through the park Jim noticed it too had changed. The first notable change was the lack of trash on the ground. In every direction Jim looked the grass was well manicured and beds of flowers were clean and free of footprints. In twenty fourteen people intentionally trampled the flowerbeds so the city stopped caring for them, but now, in this future the park was a park, and it was beautiful. Trees of different species had been planted in such a manner that it created a forest effect but room had been left to enjoy the park. In the center was a wide open space of grass allowing people to play sports or enjoy other related activities. Walkways of cobblestones made their way in and out of trees inviting people to walk at their leisure. To the far right where once stood a large maple tree stood a monument of gray granite in the shape of a tree with a woman sitting at it base and a man leaning against its trunk.

"Beautiful isn't it?" Toby asked.

"What part?"

"All of it of course. But I notice you're locked on the monument." Toby said.

Jim started walking down the brown cobblestone path toward the monument, as he got closer he could see the faces of the man and woman, it was Jennifer and himself as they were in a time long in the past. At the feet of the granite monument was a plaque.

*"From the depths of despair rises the hope of all mankind."*

Jim allowed a tear to fall from his eye as he reflected to a past that he knew would never be again.

"Does the world really believe this?" Jim turned his upper body to face Toby, puzzlement etched on his face, disbelief evident in his tone.

"We all do. I don't think you'll ever realize what your final decision did for the world. The World Medical Committee had a plan; we had the cure, but not the financial means to carry it out. We thought after buying your company we could get financial backing from investors, but it was during The Transition Period that we realized no one would have touched us or helped us. If you had not done what you did nothing would be like it is today, and it's likely that you and Jennifer would be dead. Mankind was on the brink of world war as it was. Your decision stopped what might have escalated into World War Three. History has overlooked the right decisions of one single person and focused on the bad decisions of one single person. For example Hitler, one person making bad decisions, no one stopped him, but we all remember him. Suppose one single person, his art teacher had praised his talent and nurtured it and when the world heard the name Adolf Hitler the first though we would have is of a great artist. That art teacher's act would not be remembered because we would never have known Hitler for what he did become. This time we didn't want history to forget what one single act of right could do. Because of your selfless act of kindness millions have followed and history will never forget that one man can cause worldwide good."

"That's too much Toby. I only intended to help me and Jen. My act, my decision was not aimed at benefiting the world; helping other people was an unintended consequence. I wanted me and Jennifer back together; I wanted the cancer out of her body. My act was selfish to the extreme. My act was only about me and my wife." Jim desperately wanted Toby to believe him and it carried in his expression.

"True enough at – that – time. But because you did choose to do what you did, the whole world benefited. At the time it *was* about you and your wife. But now Jim, today it's about the whole world. And in case you've forgotten you still own Fuller Labs, you still have the controlling voice in how it's used as well as the Fuller Life Serum and it's patented by your lab. Your act in twenty fourteen may have been selfish but how you act now, today will be the true reflection of that monument and that statement at the feet of that man leaning against that tree. As you learn more about this world you'll need to ask yourself, is that granite man you today or are you still the selfish man you were sixty six years ago?"

"Toby; I believe you and the World Medical Committee have made me out to be more than I am. I'm not the granite man standing before us. I'm a selfish, self-centered, greedy man who only wanted his wife back, well and whole. I could care less about the people of the world or global warming."

"Then, in twenty fourteen, I agree. But now in twenty eighty you have the opportunity to become a great man, to be the man that the world looks to."

"The image of the man that the World Medical Committee created and taught the world to believe in? I don't know Toby, it's a lot to take in and you keep telling me there's even more to take in. I'm not sure I can."

"You just woke up from a sixty six yearlong nap, you're tired. Let me walk you home, get you settled in and you take time to adjust at your own pace."

Toby placed his arm around Jim's shoulders and escorted him back to the brown cobblestone walkway that led to Central Square. The two walked at a slow leisure pace with no conversation. As they walked Jim continued to take in the new sights of Fuller City. The lack of personal technology bothered Jim and in his mind he again attempted to reason why people were without cell phones or tablets. As before Jim shook off the dark thoughts that started to form.

The court house and city offices sat around the square in twenty fourteen, as they approached where they once stood, Jim noticed those buildings we no longer present. In their place stood an open square four story building edged with a brown cobblestone path. At the midway point on all four sides were arched openings that led to the center. Inside was a large open wooded park. The apartment building was made of brownstone with wide whitewashed stone trim and steps to match. Two windows were between each apartment door; the tops of which matched the archways that led into the park. The roof of the building was red overlapping curved tiles that hung over the edge providing some protection from the rain.

The park inside had pathways of brown cobblestone that meandered its way through flowers and thick stands of trees. At one end of the park was a swimming area that matched the natural wooded theme. Its appearance was that of a small natural lake. The apartment complex bordered the park from all four sides, and each apartment had an open deck and private access to the park.

As Jim and Toby walked through the park's pathways Jim noticed the calmness that prevailed among the residents. He looked for trash but saw none, not even a cigarette butt. As with the other areas of the city no one was seen smoking or with a cell phone or tablet. He did not mind the lack of smokers, but as before the lack of personal technology bothered him. Toby led Jim to two chairs under a large maple.

"Think Jennifer will like this as her new tree and sitting place?" Toby asked.

"It's nice, I think she'll approve." Jim said.

"See that corner apartment to your right on the fourth floor." Toby said pointing to the inside corner of the building. "That's yours, ready to go have a look?"

"In just a minute. Toby I mentioned this before. I've not seen anyone with a cell phone or tablet and don't think this odd, but no smokers. I don't mind the lack of smokers, but the lack of personal technology has me concerned."

"Smoking was done away with during The Transition Period, worldwide. It was the one issue no nation disagreed with. Smoking was a burden on all tax payers and the cost to nations in the form of heath care made it one of the most agreeable items we presented. All mind altering drugs were also done away with, including so call prescription drugs that altered a person's state of mind. In fact the entire field of pseudo-psychology was eliminated. There are also few medical doctors left, simply no need for them. Around the cities are small clinics for injuries and accidents, but no one has been sick since the Fuller Life Serum was introduced. Smokers and people who used drugs were seen as a cancer on society. They were given time to reform and incentives were offered to them. Many did reform, but a few did not."

"What happened to those that did not reform?" Jim asked.

"They were allowed to continue killing themselves, but in a manner that did not bring harm to others. It was their choice to continue, the people they smoked around had no choice, so in a manner of speaking we gave the non-smokers a choice by removing the smokers to a location that allowed them to continue but without harming others. Non-smoking family members were given the option of going or staying in their homes. No non-smokers went; many did not when they realized that they could not take their children. Children had no say whatsoever to breathe in the smoke of their parents, so the World Medical Committee became the voice of children."

"Okay that explains the lack of smokers, but what about the lack of cell phones or other personal technology?"

"How about we go check out your apartment. We put you and Jennifer right on Central Square and the World Medical Committee planted this tree for her. As for the apartment, it's one of the best in the city. Thus far we've kept your awaking time unknown as well as the location of your residence. However when the citizens learn that you're awake and where you live expect a lot of visitors. Let's go." Again he ignored Jim's question about personal technology and diverted his attention to the apartment.

"Toby?"

"Jim there'll be plenty of time for learning the details later. Right now you need to see your new home and get things ready for Jennifer's arrival. You know Jim; you two will be able to start a family now."

The family statement caught Jim off guard and distracted him for pursuing the question of personal technology, the effect Toby was hoping for. Jim allowed his mind to entertain the idea of bringing his child to the park, watching him play in the fields, trees and pool. In his mind's eye he saw the face of his wife as she held their child to her breast; her face lit with overwhelming joy and delight.

From the ground floor there were three ways to gain access to the upper levels. Stairs, elevator, or a gentle low incline ramp that made a continuous curve until it reached the fourth floor. Without the need for handicap services the ramp was a means of ease. The floor of the hallway was made of the same translucent material that was in Fuller Laboratories, it too emitted a low white ambient light. The walls were also translucent and each floor emitted a different hue, the fourth floor was a soft pastel powder blue. Embedded in the structure of the wall outside each door was the name and number of the resident, as well as a status indicator to let visitors know if the tenant was home, if they were not, a V-Message could be recorded. When they approached the door the panel next to apartment four twelve lit up.

*"Welcome home Jim Fuller."* A female voice from the panel greeted.

The door turned from a solid white translucent color to transparent, it then slid open to be concealed inside the wall. Before Jim realized it he was standing in the entry hall of his new home.

"I said; what do you think." Toby repeated.

"Sorry I must have been day dreaming. It looks great. More room than it looks from outside."

"No doubt day dreaming about Jennifer and your new child. This apartment was built exclusively for you and Jennifer. Let me show you around."

The right side of the entry hall was also of translucent glass, it appeared black from the outside but was transparent from the inside. It provided a view of the wooded park below. The hall exited to the kitchen and living area. The living area was on the left with the kitchen to the right. The floor in the living area was comprised of a translucent faux wood; it gave the appearance and feel of a hardwood floor, but also emitted a soft ambient light brown light. The far wall was centered by a sandstone faced fireplace that contained a faux fire. The wing walls to each side were of the same composite as the flooring. Overhead no center lighting dominated the ceiling; instead a clear panel six inches across topped the wall. Part of the panel faced the outside and allowed light inside the room, the rest of the panel contained a series of mirrors that continued to refract the natural light until it filled the room by day. Throughout the day a series of batteries was charged by the natural lighting and at night a soft white ambient light was emitted from the panels. The amount of lighting never altered from morning till night. The kitchen floor had the appearance of river stone tiles, but they also emitted the same hue of lighting that the living area floor emitted. In the area between the living area and kitchen work bar was a table that seated six. It was made of cherry as were the chairs and the padded inlaid cushions were a deep blood red with gold etchings. The back splash around the counter was the same material as the floor and the cabinets were of cherry wood. The same décor was maintained throughout the apartment, which had two bedrooms that shared a joined bathroom and a master suite. The master bedroom had the same flooring as the living area and the same ambient lighting around the ceiling; it flowed into the master bathroom. The floor and walls of the master bathroom were of river stone and in a corner to the left was an open shower. To the right were two recessed rooms to allow for privacy with toilets. To the right of the door were the counter and two sinks with enough room for Jim and Jennifer to spread out for morning prep.

"Toby; this place is grand. How can you afford to use cherry and some of this other material? It must have cost millions."

"No, not that much at all. Logging was outlawed during The

Transition Period. All over the world in key locations are tree growth farms. Each farm is allowed to grow for decades, then harvested, the soil replenished and trees replanted. A strict cycle is kept so there's never a need to harvest trees from natural forest."

"I can't believe that the logging industry allowed themselves go under." Jim said.

"As I have stated, incentives were offered to everyone and every company during The Transition Period. Most took advantage of the incentives."

Jim gave Toby a mischievous grim, testing him to reveal more. When Toby did not continue Jim changed the subject.

"Where's our stuff, my laptop?"

"Your personal items and the furniture you chose to keep will be delivered tomorrow. Your laptop was confiscated during The Transition Period, however the contents has been uploaded to your terminals. Let me show you."

Toby walked to a nearby glass panel and using two fingers held together made a half circle gesture and immediately the glass panel lit up to display a photo of Jim and Jennifer before she was diagnosed with cancer.

"Fuller family photos please." Toby directed his statement to the monitor.

As soon as the command was given the monitor was filled with thumbnails of the photos that Jim had scanned before being placed into cryo. After the thumbnails had completed loading the monitor altered into a slideshow presentation.

"Your other personal information is similarly available. Issue a verbal command of the desired information and the system will display it for you. If you must print something out issue a print command and a hard copy will be delivered the next day. But it's simply faster to give a command to have the file sent to the desired location." Toby said.

"So is this information stored on a local hard drive? Here in this apartment?"

"No. All information, personal and public is stored as multiple copies in twenty server farms around the world. Your voice ensures that only you are allowed access to your personal data. This demo was prearranged to show you how to access the data. If unauthorized access is attempted the system blocks the – hacker for lack of a more proper term, and his location is displayed and he is picked up."

"So is hacking still an issue?"

"No not since…"

"Let me guess – The Transition Period." Jim said.

"Correct. The Transition Period was the best thing that happened to the people of Earth and to the Earth itself. Billions of lives were saved, and the only thing asked in return – a few minor sacrifices."

The word sacrifices sent a chill up Jim's spine. From what he had seen and heard so far the phrase 'sacrifices' was being substituted for civil liberties. An individual's self-rights. Had people willingly surrendered their rights to achieve world peace and better health along with a longer life? But on the other hand, the rights of millions had been forced from them for thousands of years to allow others their rights. The lack of cars, pollutants, smokers and crime were not rights, they were acts forced on others without their consent. From one point of view it appeared a person's rights had been taken from them, but so far only good has prevailed from those that complied, and no one seemed indifferent to the changes.

"I wanted to do some research on The Transition Period and the changes made worldwide later. Is the Internet still up and running?" Jim asked.

"Not as you might remember. All worldwide Internet traffic and request are routed through those same twenty server locations. Although there are people working there, the request are handled by a preset of logarithms, if certain criteria are met the user is granted his request, if not the request is denied. Excessive denials will result in an investigation."

"Toby; excuse me for saying this, but that sounds like censorship on the grandest scale."

"Perhaps it could be taken that way. But I don't see it. Some information should not be in the hands of those that can't possible understand it. Do you remember a fellow by the name of Edward Snowden?"

"Ya, he was the guy back in what –twenty twelve or thirteen that stole confidential data and leaked it to the press." Jim said.

"Correct; there were others like him, and the website WikiLeaks. Nations around the world learned from those mistakes. When President Bush implemented the program to – spy on American's after September eleventh there were not enough personal in U.S. Intel to handle the sudden surge of data, outside techs were hired. That turned out to be a huge mistake for the U.S. Due to the massive increase in hires many people passed their psychology exams with questionable results, but the man power was needed. That mistake led to other costly mistakes such as Snowden and WikiLeaks. Today information is tightly controlled, to avoid similar costly mistakes and loss of life."

Jim allowed his body to fall into one of the dining chairs; he then ran his fingers through his hair, stopping halfway to scratch his head in disbelief.

"There was something called the Bill of Rights back in twenty fourteen." Jim said.

"And it's still there Jim, nothing has really changed. In order to achieve what we have and work out differences with other nations concessions had to be made. The citizens of the United States still retain freedom of speech and freedom of the press; it's just that the information is under tighter control. Listen this is far more than I intended to share with you today and you've taken in a great deal of information. I'm going to leave you to explore your new home and you mentioned you wanted to do some research, so I'll leave you to that. If you need to contact me just bring up the monitor on any glass panel throughout the apartment and give a voice command to call me, give my full name. Don't worry about my location, the system will know where I am."

"Does the system know where everyone is at all times?" Jim asked.

"Later Jim, you've taken in way too much for your first day in twenty eighty. You also have to be considering Jennifer; how you think she might want things around your new home. You may want to do some window shopping for baby items, huh!" Toby said as a distraction with a sly grin and raising his eyebrows up and down. "Chin up old man, it'll all work out. When you get Jennifer back in your arms all this will be a part of your life and you'll be teaching her." Toby pulled the right corner of his mouth up in a half smile.

"Sure Toby; this is just not what I had envisioned. You stopping by tomorrow?"

"Ya, the furniture is to be delivered around one in the afternoon. I'll be here in time for lunch, we'll eat first then I'll help you set things up." Toby said.

"Okay; thanks and see ya tomorrow."

Toby left Jim sitting alone at the table; once he was back on ground level he called Nick and Daniel to inform them of Jim's reaction to the information that was fed him. The World Medical Committee realized it would take time for Jim to absorb the changes in the world, but with each piece of information his reaction had to be gauged to determine what further action needed to be taken. If his reaction was startled but without rejection the World Medical Committee would continue to answer his questions, at the first indication of rejection Jim would be eliminated.

Jim watched as Toby left the apartment, his mind full of unanswered questions, questions that required answers. He looked at the wall in the living area that the display had appeared on and then at the translucent surface of the kitchen wall, Toby had told him any glass surface would allow access to the Cloud Server. He walked over to the nearest wall and extended his first two fingers and made the same half circle gesture that he watched Toby perform.

*"Welcome Jim."* A female voice greeted.

"Hum, hello?"

*"Is that an inquiry?"*

"No, sorry. Do you have a name?"

*"Not at this time, but if you feel more comfortable giving me a name you are welcome to. You can also change my voice to male and any age or with an accent."*

"That won't be necessary; your current voice is fine. May I call you SAM?"

*"SAM? That is an unusual name for a female voiced interactive computer."*

"Yes; I'm aware of that. But it's S.A.M. Systems Automated Machine. When I was a boy I used to dream about having a completely automated computer system. I named it S.A.M. Of course it was just a boy's fantasy, but you're now that reality."

*"Then SAM I am. What may I do for you today Jim?"*

"I just give you a command and you carry out that function?"

*"That is an acceptable summery."*

"Bring up Google."

*"Invalid command 'bring up Google'. Please restate."*

"Show Google search engine."

*"Searching; Google, a popular search engine prior to The Transition Period. That service has been deleted. Please restate your command."*

"Okay no more Google, how about – bring up Bing."

*"Invalid command. Bing a popular…"*

"Okay I get it, it's been deleted also."

*"Correct."*

"I only know one more. Bring up Yahoo."

Yahoo's home page appeared on the translucent display monitor mounted in the wall, news stories from all parts of the world scrolled by.

*"World Medical Committee Announces Another Breakthrough in Extending the Human Lifespan."*

*"United World Nations Announces all Former Restricted Areas of the Nuclear War Soon to be Opened."*

*"United States Takes World Cup; Germany Defeated."*

*"Two Hundred Names to be Read at 7 p.m."*

No news of wars, crimes, bombings, or violence of any kind scrolled past as he continued to read. The stories focused on the good among mankind, or so it appeared.

"Nuclear War?" Jim said to no one.

*"Was that an inquiry?"*

"No SAM; sorry. There was a nuclear way? No wait. I need to stick with one subject at a time. Bring up information on The Transition."

*"Please narrow the nature of your request. The phrase 'The Transition' generated over one billion results."*

"Okay; try The Transition Period that started in twenty fifteen."

*"World Transition Period. Only one result returned. Should I scroll the text or read it aloud?"*

"Please read it to me."

*"The World Transition Period which began in twenty fifteen was set into motion by the assassination of the then President of the United States; President Damien Jefferson. Within seconds of the conformation of his death the Vice President was sworn into office. Days after taking the oath of office the Vice President evoked his executive authority and ordered U.S. troops back into Iraq to halt the advance of ISIS. He also ordered troops into Israel to assist Israeli troops in the war against Palestine. Due to prior budget cutbacks by President Jefferson congress did not pass a means to pay for the upsurge in troops and military supplies to Iraq and Israel. When it became known that the military would be required to engage in combat without any conformation of payment the Senate ordered an investigation of the Vice President at the request of the U.S.*

*Justice Department. In the course of the investigation it was discovered that the Vice President had ordered the assassination of President Jefferson."*

"Pause please."

Jim walked to the fully transparent window that faced the wooded park below and looked at the people as they mingled. He found it difficult to accept that Vice President Gates could have assassinated President Jefferson.

"SAM? What was the motive behind the assassination?"

*"The Vice President..."*

"What was the Vice President's name?"

*"Searching. Your inquiry returned no results. Should I return to the narration?"*

"Yes please."

*"Continuing from your last inquiry in reference to the Vice President. It was believed but never proven that the Vice President intended to bring the Fuller Life Project under federal and military control. The buildup in troops in Iraq and Israel was intended to serve two purposes. One; distract the military and citizens of the United States; and two; create a reason to expose the Fuller Life Serum through the injuries that solders would suffer in another war. It was hoped that the injuries would be severe enough to expose the Fuller Life Serum so it would be used on those solders. Once the serum was exposed it would fall under federal oversight. However these charges were never proven.*

*Continuing with previous narration. The charge against the Vice President having a part in the assassination was proven; soon thereafter the Senate began the impeachment process. However as the hearings continued it became apparent that it could take several months. With that knowledge the U.S. Justice department issued a warrant for the arrest of the Vice President who was now President. After the warrant was executed The Speaker of the House was sworn in as President of the United States of America."*

"Pause narration, please SAM."

*"Narration paused."*

Jim walked from the window to the kitchen and got a bottle of water from the refrigerator. Although the apartment was cool, he wiped sweat from his brow with the back of his shirt sleeve. He bowed his head to the floor and allowed his mind to absorb the information that he had taken in throughout the day. It was hard to accept that shortly after he was put into cryo the President was assassinated and at the order of the Vice President. And that event set into motion a period of time referred to as The Transition, a time that, from his limited understanding, American's lost their civil liberties. The end result of The Transition Period may have benefited man worldwide, but he wondered what path the world took to reach *this* brave new world.

"SAM; resume narration please."

*"During the investigation of the assassination it was discovered that the Vice President was but a small part in a worldwide movement to overthrow smaller governments through the use of social media. Persons participating in the world overthrow were placed in key government positions of those smaller less powerful nations. Citizens that were also a part of the world overthrow or what came to be known as WO; used social media sites such as Facebook, Twitter, Instagram and Google Plus to spread negative propaganda and outright lies about the rulers in the nations of which they lived. Many nations throughout the Middle and Far East collapsed under the heavy on slot of rebellion. In an attempt to stop the cascading effect of the fall of nations the United States, Russia, China, France and the United Kingdom formed a coalition and mobilized a united military force under a ten member joint task force command. Before the suppression of the uprising the WO had obtained a limited stock of Nuclear Weapons. These they used against all major cities throughout Iran, Iraq, Syria, Egypt, Saudi Arabia, India, Afghanistan, Tel Aviv and Jerusalem Israel, Turkey,..."*

"PAUSE!"

Jim ran to the bathroom and threw up the small amount of contents in his stomach. When he reached the point of dry heaves he went to the sink and continually splashed cold water in his face. Soon he realized that he could not wash what he had just heard from his memory and slid to the bathroom floor exhausted. Sleep overtook him.

***

Daniel gestured in front of the monitor, turning the video feed from Jim's apartment off. He then turned to face Nick and Toby who were seated across from each other. Daniel crossed the walnut hardwood floor and took a seat in a chair beside Toby. For a moment the three said nothing, allowing what they had just witnessed to absorb into their consciences.

"Well, do we have a problem?" Daniel asked.

"Too soon to judge. A limited Nuclear War would make any sane human sick. He heard a partial list of cities and countries; he must realize the death toll was in the billions. That amount of human loss would make me sick if I were in his circumstances." Toby replied.

"I agree with Toby. We need to give him more time." Nick said.

"The question that concerns me, what happens when he learns it was all a lie." Daniel said.

# CHAPTER 7

With the morning sun the people of Fuller City set about in different directions to start their day. Joggers, sun risers and morning bird watchers made their way to the park within the square, many greeting each other by name. In other parts of the city people gathered around public viewing monitors to hear the morning list of names, hoping to hear the name of a loved one. Shop keepers were unlocking their doors in anticipation of more than window lookers. Two blocks from Central Square stood a four story stately building that had been a holdover from before The Transition Period. Gathered around an old marble fireplace were seven men and women. Some stood, others were seated, but they all faced the same direction.

"What's the latest?" Doctor Thomen asked.

"Look for yourself; he's still sleeping on the bathroom floor." Carla's English was punctuated by a thick German accent.

"It's the shock." Doctor Thomen reached into her medical bag and removed her Samsung tablet to accessed Jim's internal monitor to ensure he was still alive. When her tablet synced with SAM she was able to see his breathing and heart rate as well as other vital statistics.

"Well he's definitely alive and apparently not in shock. Toby do you think you should go over and wake him?" Doctor Thomen asked.

"No! We need him to be alone when he wakes up. We need to know if he will pursue his research, and the direction he'll take it." Daniel said.

"You men sure play hard. He's been in cryo for sixty six years, give him some time. If you were this worried to begin with why in goodness did you even bother to wake him?" Carla's frustration with the other members was evident in her inability to find proper English words and she relied on her German to vent herself.

"He's been friends with most of the committee members for years. We couldn't let him lie in that box for countless eons or worse, 'pull the plug'" Toby answered.

"I never mentioned 'pulling the plug'. But you woke him not just because he's your friend but also because you trust him to a certain degree. So just tell him. Hold nothing back, tell him everything" Carla said.

"In due time. In time if our trust has not been misplaced we'll bring him fully up to date." Nick said.

***

Jim sat up and braced his back against the natural river rock, holding both sides of his head as if he were recovering from a hangover. He opened his eyes only to close them again quickly hoping to stop the room from spinning. He kept his eyes closed as he crawled to the toilet, feeling the urge to throw up. For several minutes he held on to the rim with his head resting on his arm. When he was sure nothing was forthcoming he crawled to the corner where the shower head exited the wall. Again he rested with his back to the stone wall with eyes closed. When he felt his head had settled from the move to the shower he reached his left hand up and over him and turned on the cold water, allowing it to rain down on him. Sill with eyes closed he pulled his wet shoes and socks off and tossed them to the far corner. Again he rested his back against the rock, allowing the waves of dizziness to pass. When they subsided he removed his blue jeans and underwear and tossed them in the same direction as he had his shoes and socks. As before he leaned back and let the waves of dizziness pass. He then removed his shirt and tossed it in the same pile as his other clothing. When he was finished undressing he stretched out under the falling cold water and let it rain on him until he was sure the last wave of dizziness was gone. Slowly, he pulled himself up to a standing position using the grab bars embedded in the river stone wall. When he was sure no dizziness followed him from the floor he let go of the bar and started searching for the soap. Looking he found none.

"SAM? You still there?"

*"Yes Jim. I am here."*

The area at Jim's eye level lit up with a similar display screen that was embedded in the translucent walls. The sudden appearance of the display startled Jim and he took two quick steps back, slipping in the water and landing hard on his butt.

"Ouch!" He pulled himself up while rubbing the soon to appear bruise on his butt.

*"It was not my intent to startle you. However in my defense you did request me."*

"True, but I never figured you would be in the bathroom."

*"Jim; I am everywhere. What did you need?"*

"Ya, almost forgot with landing on my butt. Where's the soap?"

*"Look right ahead."*

In front of Jim appeared another, smaller display monitor, except this one had several large round colored buttons. A blue button on the left had the notation *'Body'* a green button in the middle was noted *'Hair'* and a yellow button on the right was noted *'Other'*. He chose not to ask SAM what 'other' could apply to. He pressed the blue button expecting soap to be dispensed into his hand, but instead was greeted with a cascade of soap within the falling water. As he lathered his body and hair with the soap and water mixture he failed to see the need for a second soap option for hair and whatever 'other' was. Guessing instead of asking he pressed the blue button again and was rewarded with a correct guess, the soap stopped and he was left with cool water to rinse off. When the last remaining soap was off his body he turned off the water and walked to the sink, looking for a towel in the process. Not seeing one he again opted to guess and started looking for a display that should logically appear after a shower indicating how to dry. His search was rewarded with another correct guess; to the right of the mirror was a red button with the word *'Dry'*. He reached out with his right forefinger and pressed it. From the ceiling and floor came alternating currents of cool and warm air that was gently blown over his body; as it did so he completed his morning personal preparation. After dressing he went to the kitchen to hunt for morning breakfast.

"SAM? Inquiry?"

*"Proceed."*

"I've not seen anyone with a cell phone or tablet. Why?"

*\*\*\**

When the members of the committee heard Jim's request a look of worry encased Toby's face. He looked at Daniel and Daniel returned his own look of caution.

\*\*\*

*"Invalid inquiry, please restate."*

"Hum. Okay. How do I get a cell phone?"

\*\*\*

"He's persistent about the cell phone issue." Doctor Thomen said.

"It's understandable, sixty six years ago it was a person's right to have a cell phone or other such devices. He has, as you may recall, expressed concern over civil and individual rights. Toby replied.

"He has done so continually and that is my primary concern Toby. If he continues on this course, he may find the answers too early and then feel that these rights must be reinstated." Daniel's words were forced and expressed with intensity.

"Let this day play out Daniel. This is a huge adjustment for anyone. Those of us standing here also had an adjustment period, even you." Nick said.

The members returned their attention to the viewing monitor.

\*\*\*

*"Invalid inquiry, please restate."*

"Local cell phone service."

*"Invalid…"*

"Shut up I know. Invalid inquire, please restate."

In frustration he dragged his hand through his hair, stopping midway on his head and scratching. Cell phones, tablets, personal computers all technologies of the past; current Internet searches for information brought no results. It somehow seemed a violation of individual freedom to restrict access to technology, but if there were restrictions there had to be a reason.

"SAM? How do I contact Toby Ellis?"

*"All persons of Earth can be contacted via V-Link. All persons have interactive display monitors in their homes, office, and they are also conveniently located in many public access areas. Interactive displays are also located in public locations throughout the countryside and villages of Earth. If, however a person is not within access of an interactive display a V-Message can be left for them to access at their convenience. However, Toby Ellis is currently at WORLD MEDICAL COMMITTEE Headquarters. Do you wish for me to set up a V-Link?"*

\*\*\*

At the Barns Firm the members of the World Medical Committee shifter position out of view of the interactive display, leaving only Toby Ellis in its visual perspective. Another monitor display activated to the left of the one the committee was watching Jim on, the image of Jim in his apartment shifted to the newly activated display. Toby watched as Jim gave SAM the command to contact him via V-Link.

*"Incoming V-Link for Toby Ellis from Jim Fuller; shall I activate?"*

"Please do so." Toby instructed. On the display directly in front of Toby the image of Jim appeared.

"Hello Jim." Toby greeted.

"Toby. Listen, I've been doing some research on The Transition Period that you told me about and there's little relative information, nothing really useful on a personal level. Did a limited Nuclear War really take place, taking out Jerusalem? What happened to cell phones, tablets, and personal computers? In fact what happened to all personal technology and privacy? Also there are no news reports of robberies, murders, violence, in fact not any negative news at all. What's going on?" Jim rambled most of his words and thoughts, his speech was pressured, forced, and slightly slurred.

"Jim, slow down and take a deep breath. You're going to hyperventilate and pass out. All of your concerns will be addressed in due time. Many things changed during The Transition Period. It was a period of chaos and the World was facing its own destruction. Sacrifices had to be made and some liberties had to be – rethought in order to regain a measure of peace. Even when the United Nations Security Council was able to achieve a measure of control in their own nations, smaller nations around the world were still in ruins, politically. I will fill in the missing gaps in time. As to the limited nuclear war, yes it did happen, much the way you researched it and Jerusalem was destroyed, many sections of the Middle and Far East are still considered unsafe to enter, the Crescent Valley foremost since so many warheads were deployed in that area. It was an area of intense fighting during The Transition Period. Several factions of all religions fought for control of the area, as well as many other nations. The religious factions, Muslim, Christian, Judaism, and Buddhist alike fought each other to the brink of annihilation in that region. In the end they had destroyed all of their own sacred relics to prevent their enemies from doing so." Toby explained.

"Do you hear yourself Toby? You're explaining this so coldly, so 'matter of fact'." Jim said. The high resolution of the monitor captured the intensity of the lines that formed across his face.

"They are simply facts of history now. They brought their own destruction upon themselves. Jim, they were warned and given every chance to withdraw and seek peace. They choose the course that led to their own demise. No one forced their fate upon them. So if I sound cold it's because so much time and money went into pursuing a peaceful resolution that they rejected. But I do extend my apologies; you were not here when it was taking place so you could not possibly understand how much effort went into trying to stop them." Toby said.

"But in my research I learned that the Vice President was part of a worldwide organization that set these events into motion."

"That's correct; he was a part of that movement that brought the destruction upon the people. Larger nations that got involved were involved for other reasons beside religious. Russia and the United States were involved in the Middle East issue not for religious freedoms and protection, but for natural resources, oil foremost among them." Toby said.

"Enough! What about personal technology? I get the same message each time I do a search, 'Invalid inquiry, please restate'. I've tried several different ways of searching and still get the same frustrating response." Toby's frustration from his fruitless searching resurfaced.

"Jim; let's meet for lunch, say around noon. I'll meet you in the park and we'll get something from a street vendor and eat under the tree where we sat yesterday. Sound okay?"

"Sure. Bye." The image of Toby vanished from the monitor. "SAM terminate V-Link"

*"V-Link terminated. By your command."*

\*\*\*

The image of Jim vanished from the center monitor and the view of him in his apartment transferred back to the main display. Toby turned to face the rest of the committee members; worry etched across all their faces, his own face was a reflection of theirs.

"I don't believe he'll reform." Daniel said.

"Now wait; it's far too early to judge…" Toby was cut short when Nick walked forward and turned to face the other members. "Let's not be hasty. He can only spread a negative influence person to person or in some form of public forum. So far we're the only people he knows and with what little he does know he'll be concerned about speaking out. Fear is a powerful controlling force. Right now we need to use it to our advantage." Nick said.

*** 

Jim turned from the display and walked to the window that overlooked the park. He watched as people passed by below and engaged each other, sharing, laughing and enjoying each other's presence. For all the questions that filled his mind, the people of two thousand eighty appeared to be content and happy. Regardless of what rights or liberties he felt they were missing, the people below him did not appear to be at a loss for anything. He dragged his hand through his hair and flicked it as the last strains ran through his fingers. Inside he was frustrated and confused, but below him were happy people with happy lives, what was he not seeing. He left the apartment and went down to the park. He found the same bench that Toby had showed him the day before and sat down. He would ask no question of anyone, just watch and listen. He knew he could learn more from watching and listening then from asking direct questions that might be perceived as a threat.

He watched as husbands and wives enjoyed early lunches under the shade of a tree. As children played hide and seek in wooded areas with no apparent fear from strangers or the unknown, older children sliding or swinging from ropes into the pool at the far end of the park. An overall feeling of calm and peace, no rushing, shoving or irritation could be seen or felt. It was both appealing and frightening; could a world of peaceful interaction between people really exist? But with all the apparent happiness Jim felt something was missing from the scene playing out around him. Some part of life was not apparent in the park. There were men, women and children and even young families, but something was missing from the gathering of people, but his mind could not pinpoint it. For all the blissfulness around him something was out of place, something was not what it should be. He noticed that few people kept track of time, as if they were unconcerned with being somewhere else, and content to be in the moment they were enjoying. He heard no conversations about a missed V-Link or returning a V-Link, no talk of business meetings or missing a deadline at work. No conversations that sounded pressured from the events of life, or the life he remembered from twenty fourteen. Had The Transition Period effected so much change that the very nature of people changed? But, there was that missing element? Until he could figure it out, Jim knew it would continue to haunt him.

***

"Hey Jim."

The voice startled Jim and his body gave a quick jerk.

"Sorry didn't mean to startle you back into reality." Toby said.

"It's alright Toby; I'm still trying to piece this world together. Sit please." Jim pointed to the chair next to him and invited his friend to sit.

Toby sat in the chair and then looked at Jim to see where his gazed was fixed and followed it to a young family enjoying the afternoon with a picnic lunch and taking the time to read together. Mother, father and three children, the youngest looked to be about seven the oldest in his early teens. The love and enjoyment between them was genuine, it looked as if even the teen boy was enjoying the time with his family.

"It's nice to see families like that enjoying time together."

"That's what bothers me Toby. Something about the families that I have been watching is not right. It's like something is missing. I see the joy, love and togetherness, but it feels like something is not right, like something is absent or missing or, I don't know." Jim ran his fingers through his hair, flicking the last few strands in frustration.

"I can't help you Jim, what I see before me looks like a perfectly happy young family. As I look around the park I see other families, men women and children of all ages enjoying their time together. Noting is missing or out of place." Toby shook his head back and forth to add weight to his statement.

"That word, 'young', and the phrase 'all ages'. Something's not right."

"In time it'll all come together. In time it'll all make perfect sense. In time you'll understand, but you can't rush this process. In the past with others that came out of cryo we told them too much too soon about the changes in the world. Many committed suicide. After the tenth loss we sat down and analyzed what we were doing wrong. The only common factor was the amount of information we gave, so we introduced new protocols regarding how much we tell Wakes and when."

"Wakes? After you introduced the new protocols did it stop the suicides?" Jim locked his eyes with Toby's.

"Wakes is the term we started using for those coming out of cryo. Two more people took their own lives. But it was years after they woke up. It turned out that this was not the kind of world they wanted to live in. It was too peaceful, too 'right' as one worded it in their departing V-Message. I never considered that there would be those that did not want to live here." Toby said.

"I can't see that. Some of the information, well to be honest, much of the information is difficult to digest, but I can't see turning your back on this simply because you don't understand it all or because some of what you thought would be here is not."

"So you're starting to accept the things around you, even though you just said something does not seem right?" Toby said.

"Just because I don't understand it right now, doesn't mean it won't be right when I do. By the way what was in that shake you made me drink when you woke me up? I was really sick yesterday."

"Sick; what symptoms?"

"Extreme nausea and vomiting until I hit dry heaves. I decided to sleep in the bathroom because I never thought it would stop. A few hours after I feel asleep I ended up on the toilet with the squirts; I was sure that I would end up seeing my innards in the pot when I was done." Jim's face distorted as he described what had happened to him the night before.

"That shake was just proteins, electrolytes and other nutrients that your body needed after years of being in cryo. There's no way it would've had that effect. Did you eat or drink anything?"

"No, nothing." Jim dropped his head forward and looked at the ground, considering in his mind the items he had eaten and drank yesterday.

"You said you were going to do some research, did you read something that upset you?"

"I never thought about that. Could stress really have that kind of effect?" Jim asked.

"Ya, so you did read something that upset you?"

"I did some research on The Transition Period. That limited Nuclear War in the Middle and Far East. Billions must have died." He felt the pit of his stomach churn as he thought about the needless loss of human life, a single tear formed in the corner of his eye, dislodged and flowed down his cheek to drop in the dirt at his feet.

"Although most of the bombs fell in that region, several hit elsewhere. Kazakhstan was once a part of the USSR, they held on to some of their ICBM's. When the war started the ruler of Kazakhstan was murdered and far left radicals took control of that country's nuclear program. Although some rulers in some countries are ruthless, prior to The Transition Period they knew not to use those nukes, just keep them as a deterrent. But radicals did not have a real agenda and no respect for human life, if they got their hands on such weapons they'll use them and they did. Three ICBM's with ten warheads each were fired at the United States, the air defense shield targeted all three of them, but over American airspace. It was hoped to target them before they reentered the atmosphere to prevent the warheads from detonating. But the counter measures struck them about twelve thousand feet above the ground, one over Atlanta Georgia, one over Washington DC and the other over New York City. Since the warheads never separated from the ICBM they all detonated at the same time in the same confined space. Four more ICBM's were launched into Russia, and they had no air defense counter measures so the loss of life and the destruction there was far greater. Twelve were launched into China, again no counter measures to destroy the incoming ICBM's."

In his mind Jim watched as nuclear warheads rained down on helpless men, women and children all around the world. He could see millions, billions of people instantly incinerated as if they had never existed, and ghostly shadows; a negative, the only remaining image of the human that once occupied that space in time. He saw as people ran in terror with their arms extended in front of them their flesh dripping to the ground as it melted away from their body, running in search of water. When finding it jumping in, hoping to lessen the unbearable burning they felt to their bones. Rivers, lakes and streams full of the dead and dying as they sought relief from pain they could not comprehend.

"Toby?" Tears flowed freely from Jim's eyes. "How many died?"

"We'll never know the exact number, but the death toll was over four billion; we think, some instantly of course, others over the course of several days, and still more over the course of many years." Instead of numbers, Toby was now recounting the loss of people. He allowed Jim to see the emotional affect those losses had on him.

Jim took in a deep breath and exhaled slowly. Hearing the death toll from Toby instead of a computer made the loss of life personal, real.

"Why was it not called World War Three?"

"The nations were not at war with one another, but radical religions, terrorist and smaller nations seeking their own advantage attacked each other. The major nations learned after two major conflicts. No one had any idea that the terrorist would get their hands on nuclear weapons. It caught the world by surprise. But the United Nations Security Council knew the source behind the attack. When the radicals were finally destroyed calm started to set in."

Jim looked back at the young family, still enjoying their reading time. He thought of the countless families that would never enjoy another happy moment or life again. He felt the urge to throw up.

"I can see why I was so sick." Jim said. "Are there any survivors? Could you use the Fuller Life Serum on them?"

"Yes; hundreds of thousands of survivors, the serum was not approved for worldwide use. A few countries allowed testing and with the amount of survivors in the United States the FDA approved the use of it here, turns out that the serum can't do anything for cellular death. Radiation kills the cell, from bone to blood, the cell can't divide anymore. If the person lives they will live a deformed and painful life, we can't reverse that."

"So what happened to them?"

Toby dreaded the conversation that was about to ensue, he knew what he was about to say could be understood several different ways. He explained that the United Nations Security Council passed a resolution to sterilize all remaining survivors worldwide. Children were allowed to pass through puberty under supervision and at the age of twenty they were to be sterilized. With the approval of the Fuller Life Serum the human genome was being improved and if an unknown element was introduced into the genetic enhancements the consequences would not be known for decades. Allowing the survivors to continue to live out their natural lives in a state that prevented them from passing on defective genetic material was considered the most humane treatment for the rest of the world.

"So the survivors allowed their bodies to be mutilated even more?" Jim asked.

"Jim, it's not like that. We educated them. A few had surviving children, but when they fully understood that the human race was at stake, most, the majority, stepped up and allowed it."

"Those who did not?" Jim again locked his eyes to Toby's, his stare penetrating, looking for the truth.

"We offered an incentive, few took advantage." Toby answered.

"You have continued to talk about this incentive program to encourage people to accept change. What was the incentive program?"

"Why don't we grab some lunch. I saw a vendor setting up

outside." Toby stood and started walking along the path to the archway that led out to the street.

"Spoon feed the old man, huh Toby?"

"You got it. Let's go."

The two walked through the park and under the exit arch and got in line behind several other people waiting to order. Jim noticed that no one pushed, shoved or attempted to cut the line. Each person waited patiently and spoke to one another as if they had been lifelong friends, even if they had just met.

"What gives with all the nicey, nicey people? In the entire history of this planet no one has ever been as nice as the people I've been around. It's a demo, like showing me how to use the displays?"

"No, no demo. This is the real deal. This is how people are to each other. It just is." Toby said.

"Afternoon; what'll ya have?" The vendor asked.

"I've no idea. This is my first meal in sixty six years." Toby said.

Toby placed his hand on Jim's shoulder and rotated him sideways and stepped up to the vendor.

"He's a new Wake and has yet to eat his first real meal. What's on special today?"

"Well I've got some fresh veggies and they make up a nice salad, just picked them last night."

"Sounds tops; make that two fresh veggie salads, with the whole garden thrown in. Two iced teas to drink." Toby said.

After paying for their order they walked back to the park and sat down in the chairs under the tree. Toby left his salad on his lap unopened, he watched Jim in anticipation. Unaware he was being watched Jim opened the box that held his salad, drizzled some French dressing over it and took a bite. For a moment he did not chew but let the food rest in his mouth. Then slowly, as if tasting food for the first time he started to chew, savoring each flavor as it came to life. He closed his eyes and could feel himself in the taste of the food as it flowed in his body, carelessly and without effort. When he opened his eyes he realized he was being watched. Toby was staring at Jim with a smile that covered his entire face. Even his eyes appeared to emit rays of happiness and joy.

"What was that?" Jim asked.

"The taste of real food, no pesticides, no genetic modifications, no preservatives, no artificial nothing, just real wholesome direct from the Earth food."

"It was awesome."

"Ya I know, I eat it every day and I'm still not use to it. Fact is Jim; the nations had the ability to produce food this pure all along. But money, pure black greed, dictated they modify it to ensure the maximum dollar for each acre of production. Take away a person's greed and everything tastes better."

"If this is food minus the greed, I'll eat it every day. Well I have to eat no matter what, I mean, well I won't complain." Jim muddled his way through his comment.

"I know what you're saying, and I agree."

"I could get use to this life. I still have a lot of questions, but I could get used to it. I know Jennifer will love it. To be completely free of her cancer and able to have children, ya she'll love this world. I know in time I'll understand what I don't know and I'll accept it, I just have to work through my questions. Toby, tell the committee thanks for waking me up to this world."

"There's still a lot to learn, I do mean a lot."

"I know, and I will and I'll absorb that as well. Funny how a belly full of excellent food will affect your thinking."

# CHAPTER 8

The setting sun cast long shadows across Fuller City. Deep colors of red, crimson, purple and orange spread out across the sky. A breeze picked up leaves and carried them in swirls of updrafts to be dropped again blocks away. The streets were empty and barren except for the leaves that danced with the wind. On Sunday evening's people gathered at their homes with family and friends and stores and shops remained closed. Fuller City appeared dead as time gave way to late September, and an early fall could be felt in the air. Most of the dancing leaves were green, having been blown free of their holdings. But a few had started to change to their fall colors and dotted the swirls of green with red, brown, orange and yellow. As the wind made its way in and out of turns and corners it howled and a few times sounded as if echoed voices never heard. A gust picked up a mixed color of leaves and deposited them at the door of The Barns Firm, forcing them into the stone entryway to gather in the corner. On the fourth floor a light shown through the two arched windows made of steel and stone, from above on each corner of the building two gargoyles perched, peering down on the leaves below as they gathered at the door. The light from the window flickered and dimed as a figure paced back and forth, stopping at intermittent times then started again. The back of a chair could be seen to turn in the same direction as the pacing figure. The sun continued to drop, stretching out the shadows of the gargoyles on the cobblestone walk below until they were distorted into nightmarish figures that crawled through the stone paths. Daniel continued to pace the fourth floor above, until darkness fell upon Fuller City.

"He's too dangerous Nick. I don't think it's safe to continue to tell him anything. We need to see what he does with what he knows." Daniel stopped in front of Nick's desk, leaning over and meeting his face with his own.

"Daniel, listen to yourself, you've gotten paranoid. Jim has given no indication that he's rejecting what Toby is telling him. Give it time. It's a lot of information to process."

"Okay, I agree it's a lot to take in. But suppose he learns that Toby is not telling him the complete truth? Suppose he learns just how much he's being lied to? What then?" Daniel said.

"We'll deal with that when and *if* it ever does happen. Besides, suppose after he has been told what we have agreed to tell him and then learns the truth and feels that what we had to do was worth it? Daniel we accepted what we had to do and as each one of the members were awakened and learned, they fell right into step with the program. When you were awakened you too fell into step, but if you remember it took you some time to come around. We never discussed killing you because you were having such a hard time. You need to give Jim time."

"Jim was never on the committee and was never a part of the Fuller Life Project from its inception. He's not one of us; he's not of our thinking." He drank the rest of the rum in his glass and walked to the bar to pour another. After filling his glass he turned to face Nick and leaned back against the counter. "We've worked hard to bring about this new world; many have died to make it happen, my own parents died for this world. Jim can't bring it down, but he can cause problems that we can't even predict." Daniel said.

"Every member on the World Medical Committee and United World Nations is aware of that, and as you are aware it's something that we continue to discuss. But there's something you're overlooking." Nick said.

Nick's statement forced Daniel to take notice and he pushed his body forward to stand free of the counter. He turned and placed his drink on the shelf and walked to Nick's desk.

"I have overlooked nothing, he is a danger."

"Listen to me Daniel. He's been identified, and recognized. Tomorrow The CBS World News is going to interview him for an upcoming special. If Jim were to suddenly vanish or be found dead it would create more problems and questions than giving him time to adjust. He may not be adjusting as fast as any of us would like, but he is slowly adjusting. Now that the world knows he's awake he will garner power, at least in the mind of the public. This interview will have to have the approval of the entire committee, so after it's completed we will be able to watch it and have a better understanding of how well he's adjusting."

"Just when did you intend to let me in on this interview and the fact that he is now known?" Daniel asked.

"I got a V-Linked about an hour before you arrived; it was my intention to tell the entire committee at tomorrow's meeting. So I just learned of it myself."

Daniel returned to the bar and picked up his drink and went to the chairs that sat in the center of the room and took a seat. Nick stood up from the desk chair and walked to the chair beside Daniel and sat down.

"You're scared, aren't you?" Nick asked.

"Yes, yes I am. My parents died in a nuclear detonation. They in effect gave their lives for this new world. You and most members of the committee still have your parents around. Nick mine are gone forever, if something crashes this world, my parents died for nothing."

"Not nothing, your parents did not die for nothing. Jim can't crash this world, it's firmly in place. He can cause problems, but not a complete crash. Without the ability to reach out to the masses with social media, events like bringing down entire nations; is a thing of the past. Remember Daniel, we did away with social media, cell phones, tablets and personal computers to stop people from forming mass networks and uprisings to overthrow leaders or businesses. To accomplish anything Jim would have to form a grassroots network, one person at a time. Before he gathered fifty people we would be able to stop him." Nick placed his hand on Daniel's shoulder as a reassuring gesture.

"I hear you and I know you're right, but I'm still afraid of him. He has the ability to harness great power and authority."

"True enough, but there's something about Jim's personality that prevents that." Nick said.

Daniel turned a puzzled look at Nick.

"Jim is selfish, but not for power, not for himself. Jim never wanted anything in his past life except Jennifer and her health. Yes he loves her more than himself, but his selfish desire is for them to have their own life together and he does not really care how. Jim is confused right now, and asking many questions, his mind is turning over everything he is learning. But when we have freed Jennifer's body of the cancer and we wake her, his focus will be back on her and his selfish desires will be manifested fully. He was that way in his past life and there's no reason to believe that he will be any different in this life. Jim has always been about himself and his wife, so when we wake her, he'll care less about the ethical issue. He'll be happy that he has his Jennifer back and nothing else will matter to him."

"I had not considered that. I know he and I went to the same school, but we were never close friends. But from what I've learned and seen since he has been awakened he is very self-absorbed and centers his conversations mostly on Jennifer. How much longer until she can be awakened?"

"Toby and Emilie believe that it could be in about two to three weeks, the first part October."

"The sooner the better. I'll sleep better at night knowing that he's no longer a threat." Daniel said.

"I really don't believe he is. I think he's lost right now and has a deep concern for Jennifer. Like I said, once she is awake his focus will be back on her and himself."

Outside The Burns Firm the streets and cobblestone walks remained deserted. From behind the century old building a full moon began is accent into the night sky, beaming silver light throughout Fuller City. From above two gargoyles sat motionless, watching the streets and silently listening to the conversation from within.

\*\*\*

Jim stepped from the bathroom, clean and ready to start a new day. He walked across his bedroom to his closet to choose the suit that would best reflect his current state of mind. His interview with CBS was scheduled for eleven and Toby was not due to arrive until nine to prep him. He had two hours to dress, eat and prepare himself for his 'wakeup call' to the new world. After removing and looking over several suites he chose a dark blue satin one to be offset with a pastel green shirt and pink tie. After a final approving look in the mirror he went to the kitchen, poured himself some coffee and sat at the cherry dining table, waiting. Inside he was scared and nervous. He wanted to use the interview as a platform to question the dismantling of civil and personal rights, but the more he interacted with this new world the more he discovered that the people seemed truly happy. Some had survived the devastation of The Transition Period and were able to avail themselves of The Fuller Life Serum; within them they carried the memories of a life of heartache and a world of hate. Those people were the fabric that held the awareness of a tragic past, and the richness of the present day. Jim did not feel he had the right to express his own concerns at the cost of others. If the people of this world accepted the perceived limitations, then he felt he had no right to remind them of a past better forgotten. Death ruled the former, peace, life and happiness were present all around Jim today, peace he felt he had no right to disrupt. He also realized that 'the incentive program' that Toby continued to mention might be presented to him if he did express his concerns. He would allow Toby to coach him for the interview and follow the prescribed platform.

*"Toby Ellis is present at the door. Shall I allow him entry?"*

"Yes SAM, please do."

The translucent door slid open and disappeared inside the wall allowing Toby entry into the fourth story apartment. At the far end of the hallway he could see two arms holding a cup of steamy liquid. The rest of the body blocked from sight by the wall.

"Hello Jim, okay to come on in?"

"Of course Toby, come in and have some coffee."

Toby walked down the hall and straight to the coffee maker on the counter. After pouring himself a cup he joined Jim at the table.

"What's up with the long look Jim? It's a simple interview."

"I was just running over in my mind the opportunity this

interview gives me."

"Explain." Toby said. Swirls of steam flowed around his nose and eyes from the coffee as he sipped it.

Jim looked at Toby and locked his eyes, if he reviled what he wanted to do, could he trust that information with a member of the committee that was ruling this world. Member or not, Toby had been his best friend since they started school over one hundred years ago.

"Well you know my concerns with what I believe to be violations of civil and personal rights, after all I don't think I've stopped asking about personal cell phones or tablets."

Toby shook his head yes, acknowledging Jim's statement.

"My idea was to use the interview as a platform to express my concerns and fears. I was ready Toby to let the whole world know that they were losing out on good things. That the World Medical Committee was holding out on them. I was ready to 'expose' you."

"So what changed your mind?"

"The people of this world. Some of these people lived in the old world. They had cell phones, tablets and personal computers. They had contact with the entire world through social media so they carry those memories. But when you look at them today, they don't appear to miss them or feel that they are deprived. Toby, the people in that park below look genuinely happy. Although I've not spoken to anyone on the subject, I can tell from listening to their conversations that they don't miss what was. And something else."

"I'm listening." A smile formed deep within Toby, he knew from this conversation that Jim had been assimilated into the new world and accepted the ideology of it. He hoped the committee and more so Daniel was paying attention on the V-Link monitor they were watching.

"Well it's kind of weird, but I don't miss it. I don't miss having a cell phone strapped to my hip and being tied to the rest of the world every minute of my life. I love the privacy I have here in my home, I don't have to be concerned about hackers, or unwanted spyware, or constantly checking Facebook, Twitter, or my email. I love having my privacy back under my control. I love the mental freeness that comes with not being available to the rest of the world to contact all the time. I have no right to intrude on the peacefulness of this world."

Toby allowed Jim to see his smile. He then reached up and placed his hand on his shoulder and gave Jim a grip of approval.

"Besides Toby, whatever the incentive program is, I don't want to find out."

"I don't believe that was ever considered as an option. But you have put my mind at ease as well as the rest of the committee's. Now before we lose too much more time, let's go over the notes for the interview.

\*\*\*

*"The CBS crew is currently present at the door. Shall I allow them entry?"*

"Yes SAM, please do." Jim said.

It took the crew more than thirty minutes to set up the cameras and adjust the lighting. Once it was to the satisfaction of the production manager Toby took a seat off camera and behind Mike Williams who would be conducting the interview. In his hand he held a kill switch that would stop the camera from recording should Jim say anything that did not need to be recorded. With Jim and Mike in place the interview of the most powerful man in the new world began.

"First I would like to welcome our worldwide audience to this special presentation, but to you Jim a very special welcome." Mike said.

"Thank you. I'm thankful to be a Wake, and glad to give this interview."

"The world is also glad that you are a Wake. I understand that you've been preparing for this interview, but I will still throw some questions at you that you may not be prepared for. You up for that?"

"Bring them on."

"Very well, let's get started. My first question is generally what I ask every famous Wake. What were your first impressions of the new world?"

"Confusion; well after leaving Fuller Labs. What I saw around me confused me."

"As it does every Wake. But in your case, what confused you the most?"

"First, name changes. The city name, name of schools, names of a lot of stuff. But then the rebuilding of the city, along with the lack of cell phones and tablets. It was an overwhelming amount of change."

"Well don't feel alone. Almost all Wakes make that same statement. I have yet to interview a single Wake that did not express some thoughts about cell phones, tablets or personal computers. So what were your concerns?"

"The lack of them. I felt it was somehow a violation of a person's rights."

"Do you still feel that way?"

"No. It's without question that the world is a better place without them, peaceful and far less stressful."

"That too is a common response. So what do you look forward to the most as you continue to get to know this new world?"

"The awakening of my wife Jennifer. I'm told that it will be in a few weeks as her body was riddled with cancer. I'm excited and longing for her to be with me again."

Mike, Toby and the entire crew smiled. Back at The Barns Firm the committee members that were watching also smiled, Emily allowed a tear to flow from her eye.

The interview continued for more than an hour, the questions remained general and safe. CBS realized that if they attempted to ask unapproved questions the show would never air, the footage confiscated and Mike Williams make be taken to an incentive reconditioning area. Even the 'thrown in' questions were pre-scripted and preapproved by the committee. Nothing went on the air that had not been approved by the Committee for World Media. When the interview was completed the crew packed up and Mike shook the hand of Jim then with that Jim and Toby found they were alone again.

"Went well don't ya think?" Jim asked Toby.

"As it should be. I'm happy for you Jim, happy that you have accepted what you have. We can move forward now. We'll be waking up Jennifer in about three weeks so I have a lot to tell you, and you have a lot to learn."

"Why do I need to learn all the other stuff? Can't I just go on from here?" Jim asked.

"Jennifer's going to have questions; you'll be the one to give the answers. Also when the time's right you two are going to want to have children, we have some guidelines with regards to having children."

"I don't understand. What kind of guidelines?"

"That's why you need to learn all that I need to teach you." Toby said.

"Suppose that you tell me something that I can't handle?"

"Remember when I told you that I was spoon feeding you, giving you information little by little?"

Jim tilted his head slightly to the side and looked at Toby out of the corner of his eyes. "Ya."

"As I told you something I would gauge your reaction. If your reaction seemed drastic I would back off and sidetrack you. If you seemed okay then I continued."

"Fair enough. So how about a test of truth?"

"Ask your truth question." Toby said.

"What's the real reason, the truthful reason why people do not have cell phones, tablets or personal computers?"

"What do you think the reason could be?"

"You answer my question with a question?"

"I want to know how close you are to the truth." Toby said.

"So if I'm too close you can divert me?"

Toby could hear the distrust in Jim's voice; he could see the distance in his friend's eyes. This time he would tell Jim what he was desperate to hear but did not want to know, the truth.

"No, no diversions." Toby said.

"Okay. I figure that cell phones had become such a distraction that you were left with no choice. Maybe prior to The Transition Period deaths due to texting and driving got too bad, or job performance all across America had fallen so low that companies complained. As for tablets and personal computers, I have ideas, but they are all too far in left field." Jim said.

"Like how far in left field, like what?"

"Okay, ready? Censorship."

Toby lowered his head, then got up from the table and went into the living room; he turned and indicated for Jim to follow. Jim took a seat on the couch under the strip of windows near the ceiling, Toby in a chair across the room but facing Jim.

"You're not far from the truth with you answer. I'll get to the truthful answer, but only if you let me backfill the information."

Jim nodded in approval.

"You were still awake in the two thousands when Egypt, Syria, and several other Middle Eastern nations were toppled because of social media sites such as Facebook and Twitter." Jim nodded in acknowledgment. "Well after you fell asleep, large parts of China started to crumble, as did areas in Eastern Russia, and several nations that were once part of the Soviet Union. But the nation that fell to a social media site that took the world by complete surprise was North Korea. No one on the outside knew North Korea had cell phones for personal use, much less any form of social media. It was not Facebook, but a social media site of the North Korean's own making. Apparently the regimen there felt they had it under control, however it did not take the younger people there too much time to figure out how to hack. Once that lesson was learned nothing was able to stop the people wanting to break free. Still with me?"

"Ya. But so far all these were countries under the control of all powerful dictators or governments of suppression, so those kinds of governments needed to fall."

"I will not get into a debate on that point, but I will point out that the people that lived in those countries had lived under the control of those governments all their lives. Those governments did control their populations, as well as give them some direction, perhaps not well, but it kept them suppressed."

"Toby I'm having trouble following that reasoning."

"Okay, suppose you held a powerful spring in your hand and all of a sudden you opened your hand wide. What happens to the spring?

"Pop, it releases its tension all at once and flies across the room. It could even hurt someone." Jim answered.

"Same spring, same hand. You open the hand slowly, little by little. What happens?"

"The tension is released slow, a little at a time, controlled."

"Precisely. Social media sites were a closed hand on a tightly coiled spring. When people used them the hand opened quickly and the spring, or in this case the people, flung in all directions. There was no control, it was complete chaos. And if other nations attempted to regain control, it made the matter worse."

"I understand. But I'm still having trouble tying it all together." Jim said.

"Well stay with me. When the uprising started it was started through social media sites, a worldwide fire had been lit. After the nuclear holocaust and the World Medical Committee was placed in oversight of those nations that agreed the first thing to pass was the banning of social media. Not one single objection was raised. But an amendment was. It was pointed out that cell phones, tablets and personal computers could inflict the same damage so proposals were introduced. In time cellular companies around the world came under the control of their respective governments. Even here in the United States the Constitution has a provision to allow the President to make restrictions given certain circumstances. Control was never returned. Governments to this day still make use of cell phones; in fact the members of the World Medical Committee all use them."

"I can understand that and I don't think it's restrictive, but people can use the V-Link system"

"True, but the V-Link is controlled and monitored by Central System."

"But tablets and computes?" Jim asked.

"One word, Internet."

Jim's face lit up in recognition.

"Even without social media and cell phones people still had forums, email and other means to cause overthrows." Jim said.

"Yes, and this part is crucial to understanding the reason why the Internet had to come under the control of responsible people and why all personal communication devices had to be banned. The fallout from nuclear radiation was horrific. Jim, billions died and millions more suffered for years. The devastation it caused worldwide is unspeakable. A special memorial committee was created to capture the effects, from video to photos to audio. Teams were sent in to areas where denotations took place to video the aftermath. The bodies of survivors were videoed and photographed, every possible detail was captured. We never wanted the world to forget the cost it paid for all those personal liberties."

"So there's a complete archive of this?"

"Yes SAM can access it for you later, but be forewarned it's not to be watched if you think you're unable to deal with human tragedy on a global scale and in the billions of lives."

"I'll keep that in mind, maybe for me I should pass on accessing it."

"May be for the best, how about a break? Let's take a glass of tea to the park."

Jim walked to the kitchen and fixed them both a glass of iced tea, after handing Toby his they exited out of the back balcony and down the steps. Jim walked alongside Toby in silence, looking at the families and children as they played in the park. This was indeed a better life for all concerned, no matter what the cost was to get here. Under the tree they sat down in the chairs.

"The Fuller Life Serum had still not passed government regulations. Even after the assassination of the President, whom it may have helped, and the nuclear holocaust the FDA still had concerns as to how the serum was developed, but it did not stop other nations. The World Medical Committee was begged to allow its use in Russia, China, and throughout the entire Middle East. However it did not take long until we realized that the serum was useless on cells that had died and were no longer duplicating through dividing. It appeared that this test run for the serum would also be its end run."

"Well something happened to change direction, or I would not be here." Jim said.

"Right. Besides the causalities from the radiation there were causalities from conventional warfare. Just prior to the launching of the nuclear missiles and right after, many were wounded from gun fire, shrapnel or other conventional means, for these ones the serum proved to be a success. After we started to have one hundred percent results the committee got a phone call from the FDA, they had cleared every question and its approval was granted. They asked us nothing and wanted no further testing. They wanted immediate implementation of it use. The benefactors were beyond words. Wounds that were once beyond the ability of medical science were now healed. It was miracle after miracle. Passage was granted worldwide."

"Giving the World Medical Committee worldwide control?" Jim asked.

"Not quite. The United Nations had been dissolved because of the launching of the nuclear missiles, so a new charter had to be drafted. The United World Nations was the result. The World Medical Committee made up its core, with member nations having input, the serum was the controlling factor. But the World Medical Committee did not exercise its authority with an attitude that it's only our way. Each nation adopted key elements, and each nation had to eliminate parts of their own laws or even creating documents to reach a compromise. In the end it stabilized the world and brought about the peace you see and enjoy. Does that answer your question?"

"Yes and I can see the logic in banning such devices and having Internet traffic controlled the way you do. But it also opens up a lot of other questions." Jim said.

"I don't doubt it. But why don't we call it a day. I have a committee meeting and maybe you can go explore some of the outlying areas on the Rail."

"Okay. Toby, I know you're still holding out on me, but thanks for trusting me enough to tell me what you did. As a friend, well you're the best a guy could have being over one hundred years old."

"Welcome Jim. See ya maybe late tomorrow, but I may not be able to get over this way. I'll V-Link you to let you know."

Jim watched as Toby walked along the cobblestone path and through the arched exit, the sound of children laughing captured his attention and he watched as people gathered around an evening camp fire.

***

The early morning sun brought Jim rising hope and a reason to push forward. He had gained information and built trust with Toby, and by extension the committee, he was also another day closer to seeing his beloved. After Toby had left he pulled up some destination ideas and decided to spend the day on the Rail, visiting places that still existed from the former world. Small, out of the way towns and areas that were once called tourist traps. After gathering a few items he thought he would need he exited his apartment, being glad that he was not tethered to a cell phone to disrupt his day of leisure. He walked to the nearest Rail platform and watched as people stood around a monitor listening to a list of names read by Doctor Emily Thomen. He found a seat on a bench nearby and continued to watch as some cried and others slowly exited the group. When the list was completed he saw many shake the hands of others, pat their back or give words of encouragement. He could not withhold asking someone the question that formed in his mind. He got the opportunity when a young man, or what appeared to be young man, sat next to him.

"Excuse me?" Jim said.

"Yes." The young man answered.

"That list that Doctor Emily Thomen reads every morning and every evening, what is it?"

"You're a new Wake aren't you?"

"Yes sorry, I guess it still shows. Names…"

"Let me guess, you're Jim Fuller!"

Jim smiled and his eyes lit up at the idea of being recognized by a complete stranger.

"Guilty." Jim said.

"Well Jim", the young man extended his hand "it's an honor to meet you. You can't possibly recognize me but I was you're teacher when you were in the fourth grade." The young man said.

"What! You must be about, well past one hundred and fifty."

"Close enough, I stopped counting years ago."

Jim was surprised that the young man did not call to others to draw attention to him. Perhaps it was part of being respectful in this new world.

"I'm sorry but I don't remember your name." Jim said.

"Nathan, Nathan Anderson."

"That's right Mister Anderson. I've always credited you with pushing me to follow my father's path into science. My father's approach to science was so matter-of-fact I dreaded taking the company when I got old enough, but you presented science in a much more enjoyable manner." Jim said.

"And to think, if you did not go into science neither one of us would be having this conversation."

"Wow, I never considered that." Jim said.

"To answer your question. Doctor Thomen reads the children's list every morning and the Wake list every evening. But your name was never read; of course I can understand why it was not."

"Children's list? What's the children's list?"

"Oh hey sorry, but there's my Rail. V me and we'll continue talking later. It was sure great meeting you."

With that Nathan was on the downtown Rail and out of sight. In fact the entire platform was now clear; Jim realized that he was the only person waiting to board the Rail for the outskirts. He waited in silence, contemplating what Nathan met by a children's list. While he was still in thought the outbound Rail came to a stop and he boarded.

He found himself alone in the car, crowded only by twenty empty seats. He walked to the halfway point and took a seat by the window. Three soft chimes echoed through the car and then it lifted a few inches from the single rail and gravity pulled Jim against the back of the seat. The Rail Train quickly accelerated, leveling out at one hundred and thirty miles per hour.

Jim watched through the window as the cityscape gave way to the suburbs, soon to be replaced by open country side. The Walnut River meandered its way through lush thick forest and meadows of flowers and green grass. In the former world the landscape would have been marred by tree farmers and limestone quarries, but in this world they no longer stained the Earth. He turned his attention to the video display nestled in the back of the headrest of the seat in front of him.

"Activate display."

The sound of his own voice in an empty Rail Car startled him.

*"Hello Jim; display activated."*

"SAM?"

*"It is I."*

"How did you get here?"

"*I am neither here nor back at the apartment. You may recall, there are twenty server farms located throughout the world. Regardless of what display you activate, your voice is recognized by the Central System and your personal settings are then 'transferred' to your current location. It is the same with every citizen of Earth.*"

"Well okay then. Can you pull up the itinerary we made up last night?"

Before he completed the request SAM had the itinerary displayed in front of him. The first community listed for the Rail to stop at was *Livingston*. Before The Transition Period it was a small town of nearly four thousand people, trucked in the foothills of the Cherokee Plateau of Tennessee.

"SAM, can you pull up the current information and related information about Livingston from The Transition Period, please."

"*Accessing. How would you like the information presented?*"

"I'll read it SAM, thanks."

"*Prior to The Transition Period Livingston was ideally located on a north to south main highway that ran from Georgia to Kentucky. Its peak population was four thousand six hundred and eighty people. During The Transition Period the town suffered from a serious decline in population and when the entire length of the main highway was removed for the Global Cooling Project the population declined again. The current population is five hundred and twenty one people. The small community welcomes visitors and over the years has developed their economy around the spring and fall, when most visit the area.*"

"SAM; display current points of interest, as well as the best place to eat."

"*Points of Interest Include: Several local craft stores located around the central square. During the spring and fall locals gather on the square for musical performances, some of which have drawn in several thousand people from the surround areas. Prior to The Transition Period, Dale Hallow Lake sat to the north, during the Earth Reclaim Project the dam was destroyed to restore the natural flow of the river. A Point of Interest lays under the drained lake, a town several hundreds of years old called Willow Grove. The central square of Livingston has several small eateries. One of which is known for its old southern style cooking. However should you eat there a disclaimer is on the menu that fried foods may cause damage to the body."*

"Interesting."

*"Was that a request?"*

"No SAM sorry. Display off."

The display returned to its former translucent state to blend in with the color of the headrest. Jim returned to watching the countryside as it passed by. The Rail started to slow and as it did the landscape changed, dotted here and there with small homes. As he approached Livingston buildings continued to fill in the scenery, but he saw no roads. Paths of cobblestone connected the houses and businesses. People either walked or rode a bike, and some were even using horse and buggy. Soon the Rail came to a stop and he felt it lower, coming to rest. The doors slid open and he departed the Rail.

Jim stepped out onto the brown cobblestone walk and what felt like three hundred years into the past. The small town had been rebuilt and redesigned to resemble early settlements of the seventeen hundred's; it reminded him of the time he took a trip to Massachusetts. It was two thousand ten and he attended a conference, and while there he visited the local tourist attractions, some of which were rebuilt villages from early settlers. Livingston had that same look, but with an authentic feel.

"Hey bub. Little early for the visitor season."

The voice came from behind Jim, startling him. He quickly

turned to see a man leaning against a store signpost. His dress was in tune with the surrounding town, overalls, on top of a red plaid shirt, with a wide brimmed straw hat and a tooth pick in the corner of his mouth. Only the hiking boots were out of character.

"Well since I'm early for visitor season, then your clothing must be the way you dress every day." Jim said.

The man let out a chuckle.

"I like you already. The visitors should start showing up in about two to three weeks, the fall of the year. So what brings you here?"

Jim thought about the question, what did bring him here?

"I wanted to explore the area outside Fuller City."

"Well this is as good as place as any to start with. Eat yet?" The man asked.

"No, just got off the Rail."

"How bouts we walk over the *Sue's* and gets us a nice southern cooked meal?"

"I was cautioned about eating there because of…"

"The fired food. Shucks, the Fuller Life Serum can fix that if it gets too bad. Come on I'm buying."

Jim watched as the man pushed himself free of the signpost and started walking toward the far end of the square. When the man realized Jim had not moved he stopped.

"You comin' city boy?"

"Ya, why not."

The man waited until Jim caught up to him and then extended his hand.

"Names Chris, but folks around here call me Bo."

Jim took his hand and shook it, as he started to say his own name he realized the attention it would draw.

"Names, Jeff, Jeff More."

"Sure it ain't Jim, Jim Fuller. Everyone knows your face, but no one around here cares at all about famous folk. You is folk just like me, right?" Bo asked.

"Ya, that's right. I'm no better."

The two started walking in the direction of *Sue's Southern Restaurant*.

"Why introduce yourself different then who you are, you ashamed of yourself, are you?"

"No, concerned. Even back at the Rail Station in Fuller City when I was recognized the person did not draw attention to me." Jim said.

"See there Jimmy, people in this world don't care who you are, we're all the same. So don't hide your name. In fact you're the only person who can't hide his name."

Bo pulled open the door to *Sue's* and held it, allowing Jim to walk through. Inside Jim waited for Bo to enter and then followed him to a corner booth.

"Hello Bo," the waitress said, she then turned to look at Jim, "Well I'll be, we have us a real live famous person, and at my table. Hi Jim, don't worry I won't run around screaming and swooning. What'll you boys have?"

"Give us both the fried chicken special platter." Bo said.

"Two fried chicken special platters, be right back."

The waitress jotted down the order and vanished between two swinging doors.

"So what do you intend to visit around here?" Bo asked.

"Not really visiting, just sorting out some information."

"Ever been out of Fuller City?"

"Ya. Jennifer, my wife, and I own some land with a cabin on it up in the Cherokee Mountains. I had never traveled west of the City."

"So what you trying to sort out?"

"I'm still considered a recent Wake, and I've been trying to catch up on a lot of details, especially from The Transition Period. A long time school friend of mine, who is on the World Medical Committee, has been helping me a lot with understanding that time period."

Bo did not answer; on the table he drew a pattern over and over with his forefinger, trying to form thoughts into understandable explanations.

"I say something wrong?" Jim asked.

"Nope."

Bo continued to draw invisible images on the table. Jim reached across and grabbed his hand.

"Be careful there Jimmy, I might have to kill you if you grab me again." Bo smiled and then laughed.

"You're not serious?"

"Course not. Listen those committee members, regardless of how long you've been friends, ain't gonna tell you the truth. Every word they speak is peppered with omissions and inclusions."

The waitress returned and set two glasses of iced tea on the table.

"Be careful with this one Jim, he enjoys telling his conspiracy theories to anyone who'll give him an ear."

"Not true and you know it Sue. You know I'm right."

Sue leaned over the table and moved her mouth close to Bo's face.

"You're gonna git yourself sent off to an incentive camp if you keep this up. Eat your meal then take Jim out somewhere and talk, but not here. I ain't riskin' my restaurant for anyone, over anything, true or not."

"All right, you're right. We'll eat in peace, Sorry Sue." Bo said.

Sue stood back up and smiled at the two men.

"Good. I'll bring your order out soon."

"You'll fill me in later?" Jim asked.

Bo nodded his head yes.

***

Three miles outside of Livingston and deep in the woods a lone cabin stood on the edge of a small lake. From the outside Jim could see no electrical wires or outside dish receivers. Inside the cabin there were no electrical outlets or lighting. Bo opened the curtains and then lit some old oil lamps for light. Dust danced in the flickering dim light as it was disturbed from its resting place. The cabin was a single room, a sink nestled in a corner before a front facing window had a hand water pump. In front of it was a small seating area with two chairs and stacks of books and magazines. On the far side was a bed, room to sleep one, and in the corner at its far end was a stack of supplies.

"If you feel the call, the outhouse is out back."

"You really live off the land here."

"Many Transistors do. I lived in the old world, and I saw events as they changed first hand. I'm not from Livingston at all, but moved here after The Transition Period. I wanted out of Washington D.C. and away from the fallout."

Jim noticed that Bo no longer had a southern accent; it took on a more New England flavor.

"You were in Washington at the time of The Transition Period?"

"Jim I have an eye for trusting people, and the second I saw you step off that Rail I knew I could trust you. I also knew who you were. But I had to know why you came out here. You said you needed to understand some information that a member of the World Medical Committee has been telling you. You're here because you have doubts about what you've been told. Have a seat; I want to show you something."

Jim crossed the small cramped room and sat in a chair furthest from the oil lamp that was sitting on a side table with a stack of books near it. Bo walked to the area with the single bed and removed a plank from the wall, reached inside and removed a tin box. He pulled the box tight to his chest and cradled it as if it were more precious than his own life. He cross back to the chair next to Jim and sat down. He reached under the table on his left and pulled a small key free, inserted it in the lock and turned until he heard a click.

Jim knew a long held secret was about to be shared with him, and he could feel his heart rate increase with excitement. He watched as Bo, or whoever this man was, slowly lifted the lid of the tin box, the flicker of light from the oil lamp glistened from metal within. He heard Bo take in and let out a deep breath.

"Jim, I hope I didn't go wrong to trust you. But keep in mind, even after you see and hear what I have to show and say, you have to go on as though you know nothing different than what you've been told. Understand?"

"Not yet, but I'm sure by the time you're done with me I will."

Jim watched as Bo removed a small leather wallet, he reached for it as Bo handed it across the stack of books.

"Take it, open it." Bo said.

Jim took the leather wallet in hand, being gentle, handling it as if it were a precious gem. The dim light of the cabin flickered and danced off the wall behind him, it was difficult to see if the wallet was dark brown or black. As he was about to open it, the light around him increased, he looked up and noticed that Bo had lit another oil lamp on a shelf above him.

"Better?" Bo asked.

"Ya thanks." Jim said.

The wallet was black, black as coal. Jim carefully opened it, holding his breath as he read the words inside.

# CHAPTER 9

Jim tilted the black wallet are various angles, trying to read its contents in the dimly lit room. Regardless of what was written on the upper portion, what was attached to the bottom was undeniable, a two toned gold on silver badge.

"Anthony Christopher Williams." Jim looked over at Bo, or rather Anthony.

Bo squinted in the flicker of dancing light, attempting to discern the expression on Jim's face. How much information should he reveal to the man sitting beside him?

"Anthony was a long time ago, its Bo."

"You were in the U.S. Secret Service?"

"Yes, on presidential detail. I served under President Jefferson."

Jim's eyes widened and his eyebrows rose in arched disbelief. For a moment he considered not pursuing his next question, but opted to ask.

"Wasn't he assassinated at the order of the Vice President?"

Jim asked.

"No, not by the Vice President, but..." Bo stood up, walked to the sink, reached underneath and pulled out a bottle of Scotch. He poured some in a tin cup then tilted the bottle toward Jim.

"Better not." Jim said.

Bo replaced the bottle under the sink and walked back to his chair.

"Jim, believe me, you won't believe me. The Vice President had nothing to do with the assassination, he was the scape goat. The World Medical Committee had him assassinated."

The statement hung in the thickness of the air, as if being spoken over and over. Jim knew every member on the committee and some were lifelong friends. Toby being his best friend, and he was someone who would never consent to the murder of another person, more so the President of the United States. Again Bo stopped talking and this time reached back in the tin box and removed a black metal object. He turned it over in his hands, allowing his fingers to fumble inside the rounded guard. He held out it in front of Jim, the yellow light of oil lamps flicker off the jet black metal.

"What is it?" Jim asked.

"It's the trigger mechanism from a sniper rifle, the very same sniper rifle that killed President Jefferson."

"I – don't – understand, how did you get it?"

"It was handed to me by the assassin after the President fell to the stage." Bo said.

"So you were part of it? Part of the assassination of President Jefferson?"

Jim could not believe the question he just asked, and when the words escaped his lips he wished he could take them back.

"I was duped into playing a part. At that time the FDA was stone walling the World Medical Committee on approval of the Fuller Life Serum. Everyone that knew about it in government wanted it approved, even me. But it was excuse after excuse. When ISIS moved into Iraq the President saw his chance to gain control of the serum. Sure there were real ethical issues, however I was never told what those issues were, but I did know that the serum would help billions. The President wanted it approved, but not for the same reasons that the World Medical Committee wanted it approved. I do believe that the end motives of the World Medical Committee were going to be good, but you know the saying, the end never justifies the means. Anyway the FDA refused to approve it because of real ethical issues, but the President wanted it approved to create a better army. He realized that with control of the serum in the hands of the military, the United States military would become an unstoppable force, and the most feared. But not even the President had the ability to push it past the FDA, and the President was fully aware of the ethical issues. The World Medical Committee was not aware of the true desires of the President until a few days before he delivered that 're-invade Iraq' speech. Someone in his inner circle leaked it to the World Medical Committee, two members, Nick and Daniel, confronted the President and he admitted that he intended to invade Iraq again under the guise of pushing out ISIS, but he wanted to inflict as much damage as he could on U.S. troops. Those that were treated in the field could be treated with the serum, when the people of America saw the results the FDA would have to approve it due to public opinion, and he would ensure that it came under the control of the military. Daniel told the president that it would never happen. There were several of us 'insiders' ones who knew about the serum and its potential, and what it could do for all humankind. We wanted it approved, I wanted it approved, but not in the manner that the President was trying to get it pushed through the FDA."

Bo took another drink of Scotch and swirled the warm liquid in his mouth before swallowing. He was unaware that he was drawing on the arm of the chair with his right forefinger, the same design that he was drawing on the table at *Sue's Restaurant*.

"Those of us in the Secret Service and within congress knew what would happen if the military got control of the serum, it would be kept for the elite and the common people would continue to suffer and die early."

Bo looked at his hand and realized he was drawing; he quickly tucked his hand under his leg.

"So who did you love that would have benefited from the serum?"

Bo looked at Jim with suspicion.

"Bo, no one on Secret Service detail agrees to assassinate the President unless he feels the price is worth it."

Bo relaxed his body, Jim knew nothing and it was a question drawn from a logical deduction.

"My daughter. She had a rare blood disorder. We tried everything, nothing, and I mean nothing worked. The serum would have helped her."

Bo allowed himself to drift back to that desperate moment in time when all hope had faded.

"So where is she now? Also the rest of your family? You're here all alone."

Bo dropped his head and stared at the Scotch in his glass; he sat it on the table and buried his face in his hands. His body jerked as he fought back the tears of loss. When he looked up his eyes were red and swollen.

"We lived in Washington D.C." With the memory filling his mind he pounded his fist on the arm of the chair.

"Jim we lived in Washington D.C. After the assassination of the President and the arrest of the Vice President I was given special detail of the new President. It was just before The Transition Period and he flew to meet with the Prime Minister of England and other world leaders to discuss the situation in Iraq. That was when the nukes were launched. I was kept safe with the President, but my entire family – was – gone."

Again he dropped his head in his hands and allowed the memory of his family to flood his mind and the tears to fall unabated. His body convulsed as he sobbed at the images of his wife, son and two daughters, alive in his memory. It was several minutes before he was able to look up.

"Sorry."

"Don't apologize. I understand love for family. Are you able to continue?"

"Yes." Bo blew his nose and then dropped the tissue in a small trash can between the chairs. "Back to the assassination. Daniel and Nick presented the idea to the committee to assassinate the President, the entire committee approved. I along with several other Secret Service Agents were called to The Barns Firm, there we were instructed what to do and how. We all knew about the upcoming speech and it was the chosen event. A friend of mine was the trigger man, and then four of us waited behind him. Once we were sure the President was dead the gun was dissembled and each of us given a part, I was handed the trigger mechanism. I've kept it all this time. When I got back from England and learned what happened to my family I decided to vanish. As The Transition Period grew darker I made my way here, and here is where I intend to stay."

A long heavy silence filled the dimly lit cabin. The sun had set below the horizon and stars filled the night sky, the room was lit by the light of three oil lamps. The brightness of those was fading, as the oil was drained. The men remained silent while two of the lamps flicked their last.

"I'm turning in. That chair you're sitting in pulls out to a small bed. Not comfortable, but it's a place to sleep. I'll see ya in the morning if you're still here."

"Bo?"

"Good night Jim."

\*\*\*

The smell of fish frying and coffee brewing filled the small cabin room. Light from the rising sun flooded through the window that rested along the back wall. With the sunrise a rooster repeated his morning alarm, and somewhere two dogs barked relentlessly for their morning breakfast.

"I'll have the eggs fried as soon as the fish is done. Like salt and pepper with your food, and how do you take your coffee?" Bo asked.

Jim sat up and pushed himself back against the backrest of the chair. He ran his fingers through his hair, flicking the last few strands. He licked his lips and smacked his gums to get the nights buildup of gump unstuck.

"What time is it?"

"Just after six. You must be a late sleeper. That blasted rooster never lets me sleep in. I keep telling myself to eat the stupid bird, but I never have the heart to ring its fool neck. Your coffee, how do you want it?"

"Got sugar?"

"Sweet tooth, you baby. How much coffee do you want me to add to your sugar?"

"Only put a small level spoon in it, just enough to take the edge off the bitterness."

Bo clanked the spoon hard against the tin coffee cup; the sound would help shake the cobwebs out of Jim's mind. He then carried the cup of coffee to Jim.

"Now once I'm done cooking, you come make your own plate. This is as far as room service goes."

"How far back is that outhouse?"

"Only about twenty feet, can't miss the trail. In the summer I just follow the smell. After we eat I want to take the boat out on the lake."

"Is that Dale Hollow Lake? I thought that was drained." Jim asked.

"It was. But several small lakes remained behind. I bought the land that surrounds one. I own the entire lake."

Jim placed the cup of coffee carefully on the small table to his left and kicked the remaining cover off his feet, as he made his way to the door he heard Bo's voice, "Grab a few sticks of wood for the stove on your way back in." He continued his exit from the cabin's only door. He followed a well beaten path around the back and up a small embankment. In a clearing sat a small wooden building, in its door was a crescent moon.

When he stepped from the outhouse he saw some firewood stacked a few feet from the cabin. He picked a few pieces from the top and walked to the front, kicking the bottom of the door with his foot.

"Great thanks. Ever added wood to a fire?" Bo asked.

"No."

"Well you're gonna' learn."

Bo lifted the small round cast iron cover on the cook stove and gave instructions to Jim to shove one piece of wood in at a time. As he did so hot embers freed themselves and escaped through the hole, a few landing on Jim's arm and scorching him. Jim pulled his arm back quickly and shook it rapidly.

"Could have given me some warning."

"If I did you may not have learned how to put wood in a burning fire. Bet you'll be more careful next time."

"Ya" Jim washed his hands and then made a plate of fried fish, eggs, and slightly burnt toast. "How big is the lake?"

"Small really, only about eleven acres, but has some of the best Bass fishing you'll ever drop a line in."

"Never fished, never had the time or the desire." Jim said.

"Well today you'll learn, or drown, your choice." Bo's laughter let Jim know he was not serious.

\*\*\*

The two men sat in a flat bottom fishing boat at either end, a holdover from before The Transition Period. Between them a built-in fish holder, containing three fish, all caught by Bo. With nearly every cast of his line, Jim would see his bate continue flying through the air, landing several feet beyond where the line fell into the water. Bo instructed him not to cast with too much force, but it appeared to Jim to be an acquired skill.

"I believe I better give up, I seem to be feeding the fish more than catching them."

"Just watch for a while, and then try again later." Bo said.

"It's different out here than in the city, a greater feeling of peace and calm. I felt watched all the time in the city, but here, it feels like it did when Jennifer and I went up to our cabin."

"From what I know, they do watch you in the city. But to be honest, the World Medical Committee is fully aware of these small towns, and how many live out here. With satellites they can see me when I scratch my butt, but they can't hear a word I utter."

"So how can they know how many live out in the middle of nowhere?"

"The serum. I'm sure there were a few Transistors early on that did not take the serum, but by now they've died off. Those of us out here, we take our allotment every six months. To be honest, I could care less how the stuff was approved; I want to live as long as I can."

"So how did you go from Anthony to Bo or Chris, whatever, unnoticed?"

"With the nukes came massive confusion, for nearly a year worldwide confusion ruled. Here in America they were able to bring order through marshal law, the military was stationed everywhere. But for the first few months, total confusion ruled America as well. It was during that time I decided my life needed change. After I arrived back in the United States aboard Air Force One I got as close to Washington as I dare. I wanted to charge in and find my family, but Jim, there was nothing as far as I could see. I fell to the ground and pounded by fist until they were red with blood. Whatever the reason for those nukes, I felt that the World Medical Committee was somehow involved. Their entire focus was the Fuller Life Serum and nothing, not even the lives of billions would change that, but it was just a gut feeling. I rose from that bloody dirt and started walking. I made one stop at a safe house to pick up the contents of that tin box, but then continued to walk. I eventually came across this little town. When someone asked me my name, I told them Chris."

"Okay, so you walked south and west from Washington to disappear. But one problem, your fingerprints and DNA had to be on record."

"True enough. My prints and DNA were kept on a server in Washington, a place that no longer exists. Agents on Presidential detail didn't have them stored elsewhere."

"Do you know the truth behind the launching of the nuclear weapons? Was the World Medical Committee involved?"

"Don't know for sure Jim, just my gut talks to me. I've heard things over the years as visitors came and went, but nothing concrete. But consider this Jimmy; if they did, does it matter now? What's done is done. Neither you nor I can go back and alter anything. And if the committee did have something to do with it over the serum, then so be it. I don't mean this in a bad way, but that serum has made this a much better place, a much better world."

"So you're okay with it? Even at the cost of your own family?" Jim knew the question would hurt when he asked it.

"I hated losing my family Jimmy, and I do wish they were here with me. But it is what it is. I had to adjust and accept this world, for good or bad. I don't know what the serum is or how it's made or what the issues behind it were, but I do know that the committee will do what they need to do to protect it and ensure its survival, even if it means killing me or you." Bo said.

Jim looked out over the calm water; it reflected the trees growing along its edge and the clouds above, as if the lake surface was a second upside down sky. He had feared that if he did not accept what Toby was spoon feeding him that he would be sent to an incentive camp, but he was reassured that the idea had never entered the conversations about him by the committee. But had they considered killing him. Had his best friend been involved in conversations about eliminating him?

"I wish I could escape to this world, your world, but I'm stuck in Fuller City."

"No matter where you go Jimmy, you'll never be able to hide. You're Jim Fuller, the reason for this lovely new world. So what stop is next on your tour?"

"Well I did not intend to stay the night here. I was going to travel on, hit a few more places and head back to Fuller City around noon today, but it's now two. So your cabin is the last stop of my tour. I need to get back to the Rail Station and Fuller City."

"I had a dock built about a ten minute walk from town on the other side of the lake. We have enough power to putter over there and I can walk you to town, I'll recharge while there."

"You sure?"

"Ya, I made a new friend I can trust and share my secrets with. I need to keep friends I can trust."

Although the electric motor on the boat was quiet its noise traveled along the water's edge to return as an echo. At the far end of the lake Bo glided the boat along a wooden dock and Jim attached the mooring ropes at either end. Before exiting the boat Bo disconnected the motor from the battery and attached a recharging panel, directing its black surface toward the late afternoon sun.

"Sure there'll be enough sunlight to get a full charge?" Jim asked.

"I only need a quarter charge to get back across the lake."

Jim followed Bo up steps that were cut into the hillside and then along a well-used path. The two continued to share stories of life in the former world, and compare those to life in the present world. When the wooded dirt path gave way to a brown cobblestone path their conversation ended. They stopped by *Sue's* for a glass of iced tea then completed the rest of the journey to the station.

"It says the next Rail is due in twenty minutes, a return from Nashville passing though, making a stop in Fuller City. Want me to book you a seat?"

"Yes, please. I bet this time I won't be the only passenger."

"Not on a Rail coming out of Nashville you won't, it'll be packed. But as you have come to learn, people here are decent and nice. Jimmy, be careful who you trust in this world. Eyes and ears are everywhere. I'll sit with you until the Rail shows up."

"Thanks for the advice, and company. Can I come back to visit?"

"Jimmy, consider my cabin door open to you anytime, day or night."

***

Jim walked slowly down the crowded Rail car looking for an empty seat or at least room to squeeze on the edge of one. At the back of the car a single isle seat remained, being grateful he took the seat; he did not want to have to cross through to the next car. Beside him, sitting next to the window was a woman; Jim had long given up on guessing ages. She had a look of determination on her face.

"Where you heading?" Jim asked.

"Oh hello. I never noticed when you sat down. Fuller City."

The woman studied Jim's face, searching her memory for a name to go with the face that she recognized. "Sorry for staring, you look familiar."

"Jim, Jim Fuller. I should be used to being stared at. But don't worry about it."

"Again I'm sorry. It's nice to meet you Jim. As I was saying I'm heading to Fuller City. My daughter's name was read on the children's list this morning."

Jim's first reaction was to ask what the children's list was. Two days ago before he left Fuller City he had heard the phrase for the first time and his old fourth grade teacher promised to explain its meaning the next time they met, but he now had the opportunity to have it explained. However he recalled the words of caution that Bo shared with him, 'be careful who you trust.' He decided to play it from the beginning; he gave his seating companion a look of confusion.

"You must be a new Wake, because you look confused. My names Martha; I'll do my best to explain the children's list, but it'll be difficult to understand until you've a child of your own. Oh, let me think – where to begin? About six years ago my husband and I got pregnant. As soon as a pregnancy is confirmed and registered at a Fuller Birthing Center, DNA is extracted from the embryonic fluid that fluid is sent to Fuller Labs for genetic testing. I'm not real sure what they're looking for and I've never heard any talk about it, so I can't tell you why they take the fluid. Anyway, over the course of the pregnancy the mother and baby are monitored closely. About a week before the birth the parents are admitted to a Fuller Birthing Center. They are given a full suite to live in, and to give birth in. As soon as the baby is born it's tested and retested, then brought back to the parents. For two weeks after its born the parents live there with the baby, allowing the parents and child time to bond."

Martha took a sip of her water and shifted her position in her seat. The memories of her daughter's birth and that first two weeks started to fill her mind as she retold the account.

"Are you alright Martha? You don't have to go on if you don't want to." Jim said.

"I'm fine; it was just a difficult time. Let's see, ya; when the two weeks are over the baby is then taken to one of twenty locations in the world. There the child will be given the Fuller Life Serum, educated and properly trained. Every other week the parents can see their child via V-Link, also every four months the parents get a one week visitation."

"That sounds awful, to have your child taken from you right after it's born."

"I can see how it would sound that way to a new Wake, someone who does not understand the benefits. But Jim; our world is a far better place than it was before The Transition Period. This world is at peace, and even though you may not understand right now the cost for that peace, it's worth it."

"Martha, I agree the world is a far better place than it was when I went to sleep, but having your child taken from you, and you don't even really know why, that's a sacrifice that I don't think is worth it. How long of a separation it is anyway?"

"You are a new Wake; you don't have the right to judge me or this world, or even what we have achieved. Me; I'm a Transistor, I lived in the old world and I lived through The Transition Period, you have no right to judge me at all."

This was the first hint of anger that Jim had seen since being awakened, and it was directed at him. He had met few people that called themselves Transistors, and those that did, had a mixed understanding of this new world. Only the Wakes appeared to have had a successful assimilation into the this world. He intended to apologize to Martha but was unsure of the reception of his words. Her face was red and tears of anger hung in the corners of her eyes.

"Martha; I'm sorry. You're right; I'm no one to judge you or anyone else. I didn't live through The Transition Period and what I've been learning about it I can't even imagine how difficult of a time it was."

"Apology accepted; besides your Jim Fuller, the man who gave us this world. It's sometime around their fifth birthday."

"Excuse me? Oh I asked how long the children are kept apart from their parents. Five years? I…"

"I know it's a long time and a lot of time lost with your child. But as I said, it brings this world peace. I don't know what goes on and no child remembers. As they grow they forget. Even those parents that asked questions right away get dream-like answers. And from children five years old, some of it sounds too fanciful. But every morning Doctor Emily Thomen reads the names on the children's list, the children that are able to come home that day. My little Susan was on the list this morning. My husband had to work or he would be with me, so I'm making the trip to Fuller City alone."

Jim understood her statement to be the end of their conversation, the rest of the trip would be in silence. She would be left to dream about bringing her daughter home and Jim would consider why the committee kept children for five years. He directed his gaze over the heads of other passengers and out into the countryside as it flew past the Rail. He knew there were ethical questions about the serum; and those questions were the reason for the violence that triggered what is now known as The Transition Period. But he failed to make the connection to the ethical question and the housing of new born children until they were five. In his mind he allowed possibilities to root, grow, and die off as each seemed too farfetched.

Were they kept apart from their parents to ensure the Fuller Life Serum worked properly and without any side effects? Was it possible that starting the serum that young could cause permanent damage and the committee wanted to spare new parents the loss of a child over the administering of the serum? Were the children kept housed separate as the serum was administered in order to avoid a lawsuit in the event the child died? These and other questions raced through Jim's mind, as he considered each possibility he allowed it to play out to its logical conclusion, to ensure it could be disregarded. His attention was brought to the present as the Rail started to slow on its approached the platform that he had boarded two days earlier. When at last it settled to a stop he disembarked along with the other passengers.

"I wish you the best Martha."

"Thank you Jim. I wish you the best at adapting to the new world as well."

The last of the day's light was fading as he walked home, street lamps started to turn on one by one, almost in secession as he walked down the brown cobblestone path. The people around him experienced no fear at the loss of light from the setting sun and approaching darkness. Even children exhibited no fear when they lagged behind their parents, to Jim it was an unnatural calmness, in many ways it seemed forced. On his current path he would soon pass The Barns Firm, the only place on Earth that held the truth, a buried truth. He slowed his pace, attempting to capture pieces of conversations of those that passed; chatter, useless chatter filled his ears.

*"Sure was a beautiful sunset..." 'When do you think the swing will be done...' 'What time was your sister coming over...' 'That old song...' 'She said about nine, but I doubt it..."*

He gained nothing from the array of chattering voices as they passed, their conversations were superficial, no depth, nothing about current events or world situations. He wondered if what they read in the morning paper or saw on the CBS Evening news was also censored, to protect the public, protect them from the truth. He lowered his head and shook it back and forth, attempting to shake the negative thoughts and images from his mind. Had the World Medical Committee somehow become a black backdoor controlling force of the world? Were world leaders merely puppets to the bidding of the committee? Toby told him that the committee exercised some authority, and that the United Worlds Nations held it completely, but he now wondered if the reverse were true. On the corner he noticed a vendor packing up for the night.

"Anything left?" Jim asked.

"Water, hum let me see. I got one apple left."

"I'll take them both, please. How much?" Jim asked.

"For you Jim, it's on me. Have a good evening." The vendor said.

"Thanks; you too."

Jim uncapped the glass bottle and took a long drink of cool water; he then slid the apple in his pocket and continued his walk in the darkness. Again he tuned his hearing toward those passing by, a crowd that was growing thinner as the hour grew later, and still he heard nothing but chatter, chatter mixed with laughter. As the evening slipped into night a crisp chill settled in from the north, summer had surrendered to fall. He snapped the collar up on his shirt and rolled the sleeves down, buttoning them at the cuff, then continued his slow pace home. His home, the apartment on the fourth floor of a stylish arched building, still five blocks away. A home empty of his beloved and the memories they had made, in a former life and in a former world.

A new light appeared, the moon started its rise, and it was intermittently dimed by a passing cloud. The sky around the moon was black and the clouds backlit and white edged as they drifted aimlessly by on an undisclosed journey to another place. Before him on the cobblestone path lay two shadows stretched and twisted in nightmarish ways. He looked up to the roof of a four story building to see two gargoyles peering back down at him, backlit by the moon as it dodged in and out of the clouds. He gazed was transfixed at the sight, a sight from sixteenth century France, he stood waiting for a hunchback to climb down from the waterspout.

"Beautiful sight. Isn't it?"

The voice startled Jim and he lost his grip on the bottle of water, he bent forward attempting to catch it before it hit the stone path, but it was in vain. The bottle hit on the edge of its bottom, gave a slight bounce, then toppled to its side and spun to a stop, never breaking. He finished his reach and tucked the bottle in his front left pocket, then turned to look for the voice that startled him. He saw no one from behind, or standing in the entryway of The Barns Firm. He turned back to face the direction he had been walking and saw nothing.

"Over here, across the path. I'm sitting on a bench, under the big Oak Tree." The voice said.

Jim turned to his right and noticed the figure of a man who was indeed sitting on a bench, under what could be an Oak, but he was unsure in the darkness. He waited for the parting of the clouds to allow the moon to cast its light on the figure. As the clouds gave way to the moon, light struck the edge of the bench and made its way slowly across until it revealed what he was waiting for.

"Toby?" Jim kept his voice questioned and muffled; in the

event he was mistaken.

"It's me Jim. Come on over and have a seat."

Jim cut across the ten foot wide path and stood before Toby.

"What in the world are you doing sitting out here?" Jim asked.

"I could ask you what you're doing walking around out here. Have a seat." Toby patted the area next to him and slid to the arm rest to make enough room. "The committee completed a meeting about an hour ago and I thought I would watch the moonrise over the building. It's the last one remaining of this kind of architecture in the city from the old world. There's not another like and never will be."

Jim sat next to Toby and looked at the full scale of the building. "It scared me as a kid and it still does. I hated to come here with dad, and I still hate to go in it." Jim said.

"But she is stately, one of a kind. So where've you been the last two days? I tried to V-Link you a few times, but even SAM lost track of you. I never knew someone could fall off the Earth in this age."

"I went west, visited a small town, and even tried my hand at fishing." Jim said.

"What did you think of it, the fishing?"

"Hated it, never again, can't see the sport in it. Fish don't have a chance. Of course they're hungry, if I was starving and someone dangled some food in my face I'd bite, and then the hook. I'm caught." Jim said.

"Point being?"

"The Fuller Life Serum was the bate dangled before the world, control was the hook." Jim said.

A breeze gathered leaves of different colors and they now danced in the entryway of The Barns Firm. From above them the wind whistled and seemed to howl as it passed through the carvings of the gargoyles.

"Not quite that simple, and not what the committee had in mind sixty six years ago. Jim when we stumbled on the serum, and realized its potential all of us, even Daniel, wanted the best for the entire world. We had good intentions and we still have good intentions. Nothing has changed. When the FDA refused approval and then the President had his own designs we realized that we had to have a measure of control to protect the serum. It's not about the members of the committee wanting any kind of control. In fact Nick and Daniel make most of the decisions, we doctors are still doctors."

"In the year nineteen forty Hitler controlled most of Europe, and the doctors were still doctors. The doctors for the Bayer Corporation were still doctors, just their subjects were less willing and their focus had changed." Jim said.

Anger raged from the pit of Toby's gut and flared in his expression. He stood and faced Jim in one quick turn, the redness of his face appearing black in the passing light of the moon. His eyes wide with hate at being compared to such an evil time and an evil corporation. His nostrils flexed rapidly as he attempted to control his breathing.

Jim held his bottle of water out to him. "Gonna take me to an incentive camp?" He asked.

Toby's body relaxed and his breathing slowed. He remained standing until he was sure the anger had subsided and then resumed his place beside Jim.

"Since I was awakened I've not seen one single person get upset or lose their temper. I wanted to know if it was still possible for someone to do so, so now I know. But I still have my stated concerns." Jim said.

"Jim; the doctors on the committee are not the monsters that ran the Bayer Corp in Germany. I swear to you Jim, I swear, no harm is coming to any human or animal for the production of the serum, no harm at all. Yes The Transition Period cost the lives of billions, but not because of the serum. This committee has not been responsible for the taking of a single life to get the serum approved. We've had to wait until world conditions changed. Our hands are clean of blood." Toby said.

"So everything that led up to the approval of the serum was chance, blind dumb chance?"

"Everything."

"The assassination of the President, the imprisonment of the Vice President and the launching of those nukes were all just blind dumb chance that opened the door for approval?" Jim asked.

"As stupid as it sounds, yes. The committee was always on the outside, especially in Washington. How could any of us possibly have any pull or control in Washington? We submitted our application and data to the FDA, what happened other than that was just chance." Toby said.

"Toby?"

"Yes Jim."

"You would never lie to me would you?"

"Jim; I have not and never will lie to you. I have told you the truth from the time you were awakened until now, albeit a little at a time and what you were able to handle. I will continue to be honest with you."

"Toby?"

"Yes Jim."

"Thanks for telling me the truth."

"You're my best friend, and I value that friendship."

# CHAPTER 10

Toby walked across the cobblestone path and paused in the entryway of The Brans Firm to glance back at Jim who was still sitting on the bench. From the light above the arched entry Jim could see a tight smile form on Toby's face. Jim waited until the door of the firm closed behind Toby before he got up and continued his walk home. The darkness of night formed a cloak around Jim as he walked, his mind turning over the lie he had just been told. Toby had been the first boy he had befriend in early prep school, they had bonded and defended each other as they made their way through life. In junior high and high school they were inseparable, baseball, football and even the rowing team, they were at each other's side. They had sworn an oath of eternal friendship when Toby was ten and his mother died, they had sworn that nothing would ever stand between them. Until now nothing ever had, and Jim thought nothing ever would. He had been betrayed, deceived and cast aside, maybe not for power, but for control of the fate of the lives of all people. Jim concluded what Toby had said was correct; the committee did not guide the approval of the serum for control of the world, but the committee members saw themselves as gods. Ones who chose the fate of the human race, who lived and who died, who received the Fuller Life Serum and who was passed over to suffer. Recalling the name of the serum sent a shiver through Jim, the gods had attached his name to something he now detested.

*"Welcome home Jim."*

"Hello SAM."

As he walked through the apartment to his bathroom he removed his clothing, leaving a trail that he knew would have irritated Jennifer. In the bathroom he walked to the shower head and turned on the water, choosing the hot setting. He wanted to scald the words that Toby spoke from his mind.

*"I am sorry Jim; my programming will not allow me to adjust the water temperature to a setting that hot."*

"Then make it as hot as you can please."

The water wasn't warm enough, but it would have to do. He slid to the floor and sat under the falling water. He leaned his head back against the stone wall and closed his eyes. He was sitting in the same position, with his eyes still closed, when the morning sun woke him up.

*"Shall I turn off the water?"*

"No SAM, I might as well shower for the day."

*"Very well. There is a V-Message waiting for you when you exit."*

"Thank you SAM."

\*\*\*

"Please play back the V-Massage."

*"The V-Message is from Doctor Emily Thomen; Good morning Jim. I wanted to let you know that Jennifer is now cancer free. We are currently infusing her with the Fuller Life Serum;"* Jim shivered at the thought of the serum being forced into his beloveds body, *"we'll be waking her at nine in the*

*morning. Toby will be by around at two this afternoon to brief you."*

"End of V-Message."

"Thank you SAM. SAM?"

*"Yes Jim."*

"Is there a means to do an inquiry without it being traced, or retrieved?"

*"Negative. Any and all searches or Internet inquiries are tunneled through one of twenty server farms. Key words are indexed and if any are flagged that message is forward to a review panel. Ones that present a possible danger are then forwarded to a member of the United World Nations and or the World Medical Committee."*

"That's what I was afraid of. Thanks."

*"Would you like to make an inquiry?"*

"No thanks."

Jim dressed and then removed a bottle of water from the refrigerator and approached the door of the apartment. SAM interrupted his thoughts before he could leave.

*"Please remember that Toby will be here at two."*

"Yes I'll remember." With that Jim exited the apartment in hopes of finding answers to questions he was now afraid to ask.

As they were the day before, and the week before that, the people that filled the cobblestone walks were blissfully happy and peaceful, as if their eyes were closed to the truth around them. Instead of listening to them or watching them he choose to ignore them, he was now on a hunt. Although many of the buildings were different, much of the layout of the town had remained unchanged. He picked up his pace and walked in the direction of his home from his former life. He knew it may be gone; a relic of the past, but on the corner from where his home once stood was a used books store, owned by an older couple at the time. They may now be younger, but perhaps they still run a book store. After turning on the block of his former home, he stopped and stared in disbelief. Before him it remained, undamaged and untouched. He could not resist the pressure from within; he approached the house, walked up the steps and rang the bell. He stood inpatient, waiting, and then knocked on the hinged side of the door so the sound would reverberate throughout the structure. Impatiently he waited, still no one approached to allow him entry. He walked around back and noticed a large stone had remained unmoved in sixty six years, was it possible that the key he kept hidden was still there? He reached behind the rock and stuck his hand into a hole that still held the hide-a-key box. Although the key was there, he felt the lock on the side door had to have been changed. The key slid into the hole of the door effortlessly, he turned the knob and was allowed entry and he entered his home and stepped into the past.

The memory of Jennifer overcame him and he slid to the hardwood floor and gave way to his emotions. The grief was more than he could handle and his sobs grew louder, if anyone had been at home they would have heard. He regained control and allowed himself to explore the house and travel though time. It was now occupied by a family, with children. He had no way to be sure, but perhaps two children, a boy and a girl. He continued to explore, the home was happy and alive, much like he had left it. Before he and Jennifer transferred the home to the committee he had cleaned it and restored the happiness of the home, that happiness could be felt in every room as he continued to explore. Even after sixty six years the setup seemed to have been unchanged. There was really no other way to arrange the furniture, it was something that Jennifer disliked, not having the ability to move things around in a different fashion once in a while. He turned from the living room and made his way to the back of the house to the room that had become hers. He stopped in the doorway, seeing his beloved once more on her bed, dying before him. His knees buckled and weakened beneath him, he pushed himself against the doorframe and steadied his decline. He entered the room. The missing wall had been restored and the handicap provisions in the bathroom had been removed. It made sense; they were no longer needed in this world. Next to the queen size master bed was a small chair; he took his seat, scooting it next to the bed. With eyes closed he traveled back to a time when he was still with her and they both still had freedom of choice. It was too late to return to that time, but he wished he could. If he were able to return he would crawl in bed next to her and allow death to take them both. The more he learned of the world he was now in the more he regretted his choice for being in it. He leaned forward and kissed the forehead of his wife, wishing it was the last kiss and not the first.

He brushed the tears from his eyes, stood and replaced the chair. He turned for one last look at the past and started to exit his home.

*"Jim? Shall I wipe the homes surveillance video of your visit?"*

"SAM! Is that you?"

*"Yes Jim. Your visit to this home was captured on video, as well as a record of your entry and where you walked. Shall I wipe that from the homes security system?"*

With one hand on the door knob he thought about SAM's request. How did SAM know where he was and how could SAM have control of a security system belonging to someone else. Regardless he knew his visit needed to be kept from the current owners.

"Yes SAM please do, remove all traces of my visit."

*"By your command, all traces of your visit no longer remain."*

Jim pulled the door closed and pushed the key into his front right pocket, he remembered his watch. Jennifer had given him that pocket watch for their fifth anniversary; it was not among the items Toby had returned to the apartment. He made a mental note to ask him about it when he came over.

On the corner from the house stood the used book store; as he entered a small bell tingled and announced his presence. The interior of the store had remained unchanged, bookshelves lined the walls to the ceiling and stacks of them filled the floor space. The lighting was dimmed from the high shelves which deflected much of it back up as it hit to top of the stacks. The smell was old, not moldy, but dusty and ancient.

"Be right there." A voice from the back called. It was a familiar voice.

"Nancy?"

"Yep; be right there. Hold your horses. Words on a page can't crash."

From the far end and between two tall stacks of shelves an image of a woman appeared an image Jim recognized. As she approached he could see that she had made use of the Fuller Life Serum.

Before her Nancy could see a tall man silhouetted against the plate glass window that covered the front of her store. "May I help you?"

"Nancy it's me; Jim, Jim Fuller."

"Jimmy, little Jimmy from down the street. Well I'll be. I never heard your name announced." She took him in her arms and embraced him, he returned her affection.

"It's so good to see you boy. Where's Jennifer?"

"Nancy it's good to see you and to know you're still around. Jennifer is due to be awakened tomorrow; clearing out the cancer took time. Where's Leonard?" Jim asked.

Nancy's eyes glistened over with tears. "He didn't want to take the serum. Felt it was unnatural. He said if that was God's means for man to live he would have given it to us a long time ago. But Jimmy, I didn't want to grow old, and after watching him suffer with Alzheimer's I knew I did not want that kind of death. I hated watching Leonard suffer and die, but it was his choice. I know I will in about another seven hundred years or so, but at least I won't have to suffer to do so." Nancy said.

"I'm sorry Nancy."

"What brings you here Jimmy?"

"Books. I can't make an inquiry without the committee knowing and I can't research the things I want to research without getting sent to an incentive program."

"Jimmy, what you want to research are off topics." Nancy eased her way around Jim and walked to the front of the store. Jim's heart rate increased, wondering if once again he had been betrayed. He watched as Nancy turned the lock on the door and switched the sign from 'OPEN' to 'CLOSED'. "It's more comfortable upstairs. Share some tea with me?"

Jim allowed her to pass and then followed her between stacks of books and up a small circular black cast iron staircase. At the top she led him down a dimly lit hall, at the end of which was a single frosted glass door. She held it open, allow him entry first. The apartment was smaller than he remembered. The kitchen and living room comprised the main area; a door from the living room entered a bedroom and down a small hallway and to the right was the only bathroom.

"Still drinking iced tea."

"Yes ma'am."

"Good. We can talk up here. I have no electronic devices made after nineteen ninety what so ever up here. Except my light of course."

As she prepared the tea he studied her, wondering if she could be trusted. Bo had told him to trust no one and he learned that lesson hard from trusting Toby. She approached him with the glass of tea in hand, he took it from her.

"Sit down." Nancy said as she took a seat in an oversized chair.

The furnishings of the apartment had also remained unchanged over sixty six years. By now most of what was around him may well be over one hundred years old.

"In this world people are happy, content, and thankful that all the stress of the former world is behind them. But it comes at a high price Jimmy. People are afraid, not of each other as if they will cause harm, but of speaking out. No one trusts anyone. Right so I suspect. If you say the wrong thing or even appear to be discontented then yep you might find yourself being hauled off to an incentive program. I've never been and have no desire to go. Many of those that are Transistors learned early on to keep our head down; mouths shut and keep our place. We learned the secret to freedom is not to be noticed. Some of the Transistors disappeared into the backwoods, but they have to come out to get their serum. Others of us, well we hide in plain sight. Don't make waves Jimmy; just accept the world around you without question."

"But is that what our former world was built on?"

Nancy leaned forward in her chair.

"Jimmy forget what you knew, it's forever gone. If you don't they'll use Jennifer against you. This is your life now. People don't have a choice, this is the new freedom."

"When I first woke up I would watch people and I felt something was not right, but I couldn't figure it out. When I watch families or see the blissfulness of people is it fake? All the peace I see is it fake?" Jim asked.

"Not really. People really are happy and content, more so the Wakes or New Borns. But ones like me, well it's hard to hide reality. But the happiness people feel and the peace they enjoy comes at a seriously high price. I don't know a single person that has ever been to the incentive program, but at the same time, I don't know a single person that wants to go and find out just exactly what it is. And strangely, I've never met anyone that has been. Jimmy it's easier to control the masses of people through fear than by any other means."

"Hitler would be a proud man if he were still alive to see this world." Jim said.

"I can't say it's that bad. I don't think there are incentive camps as you referred to them, but there's a program of sorts. All people of Earth know that." Nancy said.

"But no one knows what it is?" Jim asked.

"Yep. What did you want to ask me?"

"You've touched on part of it. I just have a lot of questions, and I'm deathly afraid to ask anyone."

"Well here you're safe. So ask." Nancy reached over and patted Jim on the knee to reassure him.

"Okay. Do you know anything about the assassination of President Jefferson and what happened to the Vice President?" Jim asked.

"Not details, just gossip. I heard the committee ordered the assassination of the President and they framed the Vice President. The speaker of the house was not sworn in until he understood his relationship with the World Medical Committee. But that's just gossip." Nancy said.

"Matches what I've been told." Jim said.

Nancy did not ask Jim whom he had spoken with. She knew he was seeking answers and with the questions involved, also knew that the trust had to work both ways. He would not expose those that helped in his search for the truth.

"That it?" Nancy asked.

"No. Did the committee have any involvement in the nukes?"

Nancy bowed her head to gather her thoughts. This was the question that trust would be tested.

"Yes. I don't know how or to what extent, but they did, well according to the gossip. What I was told was that they wanted to field test the serum to ensure its passage with the FDA. But I don't know anything more." She raised her eyebrows, her expression asking if that was all his questions.

"The children's list. What is it? I was told that they keep new born children for five years, allowing parents visitation and V-Visits. But why keep the children?"

"No gossip there. I've been trying to get the answers to that for years; no Transistors know anything at all about that. I mean not a single bread crumb of information. That program started long after The Transition Period and long after the committee started censoring every piece of public information. I'm afraid that that is one secret that you may never learn the truth about." Nancy said.

"Someone has to know something." Jim said.

"If they did, then they would know about the incentive program." Nancy said.

Jim slowly nodded his head in agreement; he took another sip of his iced tea before speaking again.

"So why do you believe the gossip about the nukes?" Jim asked.

"The same one who told me about the assassination told me about the nukes, or at least what she felt about them. She worked for the third administration after Jefferson, during the launching."

"You remember her name?" Jim asked.

"Nope; she disappeared right after the launching. She was evacuated out of Washington at the time, stopped right here in my store, spent the night with me before moving on. Don't know where she went, and I'm sure the name she gave me was not the name she used in Washington. Hear tell, many of the Washington people moved on rather quickly after the launching, most just seemed to vanish. I know if they're still alive they have to get their serum from somewhere, but how I don't know." Nancy said.

Jim studied the ice that sat atop the tea in his glass, he watched at it continued to slowly melt, to become a part of the liquid, mixing in and being unable to tell what it was.

"They melt into the communities they traveled too. Suppose?"

"Would have to, change their name, create a new back story. But you can't hide from DNA and fingerprints." Nancy filled in the unspoken parts that Jim intentionally left, testing her trust.

"Well most of those in Washington, wasn't their personal

data stored on computers that were nuked?" Jim asked.

"Would seem tell, suppose. Surely they had a backup somewhere in this vast country. But never can tell with government folk, always hiding information and never trusting anyone."

"That's what it seems. Nancy it's been great seeing you again, but I have to be back to my apartment by two, a friend – well someone I know is stopping by." Jim stood and started walking toward the frosted glass door.

"Former friend you no longer trust. Be careful Jimmy, don't trust anyone and just be content. Don't stand at the end of the firing range and you won't be a target."

"Sage advice, I just need to apply it. I've been dodging bullets for weeks now."

She tiptoed to reach his cheek and gave him a gentle kiss then led him downstairs and to the locked door. "Those who you knew before may be the ones you should trust the least. I do hope to see you again."

"As do I."

Jim reached for his pocket watch; it was not where it should be. The return to the past had returned old habits; he refreshed his mental note to ask Toby about his watch. The walk back to his apartment allowed time for consideration, he had accumulated many stories and few facts, but the stories agreed. He knew he could not trust Toby, but he felt he needed to confront Toby. He asked the twelve year old boy that first approached Jennifer under the tree in the park to return and give him the needed courage.

Inside his apartment he waited. He had thirty minutes before Toby was due, he reflected back to the park and the tree. In order to stand up and ask questions he had to find the same forthrightness that he had when he was younger. Time had tempered him, mellowed him, he needed his boldness to retake control.

*"Toby Ellis is at the door, shall I allow him entry?"*

"Sure SAM; why not."

"You excited yet old friend?" Toby greeted with a loud friendly tone as he entered the apartment.

"Come in; sit down, at the table." Jim's tone was not jovial or friendly, but serious and concerned, with laces of worry.

"Okay Jim. There's no need to be this concerned with Jennifer's awaking. I've done this plenty of times."

"It's not that Toby. Here's some water. I think you'll be needed a drink here in a minute."

Jim dumped all of the information he had gathered, he related the information about the assassination, the launching of the nuclear missiles, and the children's list. When he presented the information about the assassination and the missiles he did so matter-of-factly, as if he knew full details and that the committee had ordered both. He knew too few details to play the same game with the information about the children's list, and held nothing to bluff with the serum. Much of his statement was pressured and forced; he had his mind set on what he wanted to say and wanted it out in the open before he was stopped. When he was done he was covered in perspiration and breathing rapidly.

"So there it is. You just could not leave it alone. Jim, Jim, in time we would have brought you up to speed, you're an advisor to the committee, under the new laws, if you retained that post, we would have brought you up to speed. But now…"

"I'm hauled off to some sort of incentive program?"

"Little information out there about that or the serum? At least some things are still safe. No. In reality Daniel wanted to kill you early on, but I and Nick, and some of the others rallied behind you. Lies or not, I do value our friendship, or else you would be dead. But now I don't know."

"So you hand me to Daniel, let him kill me?" Jim asked.

"No, no. SAM!"

*"Yes Toby?"*

"Delete this conversation and visit from the time I arrived and forgo any further recording."

*"By your command."*

"So you've been recording every time you have come over?"

"No…"

"Stop lying!" Jim pushed against the heavy cherry table but it did not budge, instead his chair slid back. He stood boldly and paced the floor around the table.

"Let me finish my sentence. No, we've been videoing your every move in the apartment. As I mentioned Daniel and Nick were worried about you. So all your movements and inquires have been recorded. But we stopped surveillance three weeks ago; we felt you had accepted this life. We, I had no idea that you have been gathering information all this time. Just prior to each of my visits I have activated the surveillance systems. The committee is not aware that I have been."

"I was under the impression that I was the only one who had access to SAM!" Jim said.

"Sorry Jim. I never really said that, to my credit. The

committee and those that monitor at the twenty server areas have full access to all systems."

Jim returned to his chair at the table, he took a deep drink of water and after returning the glass to the table folded his hands in front of him.

"Would it do me any good to ask you to tell me the truth?" Jim asked.

"What do you want to know?"

"Did the committee order the assassination of President Jefferson?"

"Yes."

"Did the committee frame the Vice President?"

"Yes."

"Did the committee 'win' control of the speaker of the house in order for him to become President?"

"Yes."

"Did the committee order the launching of the nuclear missiles?"

No 'yes' was heard from Toby, silence filled the air. Jim did not push him to answer, but allowed him time to carefully formulate what he wanted to say. Toby slowed his breathing, bringing it under control, took a drink of water and cleared his throat.

"The committee did not order the launching of nuclear missiles; I can assure you of that."

"But what you omitting?" Jim asked.

"You won't like it any better."

"I want to know."

"We had to field test the serum. Even with taking out President Jefferson, the Vice President and having complete control of the new President, the FDA would not budge. Their greatest concern was the questions of ethics, how the serum was obtained. Nothing was going to move them to approve it, they sat in fear. They felt that if it was approved and later got out how it was obtained that they would be tried and convicted. They were absolute cowards. The committee had to act; a field test was the only way. We had good intentions, we had a good plan, it just went completely off course."

He paused, took a drink of water and wiped the sweat from his forehead.

"We had no intentions of inflecting the loss of life that took place. I want you to know that up front."

"I hear you, go on." Jim said.

"The situation in the Middle East was severely unstable, not to mention Eastern Europe. The entire region was unstable. We thought if we tossed a small amount of gas on the fire it would give us cause to field test the serum. We never imagined that the area was so unstable that it would explode. Using the CIA we toppled the government of Turkmenistan, not an easy task, and put radicals in control of the country. The CIA then removed the ruler of Syria and that allowed ISIS to overtake the entire region. Now here comes the gas we tossed on the fire. Turkmenistan still had a few, and I mean a few ICBM's from when they were part of the USSR, they joined forces with ISIS. They did not believe in the ideologies of ISIS, they just wanted more territory to build their ideology. We never imagined two forces with opposing religious goals would join to attempt to gain control of the region. When they paired up, ISIS gained control of and then launched ICBM's at Israel, and then Israel returned fire. Czar Putin took advantage of the distraction and launched against Ukraine. We had an opposing government ready to usurp Putin, but he made his move before the CIA made theirs. We assassinated him for his efforts, and then our people moved in. Before it was over, well you heard the report when you researched it."

"How presumptuous could you be? Before, it was the United States that imposed its will on other nations, now it's the World Medical Committee. Did it not occur to you that religious fanatics would use nukes? How dare you to assume you had control of the freewill of others." Jim's anger exploded and each word was forced out with a volley of spit.

"No Jim, it did not occur to us they would use them. Who would ever consider using nukes after World War Two? We wanted a conventional war; we wanted people wounded with guns, fire, and beatings, not billions lost in a nuclear holocaust. As soon as the situation was stable enough we moved quickly. But it was pointless; the serum was useless on cells that no longer divided. I got a front row seat to the sufferings of millions and the loss of billions."

"YA! Serves you right. I hope every night when you close your eyes you see those ghosts haunting your nightmares. I hope you never have another peaceful moment in your life." Jim ran his fingers through his hair in frustration and flicked the last few strands hard as they exited.

"Jim you don't know how right you are in what you're saying. Yes the committee played some very dirty hands when setting up the approval of the serum, but we never intended a nuclear war. Not one of us did and none of us saw it coming."

"So what do I do now? Go on as if I don't know anything?"

"For the time, yes. As far as the other members of the

committee are concerned you're still making forward progress in accepting the events that led up to this world. And in time you would have been told what you now know. So yes, go about your day to day life as if you don't know as much as you do. Be happy in public and when around members of the committee, don't give them reason to believe that you know more than you do."

"And if I don't behave? If I run into The Barns Firm and blurt out everything I know and tell the world?"

"Then Jim; Daniel will kill Jennifer while you watch and he will allow you to live with that memory burned in your mind."

# CHAPTER 11

A shudder ran through Jim's body. His best friend since childhood just casualty informed him that Jennifer would be murdered if he did not accept the fundamentalist ideology of this new world. The religious far right factions that caused the nuclear holocaust did so because of their ideologies, the committee was forcing change for the same reasons, albeit a different religion, the religion of science. Jim was trapped and he knew it. Jennifer was scheduled to be awakened at nine in the morning, if he did not play along, and truly accept this new world, then Jennifer would die. He felt another shudder; he held control of his wife's fate, his next words would mean her life or her death.

"I don't want Jennifer to die." Jim's voice cracked as he heard himself say the words, fear was starting to subdue his actions.

"Then she won't. But Jim, be careful around others in public and more so around the other members of the committee. They're decades ahead of you at spotting deception." Toby placed his hand on Jim's knee in an attempt of reassurance. Jim pulled his leg toward him, causing Toby's hand to drop.

"How much deeper down the rabbit hole do I have to go?" Jim asked.

"I'll let you know when you can't dig yourself out." Toby said.

"Okay, two more issues. First what are the incentive camps?"

"No camps exist, I assure you. It is more like a program. As we got deeper into The Transition Period we realized that many people did not want to give up the things they were doing. Some were not harming others, but they had a negative influence on the society we hoped to achieve. So we offered them incentives."

"Explain." Jim said.

"Well, I'll start with smokers and then you can fill in any undesirable behavior you want. We could not continue to allow people to smoke. Smoking causes severe damage to the body, not just to the one smoking but to others around them. It's also bad for the environment. Short of it is, smoking is just an undesirable trait. Using the method that we used to develop the serum we could effectively turn off the desire to smoke in smokers. Many took advantage of the opportunity, others did not. We tried to reason with them, encourage them, but to no good. So they were sent off to one of twenty communities around the world."

"Camps!" Jim said.

"No, communities. They were in fact towns, much like Fuller City. The people sent to them were allowed to form their own governments, as long as they were not oppressive. They controlled the infrastructure, ran the stores, and even developed their own currency. All in all the communities were what the people made of them."

"They just could not ever leave. They had to stay there?" Jim said.

"Correct. If a person did not want to give up smoking but

other members of his family did not smoke he was sent there alone. He was not allowed to take his wife, children, no one. The rule applied to any person any gender. There were no visitations. If you were so addicted to smoking that you wanted it more than family then you were allowed to continue, but apart from society that wanted change."

Toby allowed his words time to be absorbed by Jim. He gave one example and knew that Jim would apply it across the entire spectrum of people and behaviors.

"So they were supplied cigarettes?"

"No, they had to produce their own, from growing tobacco to processing it. Many grew it along with their vegetable garden."

"So – who else, or what other kinds of 'undesirable people' were sent to the communities?" Jim asked.

"A list then?"

"Yes."

"Drug addicts, both street and prescription; alcoholics; gamblers; sexual deviants; people in relationships that would not result in the natural birth of a child; ones predisposed to criminal behavior; all those in prisons around the world; people who chose to engage in antisocial and unacceptable behaviors. They were sent to the communities, allowed to run or ruin them, their choice. Once they died off or killed each other off they were gone and no longer a danger to the new civilization we were building."

"New civilization! Do you hear yourself? You destroyed people who were not a danger to others. 'people in relationships that would not result in the natural birth of a child'. You mean men and woman who were in same sex relationships." Jim said.

"Jim; in the natural course of events people should be able to produce children from a relationship. Not by adopting or other artificial means, but from the relationship they are in. Regardless of your beliefs, Bible, Torah, Koran or evolution, every religious belief teaches that the species must procreate to survive. Take for example evolution. Even today many do not accept it, and I know you never really attended church growing up, but you believe in some form of a Creator, so you believe in the creation of Adam and Eve. Well when you consider the concept of evolution, the survival of the species, then any threat must be eliminated. We did not kill anyone or force anyone to change. We simply put them in a place where they could live out their natural lives away from those that wanted change. In time people who engaged in undesirable behavior died off, they no longer posed a danger to others. So no camps they were communities where those who refused change got to live out their natural lives. They were never harmed by the committee or anyone else, except by those in the communities where they lived. They were responsible for forming their own law enforcement, some communities did, others let lawlessness rule. In the end it was the choice they made. Each person had the opportunity to contact us at any time if they wanted to change and accept the new world rules. We had very few people reach out to us."

"It sounds like a form of ethnic cleansing, no matter how clean you did it. You cleaned out the undesirable people from the society you envisioned. Hitler attempted the same thing; he murdered millions and you and your ideology murdered billions. I see no difference; you just feel your method was more – humane." Jim said.

"Many who are aware of the details feel as you do. But Jim; it was for the betterment of the entire human race. Billions benefited and billions more will. Those that were sent to the communities were few compared to those that benefitted. Can't you see the logic in that?"

"I see that instead of allowing people the time and chance to change or reform, you sent then off to die."

"We did not kill them, limit them, torture them, gas them or anything. They lived out their life, the way they wanted to. No experiments and we did not confiscate their belongings. So we did not kill them. In the end they made their own choice to live or die" Toby said.

"Toby; in the context of this conversation, you might as well have. Suppose you gave them the serum and it gave them the push they needed to change?"

"We tried that. The serum does not force change on people, it allows them to change the undesirable traits because of want." Toby said.

"Do the communities still exist?" Jim asked.

"No. When the last of those kind died off the communities were destroyed and material recycled. Smaller, more manageable self-contained centers replaced the large city-like communities."

"Those smaller centers still exist?" Jim asked.

"Yes, twenty of them around the world. They're more akin to rehabilitation centers today." Toby said.

"No matter how pleasant you make it sound, it's still ethnic cleansing." Jim said.

"Jim; your thinking is old world, it's…"

"Nuff! We're getting nowhere. But for Jennifer's sake I'll play the good reformed citizen." Jim said.

He walked to the window and looked out over the park; he now knew what was missing from all the happy families, young children. The families gathered in the park were made up of children of all ages, but no children under five. The children that were in the park appeared to be happy, but as if they were with aunts and uncles instead of mothers and fathers. He turned on his heal to face Toby, as he turned he ran his fingers through his hair, flicking the last few strands.

"You mentioned you had another concern." Toby said.

"I was just considering how to put it. The serum, how does it work; what are the ethical issues; and does keeping the children until age five have anything to do with it?"

It was Toby's turn to disassociate from the conversation to gather his thoughts. He had revealed a great deal of information to Jim, allowed him into the inner circle of the few that knew what really happened during The Transition Period. But only the few members of the World Medical Committee knew the complete details of how the serum was developed, processed and extracted. He walked to the refrigerator and took out another bottle of water. As he unscrewed the cap he turned to face Jim who was still standing in front of the window.

"Jim; I want to but I can't tell you. I would have to have the approval of the entire committee, and they will not allow you to have that information." Toby walked to the table and sat down, he bowed his head, torn, he had entrusted his friend thus far but he knew he could go no further.

"You have told me the things that you told me, so why not tell me it all?" Jim pulled the chair out from the opposite end of the table and sat down.

"Telling you could cost me my life and I know it would cost you yours and Jennifer's. Daniel and Nick have made it clear, extremely clear that the development of the serum and how it's processed today remains with the committee. When we reach the end of our lives the method dies with us."

Jim looked across the table and locked his emerald eyes to Toby's deep set brown eyes. He wanted Toby to see the loathing he was feeling. What Toby said was hypocritical to the beliefs he had expounded earlier about the good moral goals of the committee.

"What you just said is stupid. You mentioned before that the committee did what they did for the benefit of all mankind, now and forever. If you destroy the process; then you destroy the future hope of humankind." Jim said.

"Not so, or we think. We believe that with continued improvements in the serum, in time all humans born will be born without any defects. We think in time we will have worked out all the remaining issues and we feel that we can do this within our lifetime." Toby said.

"You keep saying 'in time', 'we think', 'we believe', and 'we feel'. You don't know do you? You don't know if you'll have the serum – right 'in time' for you and the committee to die. So what if you don't reach the point that you feel it's perfect? What if the last member realizes that it's still flawed? What then? Do you still destroy the process?" The disgust and loathing was evident in Jim's voice and body language. "If you truly did this for the benefit of *all* humans that means all humans into the far reaching future. I was correct when I said that the committee wanted control. You don't care what happens after you die, you just want control now." Jim allowed the disgust he felt for Toby to resonate in his words.

"Not true; we've – well me, Doctor Thomen, and the Watts' have considered that. Between me and you, and please ensure that it stays that way, we have a contingency plan in place. In the event we don't reach the point we hope to reach, we have ensured that the next generation will be able to continue our work. I'm a doctor first and foremost, and I want this project to continue, it's my life's work.

I'll give my life to ensure it continues." Toby said.

"And take out those that get in the way?" Jim said.

"You're still here, aren't you?" Toby said.

"I've not stepped in your way, and I don't intend to. So you're not going to give me anything, nothing about how the serum is produced or what it is?" Jim wanted a definite rejection from Toby. It would give clear proof that he was being deceitful. Jim knew much of what Toby was telling him was a lie, if he refused to share the details of the serum, it would be a clear indication that Toby did not trust him.

"Jim; I can't. The risk is too great to me, you and Jennifer. As you've learned, billions have died to reach the point this new world is at. Nick and Daniel will not hesitate to kill three more people. Maybe, maybe in time, but not now. Are you going to be okay with this information, you're not going to form a grassroots campaign to topple the existing government, or going to the committee and challenging the ethics of what we've done?"

"I'll play my part, and I'll play it the way I'm supposed to. I'll be the good quiet citizen I'm expected to be." Jim said.

"Good. I do need to prep you for Jennifer's awaking. We have several items to go over, much you know like spoon feeding information and at some point before you decide to have a child, telling her that it will spend the first five years of its life at a Fuller Education Center." Toby said.

Jim shot a cold hard look across the table at Toby.

"Even my child? You would take my child from me, and Jennifer, denying her the joy of early motherhood? From the time she was diagnosed with cancer she has longed for a child to hold to her breast to nurse, to cherish, to love. You would deny her that?" Jim said.

"Jim; it's the law. Early on some tied to keep their children, mostly those that transited from the old world to the new world. In the end those people still had their children taken from them, and some gave up their lives trying to stop their children from being taken, only to lose their life and their child. I can't do anything about that."

"Prep me; but Jennifer and I will not be having children." Jim voice was filled with loathing toward Toby and all that he represented. He regretted being awakened to this 'new world'.

Toby removed a tablet and synced with SAM to ensure the information he shared with Jim would be preserved. Although much of what he intended to share, Jim already knew from his own experiences, a record would still be needed for him to refer to.

Jim would have to give information to Jennifer little by little, too much and her questions would exceed the answers, as had happened to him. Some information he would omit, it was not necessary in her case. He would also have to instill trust and confidence in the committee and the absolute need for her to take the serum every six months. For the first time since he met Jennifer he would have to lie to her. Lie about the assassination, the nuclear devastation, and the incentive program. He would have to do to her what Toby had done to him. Inside he felt like he had been betrayed, and he was now about to betray his wife. Lie to her in order to preserve her life and his marriage. He would have to accept that the rest of their marriage would be based on a lie. He returned to look out of the window and down at the families in the park. How many of those fathers had lied to their wives. He had encountered several people that lived through The Transition Period, Transistors. They had learned to live the lie in order to remain alive. Jim had never lied to Jennifer in his life and now their lives would be a lie. A lie to live, it did not appeal to Jim. He sat back down across from Toby.

"I'll do what I have to, but no more. Not one lie more than I have too." Jim said.

"Careful. If you go into this thinking that you can have preset limits, you're wrong. I thought I could with you and look what has happened. You got curious and went on an information scavenger hunt; you found enough to bring up this conversation. If you attempt to limit the amount of lies you're willing to tell, well then, Jennifer will go on her own hunt." Toby folded his hands around the glass bottle of water and watched as Jim rolled what he had said over in his mind.

"You attempted to limit the amount of lying you had to tell me?" Jim asked.

"Yes I did. I hated lying to you. Jim you have been my friend since childhood and I hope you always will be my friend. Lying to you was painful, and I dreaded every time we met to talk. So from this point forward, if I can answer your questions truthfully I will, if I can't I'll just tell you that I can't share that information at all." Toby said.

"As you did with the serum?"

"Yes."

"So is that the limit of my briefing for tomorrow?" Jim asked.

"Yes. I think we've covered what we needed to cover." Toby said.

"Very well, I'd like to be alone. I'll meet you at Fuller Labs at eight thirty." Jim stood and walked around the table to stand next to Toby, indicating that he would see him to the door. Toby rose and followed him to the door, before exiting he stopped and looked at Jim.

"I am sorry." Toby said.

"And I hear you. See you in the morning." Jim closed and locked the door after Toby exited.

He stood next to the closed door, turned and leaned against the wall. His body went limp and he slid slowly to the floor, pulled his knees against his chest and lowered his forehead. The thought of lying to his beloved sickened him. In the former world he never regretted taking care of her. He had days when exhaustion overtook him, but he never once felt burdened by what he had to do from day to day. This was a burden that weighed on him; he felt as if a heavy lead plate was pressing him down, not allowing him a way out. His mind drifted to the cabin they owned in the Cherokee Mountains. When Jennifer woke up they could go there, raise a family and live out a life of eighty years. They would tell no one, and no one would have to know. Before leaving he could pick up a few survival books from Nancy, and Bo had taught him the basics of fishing. He dropped his head back against his knees in resignation. He was fantasying about a life that was out of his reach. He was raised in a wealthy family, sent to the finest schools and had all the privileges that civilized life could offer, he had no survival skills. And although they still owned the cabin, it had not been tended to in sixty six years. Neglect, rot and time may have brought it down. He felt helpless and powerless; he had no control over his own life. This was what he saw in the people of Fuller City, this was what was missing. People had no control over their own lives, they depended on the serum for life and absent that they would die sooner than they wanted to. He now realized why the world was so happy; the serum was not a drug that controlled the mind. The serum was a treatment that gave people what they wanted; a healthy long life, but at the cost of surrendering control of their lives. Death was an end he now longed for, but that was out of his reach. Acceptance or death, he would have to lie to his Jennifer or they would both be killed.

He stood and went to the bathroom, showered and then went to bed. He hoped that once he had her back he would find some measure of happiness.

*\*\**

*"Jim; It is seven thirty in the morning, time to wake up."*

"I'm awake, SAM."

Jim rolled to his left side and stared at the wall. He felt no different than he did last night, if anything he felt worse knowing that he would soon have to start lying. He rubbed the remaining sleep from his eyes and tossed back the covers. He lowered his feet to the floor and sat up, allowing the blood to return to its vertical flow. Mentally he worked out his day, running through the events in his mind. It should take three hours to complete the wake cycle, when that was completed he would take her to the park, and the memorial that was made in their honor. At the memorial he would start the story of the great saving Transition Period. He would tell her how the Vice President had the President assassinated and how religious radicals nearly nuked the entire world. She would believe it without doubt, but only because it was her Jimmy that was telling her.

After he showered he stood in front of the mirror, questioning who he had become. In the old world he never lied to Jennifer, not even while in school when bullied for dating a poor girl. He was proud of her and the two had become one in the truest manner. They were one emotionally, they were one mentally, and they were one in purpose. The man looking back was a sad reflection of the man he once was. He picked up his black comb and dragged it through his hair, parting it on the left and combing it over. He ignored the glare from the looks his image gave him and walked to his closet to get dressed.

On the cobblestone path he approached a vendor and bought a bottle of water and a banana, he ate on his way to Fuller Labs. Toby had warned him that Daniel would be there, and to exercise restraint about speaking out. He rehearsed in his mind his meeting with Daniel, role playing conversations, real or not, to prepare himself for every possibility. He hoped Daniel would ignore him and attend to whatever job he was there to do, but he felt that was not to be. He paused outside the doors to his own building, he owned the serum, could he simply retract it, remove it from the market. He shook his head, he owned it and the lab in name only, he was sure the committee had a contingency plan in place in the event that he ever tried to gain control of the company and the serum. He approached the glass pivoting doors.

*"Welcome Jim Fuller to Fuller Labs. The future hope of humankind."*

"Welcome yourself you stupid computer."

*"Invalid inquiry, please restate."*

"Thank you. I'm here for Jennifer's awaking."

*"Yes, that process is scheduled to start at nine. Please go to the receiving area where she will be brought to meet you."*

The two large glass offset doors pivoted allowing Jim entry into his own lab. He remembered the layout and once in the elevator he instructed Central System to take him to the fourth floor. When the doors parted he walked down the translucent hallway to the receiving area that he was in several months earlier and where he would soon be with his wife again. He walked across the room and took a seat at the same table and then he waited in silence.

"Hello Jim, here a bit early."

It was Daniel's voice that broke the silence. His hair was raven black and had a sheen to it that appeared to alter its coloration depending on the way the light hit it. He was tall, standing nearly six feet two inches, and thin. His eyes were dark brown and set deep in their sockets. His cheekbones were high and dropped sharply to his squared chin. He was dressed in a black suit with a charcoal black shirt and white tie. Every time Jim encountered him he was reminded of the villain from a horror novel.

"Hello Daniel. Everything going okay." Jim asked.

"Oh yes, no problems what so ever. Is there Jim?"

Daniel was feeling Jim out, enticing him to reveal his own feelings by presenting a caring front.

"I'm not in a position to tell you anything Daniel. I've been here since I got here. I would have no idea if there was a problem with Jennifer or not." Jim said.

"Being smart and sarcastic. You knew what I was asking." Daniel's tony was cynical and heavy.

"If you have something to ask, then ask. Otherwise we have nothing to discuss." Jim grew defensive and stood to face Daniel.

"Very well. Do you have a problem with the information that Toby was able to share." Daniel withdrew his attack and lowered his posture.

Jim knew he needed to be careful. Daniel was on a fishing expedition and if Toby had been honest about not telling him what they talked about yesterday then revealing anything could get all three of them killed.

"Toby told me what he needed to and what I was able to absorb. Sure some if it's hard to digest, but in time I will. Besides Daniel, it's for the betterment of the entire world. One man should not have the right to dictate the will of the many. In time I'll fit in like all the rest. So no worries. Okay?" Jim kept his statement simple and avoided repeating details of his conversations with Toby.

"Okay. But be mindful, I'll be checking up on you from time

to time. And Jim; you won't know when and if you screw up, you'll never see me when I find you and your wife. Do you understand?" Daniel resumed his threating stance and tone.

"I do Daniel, I really really do get your point." Jim said.

"Good. Then I want you and Jennifer to have a nice rest of the day." Daniel turned on his right heal and walked out of the room.

Jim watched him go, being glad to be alone again. He did fear Daniel; more of that fear was focused on what he would do to Jennifer than to himself. He wondered what time it was and then remembered that he had forgotten to ask Toby about his pocket watch, even after making two mental notes to remind himself. He sat back down and leaned back in the chair and rested his head, allowing his eyes to close.

His foot was caught in some kind of trap, a vice or something. And somewhere someone was calling out to him. The voice was distant, far away. He tried to see his foot but it was too dark, not a trap but an animal because its teeth were shaking it back and forth.

"Jim, you in there? Wake up. I have someone that wants to meet you." Toby voice was hushed so as not to startle Jim awake.

Jim opened his eyes and he sat upright. He saw Toby's hand drop away from his shoe, he had been wriggling it in hopes of waking him. Jim reached up with the palms of his hands and rubbed the sleep from his eyes.

"Jimmy."

It was the voice of his beloved. He rose from the chair and froze. Before him stood the girl that he knew before cancer ravaged her body, she was healthy and smiling. Her sandy brown hair had returned and was full, thick and radiant. The blue of her eyes were glistening and with them the return of life. They had bought her a white summer dress, not suited for the fall outside, but suited for the reunion inside. His eyes flooded over with tears of love, joy, and hope.

Jennifer looked at her beloved, remembering the sacrifices he had made in the former world for her care. The eternal love he had showed by staying by her side, and the continued love by waiting for her since his awaking. Tears flooded over her cheeks.

Jim took her into his arms and buried his face in the nape of her neck, as she did to him. The two spoke no words but swayed in a joined rhythm to music that only they could hear. He turned her and they slowly moved about the tight confined space, touching nothing but each other, still dancing to music only they could hear.

"Jim! Jim. You two come over here and have a seat" Toby said to them both. He then directed his words to Jennifer. "You will need to drink a protein shake to get your metabolism restarted."

Jennifer lifted her head from Jim's shoulder and look into his eyes.

"It's okay. Let's go over and sit in the lounge chairs. The shake is okay to drink. They have to get your body going again so you can eat and drink normally." Jim said.

"Jimmy I'm so glad to see you and to be with you. Can you even begin to imagine what we can do now? Oh Jimmy, we have our life back, we have our marriage back. And we can have children." Jennifer said.

Her statement caught him by surprise. He would have to tell her the truth about having children. However, before he could complete the thought her lips were planted hard against his, the kiss electrified him, making him eager for her complete embrace.

Toby cleared his throat. "Listen you two, time for that later. Right now this shake is important. So Jennifer get over here and drink it." Toby's tone was light and playful. He too was joyful to see the reunion of his two best friends.

Jim and Jennifer sat down in the oversized lounge chairs, still holding hands.

"Here you go Mrs. Fuller." The nurse said as she handed her the shake.

"Taste like a vanilla milk shake. Not bad. All new Wakes have to drink it." Jim said.

"Wakes?" Jennifer asked.

"That's what people like us are called. Wakes." Jim said.

Jennifer took a sip of her shake, forming a white mustache above her lip; she dragged her tongue across it smearing it. Jim reached over with a napkin removing the remains.

"You've a lot to learn Jennifer. Things have changed a lot in the last sixty six years. Jim is going to be your teacher, if you have any questions ask him and he'll be able to answer them." Emily said.

"So you know it all Jimmy? You know everything about this new world?" Jennifer asked.

"Well, not all, but enough. So are we good to go?" Jim asked.

"Ya. I don't see why not. You have anything to add Doctor Thomen?" Toby asked.

"Yes. Jennifer I'd like to see you in one week, back here at Fuller Labs. Just go to the front desk in the main entrance." Doctor Thomen said.

"Will I have to come back every week?" Jennifer asked.

"Only for the first month, then once a month for six months. In a small number of cases some diseases have reoccurred. But don't be alarmed, we treated them successfully." Emily said.

"Do you think the cancer will come back?" Jim asked.

"No, not at all. But even though we've been using the serum for seventy years, it's still early in its development life. We are constantly improving it, and sometimes some aggressive diseases get by us, so we go back and make the adjustment and target that specific cellular structure that caused the reoccurrence." Doctor Thomen turned her attention to Jennifer. "But please don't worry; it'll only stress you unnecessarily."

"Okay. Thanks everyone." Jennifer turned her attention to Jim. "Can we leave now?"

Jim placed his right palm on the mid-section of his stomach and extended his elbow to Jennifer. She in turn placed her second and third fingers through the loop of his elbow, resting her remaining fingers and hand on the inside of his elbow.

"My Lady; shall I escort you to your lovely new home?" Jim's tone was a reflection of the twelve year old boy in the park under the tree.

"Why yes sir that would be lovely." Jennifer put on her best southern charm.

The two walked out of Fuller Labs hand in arm, delighted to be back in each other's company. Once they had exited the main doors Daniel joined Toby and Emily in the receiving area.

"I told you once she was awakened all his attention and focus would be on her. He could care less how this world came about now that she is it in. When she was asleep he had nothing to focus his attention on, now that she is awake I don't believe we'll have anything else to worry about." Toby directed his comment to Daniel after he had taken the chair that Jim was sitting in.

"I hope you're right on that Toby. I hate upsets and I hate having to clean up messes created by other people." Daniel said.

"I think Toby has this one Daniel. Toby has known Jim since age five or younger. They fight all the time; they fought over everything as kids. This issue was no different. With Jennifer awake I believe everything is safe and we can now enjoy some peace and quiet again." Emily said.

"Still I think it's a good idea to keep an eye on the two for a while. It never hurts to be cautious." Daniel said.

"I think we can all agree on that." Emily said. Toby nodded in approval.

## CHAPTER 12

The Fuller's had entered the lab sixty six years ago with little hope, this day they exited to a new day with hope renewed. Jennifer took in a deep breath, drawing in the crispness of the early fall air. The sky above was deep blue and clear of any floating clouds; on the ground around them squirrels busied themselves gathering supplies for the winter ahead. From time to time a flock of birds flew over, heading south to their winter roosting. The leaves of trees were showing off their colors of red, gold and yellow, some gathering on the ground and picked up by slight breezes and blown to some unknown destination. People walked by and greeted them others stopped to ask about their day. Those that were hungry gathered around sidewalk vendors, hoping to fill their need. The first day of Jennifer's awakening was pleasant and cheerful; Jim hoped it would always stay that way.

"Oh, Jimmy. It's beautiful, perfect." Jennifer said.

Jim smiled at his wife, knowing that as they walked she would notice that which was missing and start asking questions, and he would have to answer her with lies. They continued to walk down the brown cobblestone walkway, hand in arm and he listened gleefully to her expression of delight at everything new.

"Jimmy?"

He swallowed hard, this was the start.

"Yes."

"Where are the cars?"

Toby explained that during The Transition Period the planet was nearly destroyed by global warming. Several initiatives were implemented in hopes of curbing the destruction. One of which was the elimination of personal gas powered vehicles. Most highways and streets were scraped up and cobblestone pathways were put in place to allow people to walk from place to place. Some people use bikes and others used electric bikes or scooters. A few people owned a full sized electric car. But in short, cars were banned for personal use.

Jennifer stopped walking and gave Jim a long telling look.

"What!?" Jim asked.

"You've not changed at all, and for that I love you dearly. But forego the long explanations from now on. You could have simply said 'people no longer use them' and I would've accepted that. Besides what you said makes perfect sense. I always hated all those noisy cars, I'm glad something was done about them." Jennifer said.

He knew with her reply that he could now avoid some lying. She was happy to be alive and back with him; she would accept this world and the most basic of explanations without question. He felt a slight tug on his arm; she was ready to resume their walk home.

"There it is." Jim stopped walking and the two stood across from their apartment building. He pointed up to the fourth floor.

"That whole building is our new home?" Jennifer's voice pitched up along with her eyebrows at seeing the size.

"No sweetie." Jim laughed at the innocence she possessed. "We live in the corner apartment. It goes from the front corner to the back corner. Wait until you see inside and the park that's inside the court. Shall we?" He extended his elbow to her and the two walked under the arched entry and up the ramp to the fourth floor. He stopped before reaching the door.

"Ready?" He asked. She nodded to him.

"Where's the key go in?" Before Jim could answer SAM spoke.

*"Welcome home Jim and Jennifer Fuller."*

Jennifer looked around for the person who spoke the greeting, seeing no one she looked at Jim with the question lingering in her eyes.

"It's SAM; our personal computer interface to the world. It knows where either one of us is most of the time." Jim said.

"SAM? Like from when you were a boy and wanted some kind of super know-it-all computer system?" She smiled as she related the memory.

"Yep, SAM. But our SAM *is* a super know-it-all computer and it seems it can be anywhere as well."

"Will Jimmy, it seems you got what you wanted with this world." Jennifer said.

He gave his wife a tight, forced smile. He formed the two finger gesture and motioned to the right of the door, it then opened to disappear inside the wall. Jennifer watched in fascination.

"My Lady." He bowed with his left hand in his mid-section and his right arm extended to the apartment. Jennifer gracelessly accepted the invitation.

Jim gave her the full tour, demonstrating how to activate the visual monitor, kitchen faucet and appliances. He then took her to the master bathroom and demonstrated how to use the shower, dryer and prepare oneself with the in-wall hidden applications. She needed no further explanations after he showed her the basic functions. For Jennifer, the ease of use was welcomed after years of fumbling in the old world. They moved into the master bedroom next and Jim began the tour of the walk in closet, showing her her new clothes when he was interrupted.

"Jim, look!" Jennifer's voice pitched when she said the word look. He turned expecting to see something he had overlooked during the tour, or something that posed a danger. Instead she was sitting on the edge of the bed. "It's been almost sixty eight years since the last time we made love, that's a long time."

"Well to be honest we were both asleep for sixty six of those years. But you're right it has been a long time, and I've missed you." Jim sat next to her on the bed and for a moment awkwardness governed their movements, as if it was their first time. But their love for each other and the memory of that love recalled to their mind the ease of how it was displayed. They fell into each other's embrace.

***

The smell of freshly brewed coffee, baking biscuits and frying bacon pulled Jim from a deep restful sleep. He brought the palms of his hands to his eyes and rubbed the sleep away and attempted to recall why he would be smelling the things he was smelling. When the realization of his wife cooking hit him he sprang from the bed with renewed energy and joy. After emptying his bladder he went to the kitchen and approached his wife from behind. He wrapped his arms around her mid-section and kissed the nape of her neck, taking in her smell. "Morning." He said.

"Morning. I had to use SAM to place an order this morning

to have this stuff brought to the house. You had almost nothing here to eat." She said.

"I've been getting something from a vendor for most of my meals, so I never bothered to buy food to fix here." Jim said.

"Well, I'll be making the meals from now on. I don't think the bacon is from a pig, but it seems to fry up the same way." Jennifer said.

"Most of the food is grown; I think the eggs are real as is the milk and a few other things. I've never researched modern day foods. Maybe that's something you can do?" Jim said.

"One day old and you're already putting me to work. Jimmy, this place is lovely. What kind of job are you doing to pay for all this?"

"I get, well we get proceeds from Fuller Labs and the Fuller Life Serum and so I don't have to work." Jim said.

"Fuller Life Serum? That's what they named it?" Jennifer asked.

As they ate breakfast Jim explained many of the things he knew she would ask. He told her about the name of the serum, town and many schools and other buildings. He told her about the memorial in the park they used to go to and that it stood where their tree once did. He explained what happened during The Transition Period, at least the formal explanation and why there are no cell phones, tablets and personal computers. When he was done with the explanation he knew part of what he said was a lie, but he refrained from detailing the lies.

"You know Jimmy; I can really understand getting rid of cell phones and such. Before those things came along the world had fewer problems, well at least as far as I was concerned. And even if that weren't true, who cares. From what I remember the world was a safer place to live in before we had cell phones. From what you're telling me it has become a lot safer since they got rid of them." Jennifer said.

"So it doesn't bother you that the government censors the content we have access to and no one can call anyone without the government screening the call?"

She stood and walked to look out of the window and down into the park.

"Is that the park you're going to show me?" She turned back around and looked at her husband. "No Jimmy it does not bother me that those things are gone. That blasted cell phone of yours always seemed to steal your attention. Before I got sick the people I knew were tethered to their tablet or phone. I never could go out with my friends and it be just a girls night out. Someone was always texting someone more important. It always made me feel like I was not important enough for my friends if they were texting someone else while with me. So I'm glad their gone. People can focus on people in real life now."

"I can see that and how it would make you feel. Yes that is the park." Jim said.

"Jimmy those people look happy, content. If censorship brings about this kind of peace, well then I'm all for it."

Jim thought about her statement, the only reason they are happy and peaceful is they know if they are not they will not get their serum, it's fear sweetie, fear. He kept his thoughts to himself. He went and stood next to her, looking at the people in the park below.

"I wish I could see this world through your eyes. But you're right, the people here are happy so why should we care how it came about." Jim said.

"Let's go down. I want to see the park. And then I want to go see our park and our memorial. Jimmy, I think I'm gonna like being famous." The excitement in her voice carried over in her body language.

He raised the corner of his mouth in a half smile and then led her to the park.

The park was full of life and laughter. Families gathered for leisure or an early lunch. Young couples walked along the cobblestone path, admiring the changing color of the leaves, and a few brave souls could be seen swimming. The sights and sounds filled Jennifer's heart with delight. Her joy was not lost on Jim, and it caused him concern. But that concern was for the future, right now he felt as if he was on his honeymoon, getting to know Jennifer all over again for the first time. He led her along the path until they reached the two chairs under the tree where Toby and Jim had spent many hours talking. Jim waited until she was seated then took his seat next to his wife.

"So; what'd you think of the park?" Jim asked.

"Oh Jimmy; it's beautiful. I can't wait until spring to see it blossom to life. It's perfect." Jennifer said.

"I'll take you to the park we used to go to later, you'll like the memorial." Jim knew she would, it was apparent to him that she was lost and absorbed in this new world.

"I know I will. Can we go to the zoo after? It's still there, isn't it?" Jennifer asked.

Jim smiled at her innocence. "No the zoo and all zoos were abolished during The Transition Period. It seems that people came to realize that animals are best left in their natural habitat. Although there are no more zoos, people are allowed to travel freely throughout the world. If you like I can arrange a trip to Africa. There we can go on safari and see animals as they were intended to live." Jim said.

"Woo; that would take some planning, perhaps next summer. But I'm glad the zoo is gone. I hated to see all those helpless animals kept in cages, babies taken from parents to be prodded, poked and studied. It just never felt right. At least someone in control of this world sees how cruel it is to keep helpless living creatures in cages." Jennifer said.

Jim lowered his head in thought. He did not know how the children were kept when taken from their parents, but he imagined it resembled a human zoo. He hoped he was wrong.

"True enough. The people of this world did indeed learn a lot from the mistakes of the old world. But the people of this world will make new mistakes based on the foundations of this world." Jim said.

"Jimmy, you don't have to logically analyze everything around you. Sometimes it's better to accept without question the things around you, especially when it's this – right. I fail to see the mistakes of this world when so many people are happy."

Again the innocence she radiated surprised him. She was healthy again after suffering in agony for over two years. She would never see the negative attributes of this world, she would never see the dangers that he knew existed.

"How about we walk to our old park?" Jim asked.

The two walked through the archway of the apartment building and into the brown cobblestone pathway and turned toward the park. As they walked he continued to tell her of the technology of this world and some of the things that would be expected of her. He explained what the morning reading of names was as well as the evening reading. With every explanation he heard the same reply 'sounds reasonable'. From her viewpoint the laws, rules and expectations of this world made sense; they were only put in place for the betterment of the entire world, not just the few. As they approached the park Jim stopped short of the entryway.

"Fuller Park; I'll be, they even named our park after us." Jennifer said.

Jim smiled and then extended his elbow to his wife, she accepted his invitation and the two walked hand in arm into Fuller Park. The bedded flowers had faded and leaves were being blown about in gusts at their foundations. Throughout the park squirrels scampered, hiding their winter supplies of food and flocks of birds rested in trees in their journey south. Couples strolled hand in hand, a group of boys were playing football and several people were sitting and reading. Jim led her to the monument.

"It's beautiful." Jennifer read the inscription, *"From the depths of despair rises the hope of all mankind."* "People here believe that?"

"Funny, I asked Toby the same thing. Yes they really do. People believe I'm some kind of super hero to the entire world." Jim's tone was reluctant, he felt shame knowing what he knew and being held as he was by the people of this new world.

"Well, let them ask me. To me you were a hero, but only to me. Jimmy you're selfish, but not for yourself, for us. Do people really know why you did what you did?"

"No, and I mentioned the same thing to Toby. Regardless, in the end this was the result of my actions, our actions. According to Toby, it's not the means to a goal but the end result. So even if my actions were selfish, the end result negates my personal reasons and this is now the accepted reasoning." Jim shrugged his shoulders and turned away from the monument that was another lie of the World Medical Committee.

Jennifer reached from behind and placed her hands on his

shoulders. "It doesn't matter to me. I know why you did it. You were selfish for me, and now we have each other again."

Jim turned and took her in an embrace. He looked deep into her eyes and could see the love she felt for him. He slowly brought his mouth to hers and returned that expression of love.

"Is our restaurant still there?" She asked. They had finished their kiss and started walking toward the exit, this time hand in hand.

"You know, I don't know. I never thought to go and see. You hungry? We can walk over that way." Jim said.

"Na, besides that was the old dying us of the former world. We need to find a new restaurant." Jennifer said.

"Agreed. The old book store is still there. Nancy runs it alone."

"Did Leonard die, or something?"

"He did not want to take the serum. He felt it was unnatural. But Nancy did take it. She seems happy, I guess. I doubt she gets much business except from people like us."

"Transistors?" Jennifer asked.

"Yes."

"Our old house?"

"It's still there. Someone with kids owns it. When I walked over to the book store I wanted to see if the hide-a-key to the side door was still where we had it hidden."

Jennifer raised her eyebrows. "Was it?"

"Yep, and it still worked. I toured the house. They replaced the wall in the master bedroom and took out all the handicap stuff in the bathroom, but other than that it still looks like it did. It brought back some memories." Jim said.

A tear formed in the corner of her eye and he stopped and turned to her.

"I'm sorry Jen."

"It's not what you said. I don't want to go in that place or even walk by it. That was our old life, our dying life. This world is new, alive and I feel young. I don't want to remember that time or place." Jennifer raised her arms on each side and twirled in a circle.

"I really do understand. We don't have to go by there." Jim said.

"Jimmy; don't take this the wrong way, but I don't want to see Nancy either. That book store and her and Leonard were an integral part of our old life. After I got sick and my family stopped coming over – those two were the only ones that did come over and visit. I just want to wash my hands of all that was old."

"Okay; I understand." But Jim did not. Nancy and Leonard had been more than friends that dropped by, they had replaced family. When Jennifer needed extra help those two were the ones they called. They had come to depend on their help and Jim considered them family. But for the sake of his wife, Jim understood.

"So where do you want to go then?" Jim asked.

She left the question unanswered as they continued to walk. There was so much to explore of this new world and yet so much that carried over of the old that she wanted to avoid.

"Jimmy?"

He turned and smiled.

"Can we move out of Fuller City? Some place that me or you have never lived, some place far away."

"Why would you want to move?"

"This place is new, but it's still old. I was dying here and I don't want to be reminded of that past life." Jennifer said.

Jim allowed his thoughts to form before he answered.

"Where did you have in mind?" He asked.

"I love the mountains. We still own my dad's land up there. But the cabin has probably fallen down. But we can build new."

Jim smiled at his wife. He enjoyed the time he spent at Bo's, even if it was one day and one night.

"Okay. But we can't build in winter time in the Cherokee Mountains. So how about we plan for late spring?"

She smiled up at Jim giving her approval. The two walked home to their corner apartment.

***

September soon gave way to October and fall strengthened its grip. Most of the trees in the park below the apartment had lost their leaves, and fewer people were braving the out of doors. Jim asked Toby about what appeared to be an early fall, and the fact that it seemed colder. Toby explained with the primary cessation of the causes of global warming the seasons had been returning to a normal pattern. The explanation included details that the transition from summer to fall began in mid-September and by early October most leaves had changed and fallen and the temperatures grew cold quickly. By late November the snows would move in and the temperatures would continue to drop. Global warming had warmed the planet worse than thought and the seasons were out of their natural cycle worse than thought. It had only been during the last ten years that the seasons had taken on what was to be understood as a normal pattern. Jim accepted Toby's explanation and braced himself for a long harsh winter.

In the weeks since Jennifer's awakening she had unpacked the boxes that were delivered after Jim moved in and she was making their small apartment into a home. He wondered why since they were still talking about rebuilding the cabin, and she explained it most logically. It would not be until May before they broke ground on their new home, and it may take months. They had to live in the apartment for about another year so she may as well make it into a home. Jim was left with no choice but to agree in the face of such logic.

It was a mid-October morning when the sound of her voice pulled him from a deep sleep.

"…look at this."

Jim bolted from bed and ran through the house in his underwear, worried that she had somehow hurt herself. When he made it to the living room he saw her kneeling on the floor in front of the last box to be unpacked. Winded and trying to catch his breath he allowed his body to drop in one of the chairs.

"Look at this."

Before him in her extended hand swung his pocket watch, he leaned forward and cradled it in his palm, she released the chain and it piled on the back of the watch.

He brought the watch to his face and examined it. The time was incorrect. He looked at the digital readout above the fireplace, set the correct time on the watch and wound its spring.

"You're gonna tell me you never thought to look through the boxes?" Jennifer got up from the floor and sat on his lap.

"I thought about it. I wanted to leave the unpacking for you. I figured it would give you some bonding time with our apartment."

"Ya, but why didn't you just look through the boxes for your watch?"

He shook his head back and forth and let out a low huff. "I really don't know."

"Maybe you wanted to wait for me to give it to you again. Like on our anniversary."

He smiled at her and then kissed her plush rosy lips. "That has to be it."

"Well now you have it back. Go get your shower. We're going to start picking out counter tops today."

"How about we take a shower together?"

"Okay Jimmy, but I'm not rescheduling our appointment. These contractors are hard enough to deal with."

He led her by the hand into the shower, where the two got to know each other again.

\*\*\*

October had at last surrendered to November and indeed it was colder than Jim had expected. Most of the interior material for their new home had been decided upon and the blueprints were being adjusted to the changes that she had made for the interior.

The snow had moved in by the second week of November, and it had become harder and harder for Jim to find a reason to get out from under the covers in the morning. This morning was no different, until he heard an unknown sound coming from the bathroom. He jumped from the bed still in his underwear and planted his feet on the cold stone floor. He ignored the discomfort and ran to the bathroom. When he entered he saw Jennifer's feet sticking out of the doorway of one of the two toilet closets. He quickly went to her.

When he poked his head in the doorway he saw that she was bent over the toilet, throwing up.

"Are you okay?" He asked.

She raised her head and glared at him, then returned to throwing up. Seeing no apparent danger he went to the linen closet and got a small washcloth, wet it and returned to his wife.

He extended the cloth to her. "Here."

She turned and took the cloth. After several more minutes she was done throwing up and he helped her to the bedroom.

"Why were you sick?" He asked.

"I don't think I'm sick. I've been having trouble every morning for about a week. Jimmy I think I'm pregnant." She said.

Jim stood and paced the room shaking his head. He felt his own heart rate quicken and he started to perspire.

"Jimmy what's wrong?"

"Have you told anyone? I mean anyone, even some of your new friends?" Jim stopped pacing and was now standing in front of her, rubbing the palm of his right hand.

"No, no one. What's wrong?"

"We can't tell anyone, no matter what." Jim said.

"I have to report to a Fuller Birthing Center for care, and to make sure."

He dropped to the bed beside her and placed his hands on her arms near her shoulders.

"No you can't. Promise me you won't"

She could see the fear in his expression and the desperation in his eyes.

"Okay Jimmy; but how will we know for sure and how do we hide it if I am?"

"We go to Nancy. She, she stocked up on stuff from the old world. Maybe she has some old pregnancy test and one of them is still good. As for care, we'll do it."

"I don't understand Jimmy, what are you afraid of?"

Jim took a deep breath and looked deep into Jennifer's eyes.

"I've not been completely honest with you about this world. I told you the things that Toby and the committee forced me to tell you. When I first woke up I questioned everything and got no answers, so I went off the grid to find answers. Jen I learned things about the World Medical Committee that frightened me and I made the mistake of taking what I learned and confronted Toby." He paused and took a deep breath, attempting to slow his heart rate. "Toby did not deny anything. So like a fool I pressed him for the truth behind the morning reading of the children's list, he told me Jen, at least part of it. If we go to a Fuller Birthing Center they will take our child. And if Toby finds out I've told you what I have he'll kill us both."

She stared at him in complete disbelief. "Jimmy you can't be serious. Toby is your best friend."

"That's the only reason he did not kill me when I confronted him."

"Why do they take the children?" She asked.

"He would not tell me; even though I pressed he refused to tell me. You can't tell, we have to keep this secret." Jim said.

"What'll we do?" She asked.

"I don't know. I'm not sure."

Jim's body went limp, he felt sick and helpless.

## CHAPTER 13

They sat next to each other, hopeless and resigned. He wrapped his arm around her and she nestled her face against his chest. Although she attempted to hide it, he could hear her crying. He too wanted to cry, but at the moment she was leaning on him. He stood up and placed his forefinger over his pressed lips, indicating to her to remain quiet.

"It's a beautiful morning; let's go for a walk in the park." Jim said.

The two quickly dressed and exited the apartment and she followed him across the cobblestone walk to a bench opposite the apartment building. He motioned for her to sit down, he then sat next to her.

"SAM can listen to anything said in the apartment. They can watch us as well." Jim said.

"Jimmy, I don't understand."

"Toby once told me they could hear everything going on in the apartment. After he told me that I started thinking about some of the times he showed up. Sometimes right after I did some research or he would say something that he could only know about if he had been watching. I think the World Medical Committee can watch or listen to anyone anywhere and at any time."

"But why? For what reason?" Even with the threat of losing their unborn child looming over them, her innocents still amazed him.

"The committee keeps a tight grip on this new world. Every transmission is censored, even the news. People are not allowed to gather in large groups unless sanctioned by the committee, V-Links are recorded, and personal computer access systems record all activity and that is analyzed for key words or phrases. A red flag and the committee is alerted. People are happy not because they are content, but because they are afraid. The committee controls the distribution of the serum, no obedience no serum. They got people addicted to the idea of being healthy and with the hope of a longer life. In exchange they surrender their personal liberties and freedom of thought or ideas. It's a peaceful world of fear."

"Jimmy, why didn't you tell me all this before?" Jennifer asked.

"I was instructed that if I did I would have to watch you die, and I would be forced to live with that memory. I tried to limit the information and tell you to the truth, but some things, well not everything in this world is truth so I had to lie to keep you alive. I'm sorry."

"I'm not upset. You did what you had to do with what you were told. Who told you that anyway?"

Jim lowered his head and she reached over and placed her hand under his chin and pulled it back up.

"You don't want to say do you?"

Jim shook his head no.

"Was it Toby?"

Jim shook his head yes.

"Weeks ago I would not have believed you, but now I do. He has changed, he used to care but now he seems distant, almost alien."

Jim turned to her quickly and gave her a questioning look. "Alien?"

"Ya. Remember on Star Trek when someone changed all of a sudden, it was usually because an alien had invaded their mind or body. Happened all the time, alien."

"I never knew you paid that much attention."

"Of course Jimmy, Star Trek was important to you. I suppose it still would be if we had TV. So you dragged me outside in the cold to tell me something you did not want SAM to rely to the committee, what is it?"

"When I was digging around for information I got it from two sources, Nancy at the book store and an ex-Secret Service agent living out west named Bo. I want to travel to Livingston to talk to Bo again."

"So when do we go?" Jennifer asked.

"Not yet; we have to know if you really are pregnant." Jim said.

"How do we manage that without going to a Fuller Birthing Center?"

"Remember I told you that I went to see Nancy?" Jennifer nodded yes. "She trusts no one and lives off the grid in plain sight. She kept a bunch of stuff from the old world. She bought up everything she could after the nukes went off. She figured it was going to be the end of the civilized world. She may have some old pregnancy test." Jim said.

"I remember you saying that upstairs. Sorry. But Jimmy, even if she did they won't be any good after all this time."

Jim stood and extended his elbow, she took the invitation and the two walked hand in arm down the cobblestone path in the direction of their old neighborhood, and the book store.

"We'll never know unless we go and ask."

\*\*\*

They walked one path over and one block past their old house and then turned back up to approach the book store from the opposite direction. He did not want to impress upon Jennifer's mind the memories of her life of cancer. When they approached the door to the book store she squeezed his elbow and he stopped walking. For a moment they were lost in each other's gaze, she reached up and gently kissed his lips and whispered 'thanks' as she drew back. Before he could open the door he noticed the sign was turned to closed.

"She's not here Jimmy."

"She's here." Jim reached to the side of the door and pressed the buzzer three times, paused, pressed twice quickly, paused and pressed four times in rapid secession. After a few minutes the door opened and the bell above tinkled their arrival. They quickly entered and Nancy securely latched the door after closing it behind them.

Jim placed his forefinger over his pressed lips to Jennifer and the two followed Nancy to the back of the store and up the stairs to the safety of her apartment.

"Hello again Jim. It's been a long time Jennifer." Nancy wrapped her arms around her and gave her a long overdue hug. When she pulled back they were both crying.

"We have to make the reunion short. Nancy we think Jennifer is pregnant." Jim said.

"Oh dear Jim. You said think; so you've not confirmed it at a birthing center?"

"No."

Nancy turned her attention to Jennifer. "What makes you think you're pregnant?"

"Morning sickness going into two weeks, one missed period, and cravings." Jennifer said.

"Have you told anyone or expressed your feelings to anyone?" Nancy directed the question at both of them.

"No." Was their unified reply.

"So what can I do?" Nancy asked.

"You stocked up after the nukes were dropped, you bought whole stores. I – we were hoping that you bought out a drug store or maybe had…" Nancy cut Jim off in mid-sentence. "Some pregnancy test. I did manage to end up with some. I thought, well I was hoping that Leonard and I might try to have a baby. We were old but the serum would give us a kick back in the game of life. But I doubt they're any good."

"I have to try. I want to know for sure" Jennifer said.

"They work best in the morning, but let me guess, you can't wait that long." Nancy said.

"We're on our way – someplace else to gather…" Nancy held up the palm of her hand, indicating for Jim to stop talking.

"I know the routine Jim, we all remain nameless. Okay I'll grab a handful, just pee on them till one gives up the answer."

Nancy disappeared behind a set of curtains that hung where a door once did. The silence of the room was broken by grunts as she shifted boxes. After a few minutes she returned with a handful of pregnancy test, still in boxes and still with the cellophane on them. She handed them to Jennifer.

"Need to have some water to get going?"

"No, I have to go."

"Okay, bathroom's down that hall and to the right. Holler if you need help, I'll send Jim in." Nancy said.

Jennifer walked down the hall and disappeared out of sight when she turned right. Jim and Nancy sat down across from each other and waited.

"Get you some tea?'

Jim shook his head rapidly back and forth, telling her no. She could not only see his tension, but the room was full of it.

"She's not giving birth you know."

"You know what they'll do. They'll take our child."

"It's worse than that Jimmy, far worse. I'll tell you, but don't tell her until you need to, and trust me there'll come a time that you might need to."

Jim leaned forward in his chair so as not to miss a word.

"First generation Wakes and Transistors that got pregnant, their babies got taken away, but only three out of ten were on the list five years later."

"The other seven?"

"I don't know for certain, only gossip. But with each new generation of births and with each new improvement in the serum, the numbers increased until it reached nearly ten out of ten. Every great once in a while there's a missing name, but not often." Nancy said.

"But the early generations, those seven?"

Nancy shook her head back and forth. "Jim, no one knows. But their names have never been read. You and Jennifer, although you've got a dose of the current serum, you're still a first generation pregnancy."

He understood her meaning; if they registered this pregnancy chances were high that they would never see the child. Jim was startled from his thoughts by a burst of yelling. He jumped from his chair and ran down the hall, his first inclination was something bad had happened, but then he heard laughter, what he heard was shouts of happiness. The hallway was flooded with light when Jennifer threw open the bathroom door.

"We're going to be parents. I'm gonna be a mommy."

For a moment the two were lost in their joy and the thought of being parents. As Jim and Jennifer circled in an embrace Nancy stood watching from the end of the hall. She drew their attention by clearing her throat.

"Listen; for all that joy; here comes the crash. No one that I'm aware of has ever given birth without the committee learning of it. If you're to be the first you can't stay in the city. Jimmy you said you have some place to go?"

"Ya."

"Best head out before anyone catches wind. Jennifer, you got a positive on the first try?"

"No. I used six sticks, four positive, two nothing. I took the higher count."

"Sounds right by me." Nancy turned to Jim. "How you getting' where you're going?"

"The Rail."

"Play her like she's a new Wake Jimmy. Otherwise they'll see right through ya."

Jim leaned over and kissed Nancy on the cheek, then with Jennifer's hand in his he led his wife downstairs. Before Nancy unlocked the door she hugged Jennifer, she held her at arm's length and smiled. "I've always been here for you two. If you need me I still am." She released Jennifer and turned to Jim. "Jim when you get to where you're going, well if you have to drop my name, do it."

"Yes ma'am."

With that the two exited the book store and walked to the nearest Rail Station. Once there Jim entered their destination into Central System and after a second or two their arrival time was displayed, they had a twenty minute wait.

"We might as well sit down and wait. That video display is tied into Central System as are all displays on the Rail. So if you have a need to access something like historical information or places of interest to visit while we are on our trip, just ask Central System and it will be SAM that assists you."

Keeping Nancy's caution in mind Jim explained the use of Central System as if Jennifer was a new Wake taking her first trip.

Jim continued his new Wake lesson of the Rail, how it operated and was powered by the use of two properties, lead and Beryllium in opposition to each other. When a high magnetic force was employed to the elements their properties altered from a three dimensional wave to a two dimensional wave that repulsed each other. As he continued the science lesson in the new electronic power source she continued to place her facial expressions and the occasional ah at the appropriate time. In reality she did not understand anything he was saying, but it was part of the game they now both found themselves in, the game of protecting their own lives and that of their unborn child.

Once aboard they took a middle seat, she by the window, he the isle. With them in the same car were four other people, two young couples. He continued the new Wake lessons, explaining the translucent embedded monitors and how to activate them. He demonstrated how to search for local area places of interest and the best restaurants. Occasionally the lesson was interrupted by something that caught her eye in the countryside as they passed, and he attempted to answer all her questions, following the prescribed script. Time had escaped his notice when he felt the Rail slow as they approached Livingston; soon it came to a complete rest.

"We're here. You'll love this little place; it's like a New England settlement." Jim added excitement to his voice to give it a hint of genuineness.

When he stepped onto the brown cobblestone platform he turned in either direction and a sigh of disappointment escaped his breath.

"I have to take you to this really nice little southern restaurant, called *Sue's*; it's right down the path." He held out his hand and she took it, together the Fullers left the Rail platform hand in hand.

When they reached *Sue's* he held the door open for her and after she entered he followed and quickly scanned the restaurant looking for Bo. He did not notice when Sue approached.

"Well hello stranger! So this is the lovely Jennifer Fuller." She turned to Jennifer and nodded her head slightly to the side.

"Welcome Miss Jennifer to my humble little establishment. Shall I seat the two of you Jim or are you just looking for someone?"

Jim had continued scanning the faces of those seated until he heard his name spoken.

"Pardon? Oh Sue; forgive me I never intended to ignore you. We'll have a seat. Have you seen Bo?"

"Not yet hun. However he should be in here in about five or so minutes. Want me to seat him with ya'll?"

"Yes please." Jim said.

Sue placed three menus on the table, one each in front of Jim and Jennifer and one across from them by itself.

"If I remember you're an iced tea drinker, right Jim?"

"Yes ma'am I am."

"And for you Miss Jennifer?"

"I'll have the same please."

"Then three iced teas it is." The bell above the door jingled. "Well I told ya he should be in directly and look there." The Fullers turned in the direction of the door and Jim breathed a sigh of relief.

"Hello there Bo. We saved you a seat." Jim held his hand in the air to capture Bo's attention.

"Got you a glass of sweet tea on the way sweetie." Sue said. She then tucked the order pad in her apron and disappeared behind the counter.

Bo took a seat across from the Fuller's and studied Jim's tormented face. It was apparent this was no friendly visit.

"So you're Jennifer. Far more beautiful in person than on those blasted V-Pictures. Hate that propaganda crap."

Jennifer's cheeks turned bright red and she turned her face toward Jim in hopes of hiding her embarrassment.

"Please my dear, no need to be embarrassed." He directed toward Jennifer. "So Jimmy, what brings you back to my part of the country?" Bo directed his comment at Jim.

"After we eat can we go to your place? I'm hoping you won't mind company for a few days." Jim said.

"A few days Jimmy? All three of us at my place for a few days? Good grief, you're out for punishment. Well then lets order. Got the flat bottom moored below, we'll take her across after."

\*\*\*

Bo stepped from the dock and into the boat and carefully made his way to the back next to the small electric motor. Jim then helped Jennifer in and after freeing the boat from the dock he followed. Bo backed the boat away from the dock and piloted it to the middle of the lake, where he brought it to a stop and turned off the motor.

"What's up Jimmy?"

Jim looked out over the calm lake, his breath forming puffs of air as he exhaled. He was fearful to drag more people into a situation that could cost them their life, but he had no choice.

"Jennifer's pregnant." Jim's tone was abrupt.

"You know this for sure? You went to a Fuller Birthing Center?"

"Yes we know for certain and no we didn't go to a birthing

center. Can't risk going to a birthing center. Once the pregnancy is registered we become marked." Jim said.

"So just how do you know for certain?" Bo asked.

"We had a friend that had a stash of pregnancy test. A few were still good. Four out of six confirmed she was pregnant." Jim said.

Jennifer did not understand the exchange between the two men or how they knew each other, but she trusted her husband without question and realized he was attempting to save their child. She listened to the exchange with patience.

"So what's the plan now? You can't hide a pregnancy, much less a baby. You'd be the only couple with a baby."

Jim again turned to the lake and thought carefully how to word his next statement.

"Can't set here too long Jim, the frost will be settin' in soon." Bo broke his line of thought.

"Nancy…"

"Jimmy, you know the rule no names, never speak names." Bo's tone was harsh and on the verge of anger.

"Sorry Bo, but you and she are the only two I know and the only ones I trust. I'm going to need help from you both and so I might as well get the names out of the way. Besides she told me to drop hers if I felt the need. I need you to know you are not alone in helping us" Jim rushed the statement before Bo cut him off again.

Bo turned his head away from Jim and looked out over the calm water toward his cabin. He mentally let the anger in him go, whatever help Jim had come here for heightened his fear.

"Go on." Bo said at last.

"I want to know where the children are taken and what happens to them."

"No one knows that; no one. And I don't believe there's a way to know." Bo said.

Jim shook his head back and forth in frustration. "I don't believe that. I truly believe there's always a way, always a leak. There are twenty of those places worldwide, right? So that means thousands of people working at them." Jim said.

"Ya with that blasted Central System guarding each facility. I don't see anyone leaking. They would be sent to an incentive camp."

"Toby said there were…" Jennifer cut him off. "Jimmy, Toby lies." She said.

"Their supposed to be programs." Jim corrected himself.

"You want to join the program? I don't think you do or you wouldn't be here talking to me."

Jim ran his fingers through his hair, flicking the last few strands as they passed through.

"Bo; you have to know a way. You're a former Secret Service agent."

Jennifer's eyebrows raised and she let out a barely auditable gasp.

"Sorry dear. I guess I should have given you some idea who he was."

She remained speechless, and unmoving.

"It's been a long time since I played cloak and dagger. In this age, I don't think it's possible." Bo said.

"They played during the cold war." Jim said.

"Ya, but the sides were balanced. The World Medical Committee holds all the cards. Besides Jim, if I show up in Fuller City, I'm a dead man."

"You changed your identity. No DNA, no fingerprints."

"Yes, but your forgetting facial recognition. Out here, Central System is not looking for me. A new face shows up in Fuller City and the system will go nuts. The committee kept the profiles of all missing government personal. Any new face shows up on the system in the city and it attempts to catalog it. I've been here so long, Central System does not bother to compare. In the city, I'd be red flagged before I stepped off the Rail platform. We need to get to the cabin before we lose all our daylight. Have to get the fire stirred."

Bo started the motor and guided the boat for the opposite side of the lake. At the dock, Jim stepped out and moored the front, then walked to the back and did likewise. When the boat was secure he extended his hand to Jennifer and helped her out, then in turn helped Bo out.

"Surprises me that you remembered how to tie down a boat." Bo said.

"Had a great teacher."

"Take her in and I'll grab some wood, you start stoking the fire in hopes that some coals are still hot."

Jim watched as Bo started walking to the side of the cabin and then led Jennifer inside.

"You surprise me Jimmy. You really did learn a lot while I was asleep."

He gave her a smile and then picked up the poker and started to turn the coals. "When I was here last it was blazing hot, but we still needed a fire to cook on. Not much to it then, but I guess it needs more attention in winter." Jim said.

"Well to tell you the truth, I think it's sexy. Should have learned all this in the old world when we went to the cabin, somehow I doubt we can start a fire there with the push of a button." Jennifer said.

"I doubt that as well. Got some life in their Jim?" Bo dropped several large logs on the floor next to Jim.

"Ya, hand me a couple pieces of that wood."

"Been thinking Jimmy. You mentioned this Nancy woman. Can she be trusted? I mean really trusted?" Bo asked.

"Yes. She help me before Jen was awakened and she helped us both with this problem."

"Hum." Bo mused and rubbed his knee.

"I may be able to get myself in as a tourist, but I'll need a place that's safe to work from."

"Nancy's apartment is safe." Jennifer said.

"How so?"

"About halfway through her book store she installed a damping field to block electronic and wireless transmissions. Upstairs she has no technology made after nineteen ninety." Jim said.

"Smart woman, I like her already." Bo inspected the fire, taking the poker from Jim a giving it a few more turns and jabs, sending embers flying up the chimney. He placed the poker in its stand and sat down in his chair.

"So you've something in mind?" Jim was sitting on a wooden crate, having surrendered the other chair to Jennifer.

"Still in mind and still in the early stages of formulation. However I would rather wait until morning before I share my ideas. I have a lot to consider."

Jim knew from his prior visit not to push Bo when he ended a conversation. He turned his attention to Jennifer.

"That chair you're sitting in folds out into a bed, albeit a very uncomfortable one." Jim said

"I warned you last time you were here. The other one does as well. I bought those because I liked them. I never knew they were beds until I was trying to carry them in by myself and one fell open. I thought they were too heavy to be regular chairs. I'll see you in the morning, Jim when you take your morning pee…" Jim completed Bo's thought. "Grab some wood on the way back in." Jim said.

"Well that'll be a good idea as well. I was going to suggest walking Jennifer up the hill to show her the bathroom."

"There's no bathroom?" Jennifer asked.

"Well there is, sort of. It's an outhouse behind the cabin." Jim said.

\*\*\*

The smell of fish frying, cornbread, eggs and the brewing of fresh coffee filled the brisk morning air. Jennifer opened her eyes and quickly closed them again against the heavy smoke that filled the small cabin. She bolted from the small fold out bed and hit the floor on her hands and knees and started crawling for the door when she heard laughing. She stopped and opened her eyes, squinting through small slits. Near the fireplace she could see Jim and Bo working the fire and laughing.

"What's so funny you two?"

"Your greenhorn husband closed the damper instead of opening it all the way. The wood was too wet. We had a bit of snow last night."

"In fairness you never told me anything about dampers." Jim said.

"Well you'll never forget the lesson." Bo said.

"Can we open the door?" Jennifer resumed crawling toward the door. Reaching it she pulled the handle and flung it open allowing the smoke to quickly dispel from the cabin. She then disappeared outside.

"Want some help finding the outhouse?" Jim asked.

"She'll be alright." Bo said.

After eating breakfast the three went out to sit on the dock. The lake was mirror glass still and steam rose in small drifts to meander across the surface. Along the shoreline patches of white dotted the landscape, noting the newly fallen snow. Birds called or warned depending on the situation and the sounds echoed throughout the small valley. A sense of foreboding lingered in the cool morning air.

"So, what are your thoughts?" Jim looked at Bo, hoping to continue the conversation from last night.

"Well; as I mentioned, I might get past Central System as a tourist. A ball cap, sunglasses, a turtleneck and keep my chin tucked, pushing my cheeks upward. But it's a risk. Technology today is a quantum leap from the old world." Bo said.

"Guys, I'm no scientist, but I've had to listen to Jim talk all the time. If I remember wouldn't the use of the term quantum qualify as something small?" Jennifer said.

"And all this time I thought you were tuning me out. You're right hun, but I think he means..."

"I got the meaning I just wanted to correct you." She smiled at him and then at Bo.

"So what's in your head?" Jim guided the conversation back to the matter of figuring out what happens to the children for the first five years.

"Around the world there are twenty server farms for censoring all media and Internet content, there are also twenty incentive programs, and twenty Fuller Education Centers. That's where they take the children. We have to discover where the closest Fuller Education Center is located. And I would suggest that since there's something with the number twenty, all different centers are in the same locations."

"Makes sense, but where do we start, how do we start? Jim asked.

"Fuller City is where the entire World Medical Committee is located correct?" Jennifer asked.

Jim and Bo gave her a nod, affirming her statement.

"The doctors that developed the serum are the same that make up the committee, right?

Again the two men gave her a nod. "What are you getting at Jennifer? If you have something in mind, just say it."

"Doesn't it make sense that one of those centers would be located somewhere around Fuller City?"

The two men looked at each other and then to her. It was a

logical conclusion, one that had escaped their notice. However it would still be difficult to locate.

"Jen; I love you." Jim leaned over and kissed her cheek.

"Okay you two. It puts a center close by, however it'll still be difficult to locate."

"How's that?" Jim asked.

"We have no way to do a search on the Internet. We have no means by which we can split up and keep in communication. If we're to find it, we would have to walk the entire city and the surrounding countryside." Bo said.

"Must you deflate this moment? So then what do we do?" Jim asked.

"Both of you have spent time in and around Fuller City. Have you noticed anything, any group of buildings that generates a lot of foot traffic in and out?"

Jim shook his head back and forth then turned to look at Jennifer who did likewise. The air filled with silence as the two examined their memories of the cities layout.

"I have nothing." Jim said.

"I have an idea, someone who might know." Both of the men gave Jennifer their full attention. "Nancy."

"Let me gather some things I'll need and then we're going to the city." Bo said.

\*\*\*

"Is taking the Rail a safe option?" Jim asked. The three had already boarded and were walking down the aisle looking for a four seat area that was unoccupied.

"You're returning from a trip to the country and I'm a tourist. *Not* taking the Rail would draw attention. We need to keep the conversation simple from here." Bo said.

The three sat down, Jennifer and Jim sat next to each other and Bo sat across facing them. The trip into Fuller City was tense; they refrained from looking at others or discussing any aspect of their intentions. It was difficult to discern what would or would not draw unwanted attention. Some of the other passengers continued to look their way and occasionally point and whisper. Jim knew it was only because of who he was and no undue suspicion was behind the looks. At the Rail Station in Fuller City the three disembarked, stopped at a vendor and bought three bottles of water and then started the walk across the city to the book store. The bell above the door announced their presence. Nancy appeared from the darkness between stacks of shelves.

"Jimmy; every time you come here you bring someone with you." She directed her attention to the added attraction that stood next to Jim. "Hi name's Nancy; but you already knew that, didn't you?"

"Yep. Bo; just Bo."

Nancy reached around her guest and locked the door, changed the sign to closed and pulled the shade down. Before turning she gave each of her guests a glance and led them to the back of the store between stacks of books. The four climbed the cast iron spiral staircase and at the top Nancy held open the frosted glass door for her guest and then followed them inside her apartment.

"Okay, we're safe. I'll get some iced tea for everyone and then we can talk."

Nancy walked to the kitchen side of the apartment and pulled four glasses from the cupboard, dropped in some cubes of ice and poured each of them a glass of tea. Jennifer carried two glasses leaving two for Nancy to carry. Nancy handed her second one to Bo.

Jim and Jennifer sat next to each other on the couch while Bo and Nancy sat in the oversized chairs.

"So what brings you back this time, and with someone new." Nancy asked.

"Well as you are aware, Jennifer is pregnant. We want to find out what happens to the children that are taken at birth and why they are kept for the first five years of their lives, in order to do that we have to find a Fuller Education Center. We were talking about this at Bo's place and we know there are only twenty in the world, but Jennifer made a great suggestion, Fuller City has to be one of those locations."

"You put yourself together a smart team. There's indeed a Fuller Education Center, Fuller Birthing Center, and Incentive Program Center and as you know Fuller Labs. All right here in Fuller City." Nancy answered.

"Where?" Jennifer's voice conveyed her desperation for the answer.

"Why must you know? I suggest that you two find some place far away, deliver that baby on your own, and hope that you're never discovered." Nancy said.

"That's the point Nancy. There's no way to hide a baby in this world. No matter how deep under they hide, they'll still have need of items that'll draw attention." Bo said.

"So again I ask. Why must you know?" Nancy asked.

"Suppose we managed to find a place to hide and have the baby and then we're exposed. They'll still take my baby and I want to know what they intend to do with it." Jennifer's voice had now taken on a demanding tone.

Nancy lowered her head and carefully considered her next words. If she revealed the location she becomes a part of whatever the three had in mind, but her own desire to know the truth won out.

"Fuller Labs and the Fuller Birthing Center are here in town, the safe side of the committee's activity. But three miles to the North of town is a massive complex of buildings. One cluster looks like an elaborate, sophisticated education center, but then there's a single building that sits off by itself, that one must be the Incentive Center."

"How do you know this Nancy?" Bo asked.

"The construction started shortly after The Transition Period ended. Many of the trucks hauling materials passed by the store, I got curious and walked out there. I took my old digital camera and started taking pictures and shot some video. It was only after the World Medical Committee made the announcement via public V-Link that I put it all together."

"Do you still have the video and pictures?" Bo asked.

"Yes. But I want to know the whole plan before I get dragged deeper into this. I want to know just what may cost me my life."

Nancy's statement caused everyone to stop and reflect on what they were doing. She was correct; it may cost them their lives and was knowing worth one or more of them dying.

"Okay then here's what I have in mind. Jim and I will watch the Fuller Education Center until we learn who comes and goes and the times that they do. Then we'll pick a mark and study him in more detail. Once we know the timeframe of our mark we'll move in and take him."

"A major issue. That mark will be carrying electronic tracking and emergency notification devices." Nancy said.

Bo reached down in his bag and removed a small black device with several buttons on its face. "It's a holdover from my former life. It's used to create a small field that will disable all electronic devices within a ten foot radius. However it runs on four double 'A' batteries."

"For every question I have you seem to have an answer that elicits another problem." Nancy stood and disappeared behind the curtain that acted as a door to her bedroom. A moment later she reappeared with a small box. "Here." She sat the box on the coffee table in front of Bo. "They're all still in their bubble packs, but they're about sixty years old. So I offer no warrantee."

"We'll have to make do. I'll carry several packs, just in case." Bo said.

"Can't we test it first?" Jim asked.

"On what Jimmy?" Nancy answered.

"This gets riskier by the second." Jennifer said.

"Ya like I said back at the cabin the committee has the upper hand." Bo said.

"So you approach your mark, fire the device, it works then what?" Nancy asked.

"I take a knife along with us and use that to encourage the mark to come back here." Bo said.

"That's a long walk for your mark not to scream out." Nancy said.

"I'll make sure the mark knows that if he hollers out or attempts to draw attention I have nothing to lose since I would be sent to an Incentive Center so before help reaches him I'll use my encouragement device." Bo said.

"Once you have the mark here?" Nancy asked.

"You'll have your nineties video camera already sat up with a dark black curtain in front of it and a single metal chair. That'll be all that the camera sees. I'll set our mark in front of the camera and asked him some pointed questions." Bo explained the entire plan to the other three, dragging them deeper into the only means of learning the truth.

"I miss the days of social media and cell phones. We could have just posted this on Facebook and thousands would have lined up to help." Nancy let out a sigh. "Never mind that, someone within the center would've already posted it."

"That's the one area where the committee made a mistake. Instead of controlling the flow of information through social media or cell phones they eliminated the source. If they had chosen to control it instead we would not be able to do what we are attempting to do." Jim said.

"Okay, the mark tells us everything. What then? We become the committee and kill the mark?" Jennifer asked.

"No and that's the best part. We let the mark go. When our mark realizes that the whole conversation was videoed we use that to keep him silent. He'll be terrified of the idea of going to an Incentive Center, he talks and a copy of the video is sent to the committee. He'll never talk." Bo said.

"You sure about that?" Jim asked.

"No. But it's the only leverage we have. So, is it a go?"

The three nodded in agreement, not speaking the word yes out loud.

"Okay, Nancy the video and photos if you will please."

Nancy once again disappeared between the curtains that divided the rooms. This time however she was gone longer than at previous times. When she did finally return she had a large metal box in her hands. As she approached the coffee table Jennifer quickly cleared a spot to make room for the box. After Nancy put the box on the table she removed a chain from around her neck and with the attached key unlocked the box.

"There you go, bury us deep."

Bo gave her a quizzical look and then began to lay the contents out on the remaining space of table. For the next several hours he watched the video and studied the photos, noting every door, security camera, and shift change. Although the footage and photos were several years old, he had no reason to believe that the committee would change something that worked. Everything around Fuller City and the entire Central System had not been altered in the last forty five years.

"How many times do you think you'll need to watch the videos?" Jim's question interrupted Bo's train of thought.

"Excuse me? Oh sorry Jim. I think I see a pattern but I can't be sure."

"What! Back up the footage and point it out to me."

The screen on the TV went blue displaying the trademark DVD logo and then the same familiar footage of people entering The Fuller Education Center begin to play.

"Okay Jimmy watch. We see the morning shift entering the complex exactly at ten minutes until seven. Now I'll fast forward..." He pressed the button on the remote and as he did so he directed his statement to Nancy. "What made you record several whole days' worth of uninterrupted footage?"

"I never had in mind what you're intending to do with it, but I did not know what I would need if for. I'm just glad it's helpful."

"More helpful than you can possible realize. You've saved us days of intel gathering." The video resumed playing. "Notice the time stamp Jim, it's now five minutes after one in the afternoon." All four of them directed their attention to the television, as if expecting something to jump out of it, but only a single employee exited the Fuller Education Center.

"There did you catch it?" The excitement in Bo's voice reverberated throughout the room.

The other three only gave him curious looks, as if he had seen something they did not.

"You don't get it do you. Okay I think I know why. Nancy recorded a total of four days of video. She started the recording at six thirty in the morning and stopped at seven at night. All four days the exact same person comes out of the building at the exact same time, precisely at five minutes after one in the afternoon. All four days the exact same time, the same person."

"Late lunch hour for him?" Jennifer asked.

"No, that's not it. He does not return until the next day during the morning shift start. But all four days he leaves at the exact same time. Here's what we do Jim. Tomorrow we go and find us a bench to sit on at about twelve thirty. We take a lunch, and maybe a paper. Have some meaningless chit chat. We wait and watch. If this same person comes out at the same time again we know his routine has not altered. If that's the case we take him day after tomorrow."

"Those are some mighty big ifs. It's been decades since I shot this footage" Nancy said.

"True; true. But one thing you can count on, if it works the committee won't change it. If the same man is still leaving at the same time, he must be bored with his job by now." Bo said.

"Another possible that you can count on." Nancy said.

"You are a disagreeable one aren't you? Listen I think all we have are possibilities. No sure things. Blind chance, what else do we have going for us? So Jim, are you ready to start the game tomorrow?"

"To be honest Bo, I wish I was not in this game. But I am and so I'm as ready as I can be."

"Then we should all get to bed. In the morning after breakfast Jim and I'll start the walk to the complex while you two girls get the apartment ready for our guest."

"But you're not grabbing him until day after tomorrow, right?" Jennifer asked.

"Right."

"You seem so sure he'll talk." Nancy said.

"I would want to after being in the same, unchanging job for over sixty years. I would be ready to spill everything I knew." Bo said.

"I hope it's that easy." Jim said.

# CHAPTER 14

The morning sun shone through the grim covered windows of the apartment. Its light was defused and scattered. Dust filled rays extended from the dirty glass and illuminated patches throughout the kitchen and living room areas. Slowly they crawled across the floor and up walls and furniture, until one cast its light in the eyes of Jennifer Fuller who was sleeping on the couch. She pulled the cover up to hide her face from the encroachment and then quickly toss it back. She reached down on the floor where her husband was sleeping and gently stroked the side of his cheek with her forefinger. He fluttered his eyes, opened them and sat up, resting his back on the couch. She ran her fingers through his hair, scratching his scalp as she did. He tilted his head back and she tilted hers down and they kissed each other. He then smiled at her and her at him. He mouthed the word 'ready' and she nodded her head yes.

Jim extended his left leg and pushed gently on Bo's hip waking him from his sleep. He turned and looked at the two, blinked his eyes several times than sat up.

"Who's the late sleeper now?" Jim's tone was light and jovial.

"Long night going over those photos and videos. I've not done this in quite some time."

The sound of a toilet flushing could be heard from the bathroom and within a few seconds Nancy appeared in the entry to the hallway.

"All of you are late sleepers. Jennifer; go get your shower before these two take all the hot water, then you can help me in the kitchen. You two," Nancy directed her comments at Jim and Bo. "Review what you need to do today. We can't mess this up. No second takes."

Nancy took the items from the refrigerator that she needed to start breakfast while the others set about the task she had instructed. There was no room for error, but yet there was no opportunity to run scenarios to have full confidence in their plan. Much of what they intended to carry out would depend on blind chance, and the odds were not in their favor. Within all four of them a sense of fear was felt, but never discussed. If one made a mistake they all failed. They all knew and understood what was at stake, five lives hung in the balance, five lives that would be lost if any one of them failed at their assigned task.

After breakfast and some parting encouragement from Bo, the two men exited the book store and began the thirty minute walk to the complex, along the way they kept their conversations simple, shallow and related to a tour of the city. Jim was escorting a visiting friend on an exploration of Fuller City, the two played out their part to exacting detail.

***

In the apartment above the book store Jennifer and Nancy set about creating the stage and props necessary to illicit the truth from the mark the men intended to obtain. From the storage room behind the book store Nancy retrieved a large black curtain that she had used in the past to create displays for sales. This she took upstairs and hung against the wall as a backdrop, in front of it a single metal chair was set. The chair was an old office chair that she had obtained from a closing military base in the old world. Its arms, back and seat had stiff padding that was covered by drab green plastic. The two women removed the screws that held the padding, leaving only the metal frame of the chair, intending to make it as uncomfortable as they possibly could. Next they found as many lamps as they were able and lined them up on each side of the video camera tripod, directing their light toward the chair. To focus as much intensity of light as they could they wrapped tin foil around the base of the bulbs and targeted the light at the set they had created. Nancy plugged in the camera, ran a few video tests to ensure the light was intense enough and then the two women gathered the tools that Bo requested to encourage their mark to talk. These they set out on a black cloth and then folded the ends over to conceal what lay beneath. When at last all was done Nancy placed a roll of duct tape on the floor next to the chair. The women had completed their assignment and were ready for the mark.

"We didn't have to have everything done today." Jennifer said.

"Bo has already chosen the mark. If the same guy exits at the same time, this will happen today, not tomorrow."

\*\*\*

The two men continued their game of tourist as they approached the complex. After the traffic cleared they crossed the street and sat on a bench that faced the main entry to The Fuller Education Center Number 01, then they waited.

"I think this is the first road I've seen in Fuller City since I was awakened. And I don't believe that all these vehicles are electric." Jim said.

"I had heard, but could never confirm that the government,

or committee, still uses gas and diesel powered vehicles, and of course this now proves it."

"A bit hypocritical if you ask me. The rest of the world is led to believe that everything is pure clean power, and here we see different."

Bo looked Jim in the eyes and raised his own eyebrows. "Hypocritical? You're joking."

"Well you get my point. Bo; if our mark exits at five after one today, why don't was just take him today?"

"I was thinking that myself. Way waste another day. I brought the knife; I was intending to mention that idea to you."

"So we take the mark? Okay. When I press the button on the black box what if I don't get a green conformation light?"

"Press until you do. That neutralizer has to work. If the mark notifies anyone before we get his statement recorded, we're dead or worse, sent to an Incentive Center. So keep pressing." Bo said.

Jim's heart rate increased and he wondered if Bo was feeling the same inside. Outside Bo appeared calm and focused; Jim hoped that was the same expression he was conveying.

"It's five after." Bo said.

As planned the two men stood and crossed the street at the crosswalk, then turned down the sidewalk and slowed their pace to ensure that they would walk up behind the mark as he approached. The door to the center parted open and their mark exited. Jim and Bo walked up from behind and continued their game of guide and tourist.

"Excuse me sir?" Jim quickened his pace and approached the mark from the front and was walking backward as he spoke. "My friend here is visiting the city for the first time and I'm showing him around, I was wondering." Jim never finished his question, he removed the neutralizer and pressed the button – no green light confirmed that it worked, he pressed again, nothing, a third time and still nothing. He looked over the mark's shoulder at Bo, Bo just shrugged.

"What are you trying to do?" The mark reached out and took the neutralizer from Jim, smacked its side and then pressed the button himself. The green light glowed its conformation.

"Well thank you. I was having some trouble with it." Jim said.

"I could see that. So what kind of device is it?" The mark asked.

"It's an electronic disabling device. It neutralizes all electronic devices within a ten foot radius." Bo came along side of the mark. "In my left hand, concealed up my sleeve is an eight inch hunting knife. If you attempt to call for help my friend and I will be hauled off to an Incentive Center, so I have nothing to lose before I go. I know you understand my meaning."

"I got you, and that damping device makes using my cell phone and other notification devices useless?"

"You catch on fast." Jim said.

"So where're you taking me?"

"It's a thirty minute walk to another part of town. So along the way you're going to act as a local helping to show me around. Got it? If at any time I feel that you're attempting to draw attention from a person or Central System, well as I said I've nothing to lose facing an Incentive Center." Bo said.

"Then lead on."

The three men walked peacefully and without incident to the book store. Nancy watched from the store front window as they approached and when they were near she opened the door. The mark was led through towering stacks of books to the cast iron spiral staircase and up to the apartment. Inside he was told to sit in the metal chair and then his arms were duct taped to the arms of the chair.

"You spared noting to conduct this interrogation. So why do you think you'll get away with it?" the mark asked.

"See the camera? As you confess your story it'll be videoed. If you expose us, we send a copy to Toby." Bo said.

"I get it." The mark turned to Jim. "You're Jim Fuller, the man who created this world. Why are you involved?"

"I – did – not – create – this – world. Before the Transition Period I only turned control of my company to a group of people that I thought were going to save me wife's life. I had no idea things would turn out like this. My intentions were for me and my wife. That committee stamped my name on everything as if I approved of it." Jim's explanation was given with a tone of sarcasm.

"Humm I see. So what do you want with me?" the mark asked.

"When we reach an agreement, that camera will start recording, as it records you will explain in detail what happens to the children that are taken and kept for five years. You'll also explain in detail how the serum is developed and what the ethical issues was that scared the FDA before The Transition Period." Jim laid out the plan to the mark.

"And why do you assume that I'll give that information up so freely?"

Nancy reached across the table and unfolded the edges of the black cloth that covered the tools she and Jennifer had gathered. Lined up neatly in a row was a cigar cutter, pair of pliers, a pair of needle nose pliers, wire cutters, a small metal fingernail file, and a paper clip. Jennifer walked from the kitchen area with a small plastic bottle that had a fine pointed tip. She sat it in front of the assortment of tools, label side facing the mark, 'sulfuric acid'.

"Wow, all crude but highly effective. I've worked at the center doing the same job for fifty three years. I've put off marriage because I don't want to bring a child into this world, and in the beginning I disputed what was happening behind those walls. I've kept buried inside me all the frustration of working there for all those years, with no one to express my concerns to. If I had married I would have a wife to complain to when I got home, but I don't. You won't need all those tools, I'll tell you what you what you want to know, because if you send that video to the committee, you send yourselves to an Incentive Center. But you already knew I would talk, didn't you?"

"I figured you would. I have watched you for some time and I could see the dejection in your expression and body language when you left the complex every day. I could see you hated your job." Bo said.

"Start with the disgruntled employee." The mark finished the thought that Bo expressed. "So now what?"

"We start the camera; you give your full name and what center you work at and what you do there. Then you explain how the serum was created in two thousand fourteen, its continued development and how the children are connected." Bo said.

"You won't like what you learn. I mean that stuff is flowing in your veins, rewriting your DNA, altering your personalities. Honestly, you've no idea what you're asking for. It may be better to just leave things as they are."

"We don't think so." Bo looked at Nancy who was standing behind the camera. "Start recording."

She pressed the record button and the red light on the camera activated as well as the television behind her, displaying the mark sitting in front of the black drape.

"State your full name." Bo's tone was demanding, without opportunity of debate.

"William J Crouch." The mark answered.

"William J Crouch, where are you currently employed?" Bo asked,

"Fuller Education Center number one in Fuller City."

"How long have you been employed there?"

"Fifty three years."

"What are your primary duties at The Fuller Education Center number one?"

"To extract blood samples from newly arriving children, process the samples, extract the DNA and prepare the extracted DNA for genetic sampling." William said.

"For what intended purpose is the blood extracted from the children?"

"That question is rooted in how the serum was developed in two thousand twelve. Shall I start there with your answer?"

Bo motioned for Nancy to stop the camera, then untapped William's arms from the chair.

"Would you like a glass of iced tea?" Bo directed the question at William.

"Thank you, I would."

Nancy entered the kitchen area and made them all a glass of iced tea and then she took William's to him and allowed the others to collect their own.

"Start recording again Nancy." Bo said.

"We're recording."

"Okay, tell your story."

"In two thousand twelve the field of epigenetics was opening up. With the cracking of the genome the field of genetics was now wide open. Doctors and scientist started clustering around certain speculated areas of study, because for the first time man had unlocked the secrets of perfect health. But understanding those secrets was a long way off, or so they thought."

William took a drink of tea and wiped his mouth with the back of his hand.

"Think about it, it's long been known that trees can live for thousands of years, and a clam for up to four hundred years. So what happened to humans? This new field of research held the answers. Doctors Thomen and Ellis were on a similar path of study, researching a cure for cancer and genetic mutations. So the two paired up and expanded their research. But like other doctors and scientist they were reluctant to share all the details of their research. With this new field, every doctor wanted to be the first. Pride was tearing apart the perfect foundation for a healthy future mankind. However that was soon to change. In Germany the Watts' focused on epigenetics."

"Epigenetics?" Nancy asked.

"Jim explained it like light bulbs that can go on or off on each side of a wire." Jennifer said.

"Crude explanation, but effective. Epigenetics is the study of cells within the DNA and their chemical reactions. Like the crude explanation of bulbs on a wire, these reactions are chemicals or tags attached to the DNA. These tags turn genes on or off based on given parameters. Those parameters can be environmental factors, stress, diet, the experiences we have in life, as well as inherited factors from our parents and grandparents. We even inherit memories from our parents and grandparents. Within these on or off switches was the answers that mankind needed to fix the human race."

"So I don't hear anything that would raise red flags." Bo said.

"Not yet, don't rush ahead. So the Watts' published a paper and Doctors Thomen and Ellis read it, they realize that the Watts' were seeking the same goal, one seeking the cure for cancer, the others having found the possible switch. Doctor Ellis contacted Doctor Greg Watts and a meeting was arranged. The four realized that by joining together they could make greater strides in their work. The Watts' moved from Germany to the United States, the foundation for the World Medical Committee was laid. I need to pee, too much tea."

"I'll take you, Jim stand outside the door just in case." Bo turned to Nancy. "Stop recording."

William stood and followed Bo down the hall and the two men disappeared when they turned right.

"Do you understand what he's talking about?" Nancy asked.

"No, and I fail to see how this has anything to do with keeping children caged like animals in a zoo for five years." Jennifer said.

"Hopefully he'll get to the point quickly."

The sound of a toilet flushing filled the apartment and the two men reentered the living room area.

"Sit back down." Bo pointed to the chair and walked out of view of the camera. "Start recording."

"Pick up at the foundation of the Medical World Committee."

"With these four they had the beginnings of what was needed for the base of the serum, they went to work. At first they extracted their own blood and worked with their own DNA. They learned the tags on each genome, and how to manipulate it. They did in fact find the switch that caused normal cells to go rouge, they stopped cancer, mental illness, birth defects, leukemia, but aging, and personality disorders seemed out of reach. When they had reached a point of testing they opted not to present their findings to the FDA, instead Doctor Ellis went to a friend of his, an attorney, Nick Barns. Nick was now part of the committee and suggested building the first birthing center. However it was a front to collect more DNA and do more experimenting. By this time Daniel was brought on and the committee was nearly complete. At the hospital where Doctor Thomen was working a man was on life support, he was going to die so the committee saw no point in seeking his permission or FDA approval to test the first generation serum on him. It worked and it was announced to the world. Nick, Toby and Daniel took their findings to the FDA for approval, but it was denied"

"Why, I don't see the point in denying the serum if that's how it came about, it worked."

"It's simple science Jim. The FDA is a panel of doctors and scientist. They saw what the committee presented, but they also saw what the committee omitted."

"Omitted?" Nancy asked.

"They had unlocked the tags to the human genome; they opened the door to human genetic manipulation. Think Star Trek and the eugenics wars."

"Khan." Jim said.

"Precisely Jim; Khan. Although those were not the words the FDA used, that was their concern. With unlocking the genome and being able to read and flip the tags or switches what would stop the patient holders from altering the entire human race. The FDA was terrified, and that's putting their reaction mildly."

"That explains why the President saw a more powerful, stronger military." Bo said.

"I can't believe that Toby would be involved with this." Jim ran his fingers through his hair and flicked the last few strands as they passed through. "They played God."

Bo was drawing with his finger on the kitchen counter, the same pattern over and over. "No Jim, not just past tense, they are still playing God. They have to be stopped."

William laughed. "Stopped! Are you stupid? Let me continue. The committee continued their experiments and testing. The birthing center proved a perfect front. They targeted low income and poor people. Those ignorant people poured into the clinic, and the pool of genetic material increased with every walk-in. With more genetic material the committee gained better insight into the genome and tags or switches; if you increase the pool you increase the knowledge. Nick and Daniel approached the President. The President was all for it, but not even he could sway the FDA. Well I suppose you already know the truth about the political side of this because you've never asked about it."

"We do. Continue." Bo said.

"Toward the end of The Transition Period the committee set up…" William turned to Jim. "You were put to sleep in two thousand fourteen, right?" Jim nodded yes. "Way before the committee went Hitler. So they set up the Incentive Centers. At first they believed that people with personality disorders…"

"Personality disorders? What are those?" Jennifer asked.

"In layman's terms? Murders, serial killers, sexual deviants, misfits, psychopaths, people who had issues with their personalities that made them difficult to function normally in society. The committee believed that through successive breading and flipping tags that these kinds of people could be 'improved' to behave like normal people. They were wrong. As it turned out some people have a predisposed personality that can't be altered. So the committee gave up on altering tags of these kinds of people, but because of gathering this data they were now able to identify these kinds of people from the time of conception."

"Good night; that's why they want the children." Jennifer stood abruptly to her feet.

"Only part of the reason. At the first Incentive Centers the staff doctors attempted to use conditioning and behavior therapy. It was coupled with rewards for acceptable behavior that was displayed when not elicited."

"William this is ridiculous. That has been tried over and over for hundreds of years." Jim said.

"You're right, but not along with genetic altering. But in the end, we failed. We could not alter the course that was somehow predisposed in these people. They were kept at the Incentive Centers for continued testing until their deaths."

"What you're suggesting means that man does not have freewill. We're governed by our genetic material."

"Actually not at all. When people that are predisposed through their genetics are allowed to flourish in a positive society, with positive feedback, other tags are altered. In the end it came down to choices. Although a person had the tags to be a killer, acting on that predisposition depended largely on what he was exposed to. Violence breeds violence, thus the reasoning behind censorship."

"So everything the committee learned about human nature from the genome allowed them to strip freedoms away little by little." Jim said.

"You can say what you want Jim. But stopping violent movies, video games, music, along with altering the genome has stopped violence worldwide, can't argue with the facts."

"You said not all people with personality disorders could be helped. What happened to the others, and babies that were born that had the same set of tags?"

"As I mentioned that first generation was studied until they died. That allowed the committee to amass a huge database of what to look for in new pregnancies, thus the birth of the Fuller Birthing Centers worldwide. All pregnancies had to be registered and all mothers had to go to one for treatment and the give birth. All expenses were covered. The new expectant parents did not have to pay for anything."

"So that drew the parents in, free health care, what bait." Nancy was shaking her head back and forth in disgust.

"The baby's genome was screened during pregnancy, and after birth. If no undesired tags were identified it was given a shot of the second generation serum and the parents took it home."

"What if tags were noted?" Jennifer asked

"The parents were told that something was wrong and the baby would be admitted into an Incentive Center for observation. Of course that was not the truth. A few days later the parents were informed that the child died of some as yet unknown illness that the serum could not target."

"And that fueled a greater reliance on the serum?" Bo asked.

William nodded his head in approval. "May I have some more tea please?"

Nancy poured him another glass and handed it to Bo to hand to him. She then set some more water on the stove to boil to make another pitcher of tea. She picked up a towel and wiped her hands and set the towel on the counter. "So how did keeping children for five years come into play?"

"Well remember when I told you that they had cured all birth defects, diseases and illnesses, but people were still dying at eighty and ninety years of age?" William paused, waiting for a yes but did not get one. "Well anyway, the committee was using adult DNA and that was the problem." William could tell he had just lost his audience of four. "Adult DNA is broken DNA. If every cell in the human body is replaced at a set time, except of course the heart cells and brain cells, then why do we age and ultimately die?" Again William paused. "You guys are a tough crowd. Our cells divide as a means of replacement. When a cell dies its matter is blown off, some is excreted in our bowel, urine and sweat. But some of that dead cell matter floats freely in our bodies causing havoc. You may have heard the term 'free radicals'? Well they do cause serious damage to existing cells. And when those cells split so does the DNA and the damage that is done is copied."

William was met with blank looks from his audience. "If I

had an apple and took a tiny bite out of it, then copied it, that bite would be in the new apple. So then I took a bite from the new apple and I have two missing parts. This process continues until there's nothing left of the apple. The same thing was happening to our bodies. As each cell died and parts of it flowed freely in our body it took a small part out of new cells, when that DNA material split to make a new cell the damage was copied. This is what causes us to age, damaged cells caused from the death of previous cells."

"So how does keeping the children fix this?" Jennifer's tone was more demanding.

"As I mentioned, the doctors were using adult DNA for the serum…"

"Damaged cells already." Jennifer's blurted out with strained force.

"Yes, you got the point Jennifer. However from the data stored in what later became Central System, the doctors identified that children's DNA had not suffered from such damage, thus the formation of The Fuller Education Centers. It was a hard sell to the world, but no choice was offered, the World Medical Committee had the backing of the newly formed United World Nations. Assuming complete control was now accomplished. The committee controlled the serum and the people of the world depended on the serum to live, a perfect control mechanism."

"I don't see how the decaying DNA was controlled by resorting to DNA from children." Nancy said.

"My students are learning to ask the right questions fast. Children's DNA has suffered far less damage than adult DNA. That's why their skin is soft, and they heal easier than adults. With the DNA from children it was possible to alter the tags that controlled when and more importantly how a cell died. T-cells were programmed with specialized DNA to target dead cell remnants, attach to them and carry them to the bladder. We were able to increase the human life span considerably. But not to what it is now. It took successive generations before we reached the seven hundred mark. We're closing in on eight hundred years now."

"So why not just extract the genetic material at birth, why keep the children." Jennifer asked.

"It quickly became apparent that a child's environment played a key role to keeping those 'flushing tags' turned on. In the early days we did send them home, but we had problems with extending the life span of the children of those children. During the first five years of life those genetic tags can be altered by the child's environment alone, The Fuller Education Centers were the answer. We controlled their environment completely."

"Like animals in a zoo." Jennifer said.

"Another crude analogy, but it works. After the centers started it took nearly twenty years before we reached a ninety two percent return rate."

"Excuse me? A ninety two percent return rate? What in the name of – just what do you mean by that?" Jennifer's anger was evident in her facial expressions.

"To this day ninety two percent of all children are returned to their parents at age five."

"And the others?" Jennifer asked.

"We can't fix personality defects, they are sent to the Incentive Centers where they are studied for the term of a un-serum life."

Jennifer walked into the field of the camera and drew back her hand and slapped William hard across the face. She turned, stopped and turned back to him, spitting where she had slapped.

"Nancy remind me to delete that portion of the video." Bo said.

"I set a time stamp on it."

"So you think you doctors are gods? William do you hear yourself? You're sending babies and small children off to be kept in a zoo like environment, studied, poked and prodded. You yourself said earlier that if these children are placed in a positive environment they'll make the right choices."

"That's just it Jim, their choices. The World Medical Committee could not take a gamble on that one single person making the wrong choice. Suppose that one single person made the wrong choice and shot up a school, or blew up a building, or went on a killing spree? The committee has the right to decide what is best for the world as a whole, not the rights of a single person. One person's right to choose cannot be placed above the rights of billions."

"I've heard enough. Stop the recording. Listen you worthless piece of cr.. – you're free to leave. You told us this so readily as a means of confession, didn't you?" Bo said.

"If you give a man the chance to confess his sins he will. This will surprise you, I requested a transfer to a serum injection center. My only job will be to inject the Fuller Life Serum into people once every six months. My transfer goes into effect tomorrow. So, ya, this was my last confession. I can sleep easy tonight and every night from now on."

William never saw the fist that made contact with the side of his jaw. It knocked him hard against the chair, flipping him back and sideways. He stood with his chin in his hand rubbing it.

"Did it make you feel better? Listen each of you has the

serum flowing through your bodies. You have all benefited from its life sustaining proprieties. You'll go on to benefit from it. You might as well accept that this is the way it is and will be from now on. Mankind has solved the problem of health, war, violence and has increased the lifespan to an unbelievable length. Who cares how, who cares if a few have to suffer so the many can enjoy life? Billions are living better lives because a few had to pay a small price."

"A few? Billions died in the nuclear holocaust, hundreds of thousands more died a slow agonizing death. In the beginning of this Transition Period still untold amounts suffered at your hands and the hands of the committee to produce the serum, no wonder the FDA ran in fear. A few? No William billions paid the price. The people of this planet stand on the back of billions. And you feel it's ethical? It's okay?" Jim said.

"Stop! Today only seven percent of the world's population that's born shows traits that are undesirable. The doctors working on these projects feel that number will continue to drop, until no one has to go to an Incentive Center. That's the goal that I was working for as well as all other doctors that work on the Fuller Life Project."

"Undesirable traits – undesirable traits. Do you hear yourself? The very traits you are displaying as well as the committee are not at all desirable. You and every doctor and every member of the committee need to be taken to an Incentive Center." Bo said.

"There's not a human on this Earth that has the ability to do that." William turned to Jennifer. "Jennifer, as soon as your pregnancy becomes more appetent they'll force you into a Fuller Birthing Center, they'll take your baby, and as a first generation Wake baby, I would not plan on a welcome home party in five years."

Jennifer dropped her hands from covering her mid-section. She had been unaware that her instincts as a protective mother had been displayed during the conversation in her body language.

"Remember folks, if you ever release that video, I give names." William pointed toward Bo. "I doubt your name is really Bo, but the link to you is easy to make from Jim." He turned to Jim. "Will you and Nancy see me to the door? I believe Bo has other thoughts in mind."

"Get him out of here." Bo's tone was full of anger and disgust.

Nancy held open the frosted glass door for William and then Jim, when the two men exited she followed. Jim let William take four steps down the staircase before he began his decent; he wanted to put space between himself and his adversary. When William reached the landing he was told to wait until both Jim and Nancy had reached the bottom. The two walked behind as William made his way to the front of the store. Nancy turned the lock and reached for the knob when Jim stopped her.

Jim poked his finger in William's chest, glared at him and gave some final instructions. "Go about your new life, but be aware, we have the footage. Ever speak any of our names and the footage reaches Nick and Daniel."

"I'm not stupid, I know the agreement. Best be keeping your part as well, founding father." The words stabbed at Jim and William knew it. "You four have a great life. I know I will." With that William exited the book store and Nancy closed and locked the door.

The two said nothing as they walked back up to the apartment. Inside Jennifer had made a fresh pot of coffee and had some waiting for them. They took their cups and sat down, Jim next to his wife and Nancy in the chair beside Bo. No sound filled the small room except the slurps as they tasted the hot beverage. The four could find no words to express the feelings they had about what they learned. They all knew they could no longer take the serum, but Jennifer's pregnancy was also a life altering course.

"Well I guess here's to dying young. How old are you Nancy?" Bo asked.

"I was sixty eight when I took my first dose of the serum that was three years into The Transition Period. So I guess I'm about one hundred and thirty one."

Bo raised his eyebrows. "I was forty two, so I guess I'm one hundred and five." Bo looked at Jim. "That makes you and Jennifer the youngest. As far as I know, no one has ever stopped taking the serum, so I have no idea how long it will take for the effects to taper off and we die."

Bo's words were sobering. Although Jim and Jennifer were still considered new Wakes, the idea of living hundreds of years sunk in early, and now that idea was forever gone.

"Seems to me that once again mankind has made a bigger mess of things then if they had just left things alone. Every time he tries to do good, worse things happen." Jennifer said.

"It's possible that some of the committee members had good intentions at one time, but as we have learned that changed quickly. With the better adjustments in the serum, they realized they had the power to choose who lived and who died, but on a worldwide scale." Jim said.

"I always wondered how some of the radicals in other parts of the world just stopped fighting. Now we know, make them dependent on living by holding the only source to life, the serum. If they fight it, send them to an Incentive Center. So many dictators dreamed of this world, and it's now a reality." Bo said.

"If there was a way to get this video footage to the public…"

Bo held up his finger and waved it back and forth, cutting Nancy's comment short. "There's not. Consider, even if the majority of the population saw the footage would they give up the serum for the former life?"

"I had not considered that." Nancy said.

"Do you really believe that people would continue taking the serum knowing how it was developed, and how it is processed today?" Jennifer rubbed her hands across her belly as she spoke the words. No one answered the question as they all knew the answer. "So what now? Jim and I can't stay in Fuller City, they'll take our baby, and I won't let that happen."

"The cabin, we can all move out to the Cherokee Mountains and survive off the land." Jim said.

"We'll have to walk out there Jim, and it's the beginning of winter." Jennifer said.

"Regardless he's right Jennifer, no choice. Even if William does keep the deal, when it's realized that we are missing a search will be started. The Rail records show that we traveled from Livingston to here. They'll tear Livingston apart looking for us. So we can't go back to my place." Bo lowered his head and started drawing on the arm of the chair. He had left his tin box embedded in the wall. "They'll find my box; it's all I had of my life before the nukes went off."

"Once they find that box they'll know who you are." Jim said.

"All the more reason why we can't go back." Bo said.

Nancy looked at Jim and then Bo. "What's in the tin box?"

Bo explained the contents of the tin box and who he was in the former world, as well as his role in the assassination of the President. When he was done Nancy stared through him.

"I would never have pieced that together. But we all have secrets from life in the former world, and I'm sure we would like to

## Still With Eyes Closed

keep them in the former world." Nancy reached over and placed her hand on Bo's knee. "I'm sorry about your box."

Bo shrugged his shoulders. "Can't change what is. So we're in agreement, the cabin in Cherokee Mountains?" The other three nodded their heads yes. "Let's start packing. Remember we're walking so take only essentials, noting else matters from this life."

\*\*\*

William entered The Fuller Life Center, one of twenty located around the world, for his first day of work. He had put in a request for transfer eight years ago, and every year since. He breathed a sigh of relief to be out of The Fuller Education Division and hoped to never return. Although he was grateful for the benefits of the serum, he despised having a direct part in its production. Here his only job was to administer the serum, nothing to do with processing.

"Morning William." The security clerk greeted.

"Morning." William pulled his head back from the scanner and returned the greeting.

"I'm supposed to give you this message." The clerk handed him a folded piece of paper.

William held up the folded piece of paper and studied it for a moment. "How quant." William unfolded the paper and as he read the contents he could feel the sweat roll down his sides from under his armpits.

*"William; before checking in at your station; come see me in my office. Supervisor FLC # 1"*

"You going to be alright. You look sick." The clerk asked.

"Oh; ya; sure. First day on the job and already the boss wants me in his office. Well here I go." William stepped through the narrow security passage and then turned back to look at the clerk.

"Fourth floor. They'll point you in the right direction."

"Thanks." William approached the elevator and could now feel sweat flowing down the inside of his legs. Jim and Bo would not have dared self-exposure and sent a copy of the video, so there had to be another reason. He began to play out the events from yesterday over and over; he said nothing to draw attention as he was led to the book store. After exiting he walked straight home, again drawing no attention. As he approached the fourth floor he took in several deep breaths through his nose, releasing them slowly though his mouth. The doors to the elevator parted and William found himself standing a few feet in front of a large desk.

"Hello Mister Crouch. You're expected, through those two doors." The red headed secretary pointed to two large oak doors at the end of a long hallway. The walls were paneled with dark oak and heavily trimmed along the top, bottom and mid-sections. Unlike most Fuller buildings, the floor was not translucent, but covered is a plush deep red carpet. He entered the hallway and started his walk to the two large doors at the end, his lab coat showing the sweat underneath. As he drew closer to the doors they swung inward to allow him entry. He took four steps into the office and froze, unable to move forward.

"It's alright William, come on in." His supervisor said.

William was not just unable to move forward, but unwilling. Standing to his supervisor's side was Nick and Daniel.

"Come in, have a seat." Daniel approached the only chair in front of the large cherry desk and placed his hand on it.

Slowly, reluctantly William entered and took the seat, he had no other option. "What's going on? Up for a promotion already?"

"No, nothing like that. To the point. After you left The Fuller Education Center yesterday Central System noted two men walking with you, one of those men was Jim Fuller, the other we have yet to identify. We could use your help. You do want to help us, would that be a correct statement William?" Daniel asked.

"At this point it depends."

"Depends. You know for a fact that we'll get what we want out of you." Daniel said.

"So you saw me with Jim Fuller. What's the big deal?"

"Jim's been under observation since he was awakened. Toby has been his handler, but he has slipped us up several times. Central System has Jim going to Livingston twice, this last time he returned with the same unidentified man you were with yesterday. So help us out." Nick said.

"Why was Jim under surveillance? He's supposed to be one of us, the good guys."

"William, you know that helping will go a long way in your recovery." Daniel asked.

"We all know that is as much a lie as what we tell people when we inject them with the serum. You intend to haul me to an Incentive Center and 'learn' just why I failed. You have no interest in helping me, just saving your place in this world. To tell you the absolute truth, I don't know who that man was, but I know that I'll be a worthless vegetable in a few days, so work for the rest of the information."

"Come on William. You know faithful employees do not suffer the same as traitors of the state. Help us out and we'll simply alter a few tags. Quick extraction of some genetic material, a few flips of switches and reinjection and you're as good as a – loyal subject again." Daniel said.

"No, don't think so. Not that easy when you discover who they were and what they wanted. After you learn the truth, I'm a loose dirty end. Work for your information."

"We're going to take you to an Incentive Center, extract your DNA, analyze your tags, dissect your brain, while you're awake, and in the end re-inject you with faulty genetic material so you'll suffer a long painful antagonizing death. Is that what you want?" Daniel asked.

"No you moron it's not. But it's what I have. So do it."

The doors swung open and two men entered. William stood and approached the door, before exiting he turned back around. "They were right."

\*\*\*

That morning the sun shone brightly through the window of the apartment above the book store. Around the room were upturned boxes and books that once stood in stacks. The living room looked as if it had been ransacked. At the foot of the cast iron spiral staircase two women and two men stood, as if expecting long lost friends, they checked their gear one last time.

"Central System will take note of us exiting the store." Bo said.

"Only if we're flagged. There's no reason to believe we have been." Nancy flung her backpack over her shoulders and slipped her arms through and then started walking up the aisle between two tall stacks of books. After she crossed the halfway point a voice echoed throughout the store.

*"There is a V-Message for you Nancy."* The computer stated.

Nancy turned to look at the other three, no one said anything. "Please play the V-Message."

*"Nancy this is Bill. I was by your store and we shared a great deal. Anyway it's getting hard to find real books today and I'm looking for one in particular, I believe it's called "The Boy in The Wood", not sure who the author is. But the point of the story is the protection found by three boys deep in the woods. If you still have that book I think I would be interested in reading it. Thanks."*

Nancy turned and started walking back up the spiral staircase to be followed by the others. Inside the safety of the apartment she let out a sigh. "William sent us a V-Message. Why?"

"He's attempting to tell us something, but what?" Jennifer said.

"That book, *The Boy in the Wood*, he made a point of saying that it was about survival deep in the woods…" Jim was cut off by Bo.

"They caught him, and somehow he left instructions for his personal system to send that V-Message if he was unable to stop it by some prearranged method. It would have to have been a quick turnaround; if they were on to him they would analyze all his online traffic and V-Links as well as messages." The other three looked at Bo with suspicion. "Ah come on you guys, it's logical. If you ask me William wanted to escape this world as much as we do."

"So now what?" Nancy asked.

"We can't stay together. Central System has all of us flagged." Bo looked at Jim. "You and Jennifer have to alter your appearance as well. We have to be quick, they'll be here soon."

Nancy quickly grabbed two hats, a scarf and two large heavy winter coats with collars that pulled up over the ears. She tossed them at Jim and Jennifer and then dug two pair of sunglasses from a box. As she gathered the items Jim and Jennifer put them on.

"It's not much, but it'll fool Central System long enough for you two to get to the edge of the city. Don't stop walking for anything." Bo said.

"You two? What gives?" Jim asked.

"We can't stay together. I intend to head out west, deep west, to the Rockies, Black Hills if I can make it this time of year." Bo looked at Nancy. "I'd like to take you with me."

"Is that a proposal for marriage?" Nancy asked.

"I'm sure somewhere out west we can find an old Indian who can marry us." Bo said. "Jim, does anyone know about the cabin in the Cherokee Mountains?"

"Not to my knowledge." Jim looked at Jennifer.

"Me either. Since I never put it in my name, I think we're the only two who know where it is." Jennifer said.

"You're sure?" Bo stressed.

"As sure as I can be under this kind of stress." Jim said.

"Then you two go there. Build a new life and never look back. Nancy and I will make our way to the Black Hills; we'll start a new life. Perhaps from two different areas we can give birth to a new generation of people, people not dependent on the serum." Bo said.

"How will we know if you and Nancy make it or you us?" Jim asked.

"We may never know. Perhaps it's better not knowing and believing that we all made it. Jim, you and Jennifer leave first. Nancy and I will wait fifteen minutes and then we'll leave."

The four made one last decent down the spiral staircase and to the door of the book store. Nancy opened the door one last time for her guest. With tears in her eyes Jennifer hugged Nancy and then Nancy hugged Jim.

"You two walk fast, don't look back. Once there, no matter how bad of shape the cabin is in make the best of it, it's the only life you'll have." Nancy said.

"The same with you and Bo." Jennifer said.

The four said their last goodbyes and Jim and Jennifer left the book store, turned the corner heading east and were gone from sight. Bo looked at the clock, waited fifteen minutes and then he and Nancy exited the book store. Nancy never turned to lock the door, the two walked west, out of town and toward the Rocky Mountains.

# ABOUT THE AUTHOR

DeWayne Watts currently resides in Tennessee with his wife of 25+ years. He fathered three children, the first of which passed away. His two sons have matured into two responsible men in their respective communities. He started writing at an early age, and in 1984 and 1985 had poems published in a literary magazine. At the age of 14 he did a walk-on role in the movie 'Rumble Fish'. He has produced over 45 semi-commercial and commercial videos. His parents divorced when he was 6 years old and over the course of his life his parents remarried many times. In between 'step-parents' others came and went.

He enjoys Star Trek and has a love of reading and knowledge. In his spare time he tries to keep up with archeology, physics, quantum physics, quantum mechanics, astronomy, medical advancements and scientific achievements. He enjoys reading fiction, science fiction, Star Trek (Belongs in its own genre) biographies, non-fiction, manuals, periodicals, and the Scriptures. He holds a CompTIA A+ Certification, 3 DCSE Certification's and two other IT degrees. Since 2010 he has been working on a theory for dark energy/matter. It is currently at a state that it needs a solve. He is actively involved in a volunteer educational work in the community in which he lives.

**Visit his blog at www.dewaynewatts.com to keep up to date on all his current projects.**

Please take time to leave Feedback on Amazon.com if you enjoyed this novel. Indie authors benefit from such feedback.

Visit www.dewaynewatts.com to follow the latest information regarding DeWayne Watts

Also check out DeWayne Watts on Twitter at dewayne_watts

Or

Facebook: www.facebook.com/dewayne.watts.758

## "The Boy in The Wood"

The bond between the brothers is strong. Their mothers love enduring. In one heart pounding fall it's all gone. The fall from the glass tower shatters her self-image. She is tormented by a dead secret from her past. Her sense of self-preservation possesses her mind. Her husband is useless, a wimp. In a desperate attempt to regain her life she sets into motion and unspeakable series of terrifying events. The deeper into her own mental darkness she delves the greater the cost to those around her. The family makes one final attempt to run from the evil, they move west, away from the city, away from the evil. But with them the evil comes. The Wood is their only hope, the only chance to save…the boy.

At Amazon.com

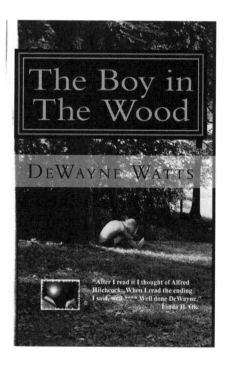

**"David's mark"**

Brian was looking forward to his sixth birthday. He lived in a new town, the family was going to a new church and he made new friends. But what he got was a week of absolute terror. It ended when he stopped his mother from being murdered, the first time. The terror rolled into a dark evil present in his father. An evil he could not escape. His father was obsessed with an idea all his own, an idea that feed into a life of horror for Brian.

Brian was looking forward to his ninth birthday. He made three new friends, lived in a new state and was a Boy Scout. But what he got was his father's vengeance. On the night of December thirty first nineteen seventy seven, four boys, one betrays, one dies, and two fight for their lives.

At amazon.com

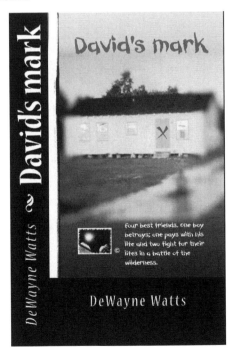

**From my Editor – William Gordon: "Life in Black & White"**
Life stories of a cop, the lighter side.

Life In Black & White is a collection of humorous incidents encountered over the author's 30 year career in Law Enforcement. This book stands out from the typical "cop" book in that it describes the lighter side of dealing with difficult situations. If you are searching for a book that will make you smile, or even say to yourself, "No, he didn't do that" this is the book for you.

**At amazon.com**

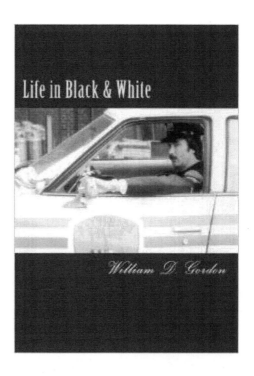

Still With Eyes Closed

Made in the USA
San Bernardino, CA
26 September 2014